The Orchid House

The Orchid House

PHYLLIS SHAND ALLFREY

With an Introduction by
LIZABETH PARAVISINI-GEBERT

Rutgers University Press
New Brunswick, New Jersey

Library of Congress Cataloging-in-Publication Data

Allfrey, P. Shand (Phyllis Shand)
    The orchid house / by Phyllis Shand Allfrey ; with an introduction
by Lizabeth Paravisini-Gebert.
        p. cm.
    ISBN 0-8135-2332-X (pbk. : alk. paper)
    1. Sisters—Dominica—Fiction.   2. Family—Dominica—Fiction.
I. Paravisini-Gebert, Lizabeth.   II. Title.
PR9250.9.A44074   1996
813—dc20   96-20720
                                                                CIP

British Cataloging-in-Publication information available

Manufactured in the United States of America

CONTENTS ✹

INTRODUCTION

It has been the fate of *The Orchid House*, Phyllis Shand Allfrey's 1954 novel, to be consistently misread, to be seen as a nostalgic paean to a colonial world gone by, a reflection of the "terrified consciousness" of white West Indians living in fear of the threatening black masses surrounding them.[1] This reading of her work—a misreading that fails to account for the novel's complexity and progressive political stand—has led to discussions of the text being always relegated to the margins of West Indian fiction, to that still uncharted literary territory of colonial texts.

Yet, few lives have been so deeply connected to the mainstream of Caribbean society and history; few literary and political careers have been as devoted to the empowerment of the peasantry and the laboring classes. Throughout long years of work as a writer, socialist activist, political leader, and newspaper editor, Allfrey waged a ceaseless battle against her own class, the West Indian "bourg high-life."[2] The struggle was the cornerstone of her identity, and was inspired and sustained by her resolve "to conduct her life as a continuum of West Indian history."[3]

Phyllis Byam Shand was born in Roseau, Dominica, in 1908, to a family whose roots in the Caribbean dated back to the seventeenth century. Her earliest West Indian ancestor, Lieutenant General William Byam, a Royalist officer who had defended the fortress of Bridgewater against Oliver Cromwell's forces in 1644, had accepted "a pass to go beyond the seas" in lieu of continued imprisonment in the Tower of London. The extensive land grants in Antigua he received in recognition of his loyalty to the Crown after the Restoration laid the foundations of the family's fortunes in the West Indies. The Byams of Antigua—a family remarkable for its continued residence on an island that had more than its share of absentee landlords—would enjoy almost two centuries of seemingly endless prosperity before falling victim, as many other wealthy planter families did, to the economic and social changes brought about by emancipation in the 1830s. As the nineteenth century progressed, the family's fortune dwindled—"everything went to pieces" was how Allfrey herself would describe it many years later.[4]

Despite the collapse of the family's fortune, Allfrey was to grow up in relative affluence in Roseau, Dominica, where her father, Francis Shand, had secured an appointment as Crown Attorney and de facto member of the Executive Council. Her mother, Elfreda, was one of the daughters of Sir Henry Alfred Alford Nicholls, a famed doctor and botanist who during his career had been connected with almost every public activity in the island. His family was regarded as the equivalent of a Dominican royal family, and indeed boasted of distant connections to royalty: Phyllis's Martinican maternal grandmother, Marianne Felicité, was related to Napoleon's Empress Josephine; Lieutenant General Byam could trace his ancestry to one of the purported knights of King Arthur's Round Table and had married a descendant of Anne Boleyn's sister.

Allfrey was always to write about her Dominican childhood and adolescence in a light, playful tone—not for her the somber descriptions of a haunted childhood we find in *Smile Please*, Jean Rhys's Roseau memoirs. Hers was, despite her father's return from World War II suffering from the aftereffects of a severe case of shell shock, the relatively happy childhood of which we find echoes in *The Orchid House*. In the early decades of the twentieth century, Roseau was but a provincial village in a small and rather underdeveloped island, but the Shand girls never lacked companionship or amusement. Their circle of friends was small, but it provided a tightly knit community with many friends their age and abundant homespun entertainment —garden parties, outings to the Trafalgar Falls, dinner parties followed by concerts, "fun-and-frolics" organized for charity, and regular visits to her grandfather's modest lime estate at Saint Aroment, the site of his botanical experiments.

There was but one thing separating this provincial upbringing from that of any small English village, and that was the racial divisions and concomitant tensions of a former slave society. Dominica had always been a relatively inefficient producer of sugar; its economy had never enjoyed the legendary prosperity of West Indian plantation society. Its rugged terrain and poor communications had kept the size of plantations small and had resulted in there being, long before emancipation, large settlements of free blacks and mulattoes who owned land or lived as squatters in abandoned or neglected estates. In the early decades of the twentieth century, the island boasted a powerful and accomplished mulatto elite, the "mulatto gros bourg," which presented a mighty challenge to continued white economic and political control.

Allfrey, whom a black political colleague would later describe as "color blind," always insisted that she had never harbored any racial prejudice as a child, although she had always been keenly aware of its existence around her.[5] She had to be, as racism permeated her society. Her own father was adamantly conservative on racial matters and tried to keep his family from any association with the colored or black. The Shand girls, a friend recalled, "kept to themselves," as then "black and white did not mix."[6] In church, for example, they couldn't have mixed, even if they had wanted to, as it was divided into two parts—one for the whites in front, one for the blacks at the back, and an open space between them. At the end of the service blacks and whites went out separate doors. As a result, whites, blacks, and colored lived in a never-ending ritual of power plays of which Allfrey was profoundly conscious: whites tried in subtle and unsubtle ways to maintain their threatened supremacy; blacks struck back by mocking whites. The mockery could be unsettling, but the Shand girls seemed to have taken it in stride.

Allfrey's bridge to the black and colored society of her home village was her beloved nurse Lally, who in time would become the narrator of *The Orchid House*. Lally was a devout Methodist who brought to her charges, the four Shand daughters, the calm assurance that came from strong religious faith. Like her fictional alter ego, she had "come fresh from Montserrat in [her] middle years [and was] an English Negress and proud of her skin, not Frenchy and Catholic and boasting of a drop of white blood." Lally, whose position in the family was more that of a family friend than that of a servant, remained with the family for twenty-five years, and was throughout Allfrey's childhood and adolescence her emotional anchor in a home often troubled by her father's emotional crises. As Allfrey's confidante and her mother's mainstay, Lally played a pivotal role in the young woman's emotional development; the level of her emotional identification with her old nurse often outweighed the bonds that tied her to her own mother. Allfrey would often refer to her as "the linchpin of my life."

Despite her awareness of the animosity many Dominicans felt towards the white elite to which she belonged, Allfrey grew up with a deep sense of connection to her island. The Shands of Antigua, their concerns with the preservation of racial hierarchies notwithstanding, were West Indians through and through, proud of their old Caribbean roots, intimately connected through kinship and friendships to many other families, white and colored, in neighboring islands. The Nichollses of Dominica, for their part, were a family particularly disposed to compromise, to meet Dominica on its own terms. The alienation assumed to be the shared outlook of white West Indians throughout the region was not a part of their—and consequently of Allfrey's—life. She imbued from both Shands and Nichollses a highly developed, intrinsically Victorian sense of obligation to her home island, which the socialist training of her young adulthood would help transform from its conservative, paternalistic roots into a political agenda for socialist change. This sense of noblesse oblige became her protection against alienation. She would always see herself as a "Dominican of three-hundred-years' standing despite [her] pale face," and always felt that her family's deep roots in the Caribbean made her a "true West Indian" and "the first Dominican."[7]

Allfrey was educated at home, where her aunt Maggie Nicholls, with the aid of tutors, prepared the four Shand girls for the School Certificate Examination. At "Miss Maggie's Academy," Allfrey was encouraged to develop an early interest in poetry, instilled in her from her nursery-school days. By the time she reached her teens her status as the family's poet set her apart from her sisters, giving her the special status she lacked as the plainest girl in a group of pretty daughters. She found an early mentor in Dominican poet Daniel Thaly, a doctor, family friend, and author whose eight published volumes of poetry abounded with beautiful images of Dominica, haunting visions of Africa, and expressions of passionate albeit unrequited love. Phyllis's own poetry would echo many of his themes and motifs. She was also encouraged to see herself as a budding dramatist, writing and directing her little plays for children at holiday soirees she organized with her sisters. Not surprisingly, given the family's support for her literary ambition, she published her first work, a children's tale, in an English children's magazine, *Tiger Tim's Weekly*, when she was only twelve.

At nineteen, Allfrey left Dominica for New York City—where her family had friends among the Morgan banking family—intending to find work as a governess and eventually establish herself as a writer. Her early experiences in New York, as the guest of J. P. Morgan II and protégée of his married daughter Janie Nichols, are faithfully recorded in the "Stella" section of *The Orchid House*, where she also conveys her awareness that, in the Morgans' New York circle, she of the royal family of Dominica was but a rather unsophisticated, penniless girl from an obscure island—and a governess at that. A budding romance with a young man in the Nicholses' set was promptly nipped, and she was encouraged by her employer to leave for England to attend her sister Celia's wedding, at which she met her future husband, Robert Edward Allfrey, an Oxford graduate with a degree in engineering. The sojourn in New York would prove crucial in two respects, however. Her experiences of near-servitude as a governess rattled any class complacency she could have harbored and laid the foundations of a socialist philosophy she would develop under the tutelage of Fabian socialists in London. Through the Morgans, moreover, she had met Harold Towbridge Pulsifer, a respected poet and editor of the *Observer Magazine* who had fostered the careers of poets like Edna St. Vincent Millay. He and his wife, Susan Nichols Pulsifer, herself an established artist and writer, took Allfrey under their wing, helping her develop her own poetic voice.

In the early months of the Depression, Allfrey moved with her new husband to Buffalo, New York, where Robert had se-cured a job through her connections with the Morgans. There, she began to write in earnest, mostly poems and short stories, as she claimed that between secretarial work and motherhood—her two biological children, Josephine and Philip, were born in the United States—there was little time for more sustained writing. In 1936, having failed to prosper in Buffalo, the Allfreys returned to London, settling in the working-class borough of Fulham. Allfrey soon found employment as private secretary to Naomi Mitchison, the aristocratic novelist, essayist, and prominent member of the Fabian Society, who encouraged her to join the Labour Party. Mitchison's essays on political moral-ity, class conflict, and the responsibilities of those with power for the abuses committed by the system were to have a pro-found influence on Allfrey's growing political consciousness. Through Mitchison, Allfrey met Edith Summerskill, a physician and ardent advocate of birth control—then a highly controver-sial political issue—on whose campaign for a seat in Parliament she would work indefatigably, thereby gaining most valuable experience in grass-roots political organization. Like many of those on the left branch of the British Labour Party, Allfrey also joined the Popular Front, established to lead the campaign in support of the Republican cause in Spain.

During World War II, Allfrey worked as a welfare officer in Fulham, one of the hardest-hit districts of London during the Blitz. She also established a communication network with Do-minicans in England, gathering clothes for those arriving in the winter, helping them find employment, housing, and often-needed medical assistance, lending her Fulham flat for wed-dings, reunions, and meetings. Among those she befriended and helped was fellow Dominican Jean Rhys, with whom Allfrey de-veloped a close friendship that would endure until Rhys's death in 1979. Out of this network grew her knowledge of the often desperate conditions of the migrating laborers of Dominica and other West Indian islands. This knowledge, together with her long apprenticeship in grass-roots politics with the Labour Party in Fulham and her growing network of friends and acquaintances in the House of Commons, would prove invaluable in her efforts to found the Dominica Labour Party in the early 1950s.

The 1940s were Allfrey's most creative and productive decade, during which she wrote most of her forty-odd short stories, the poems included in *In Circles* (1940) and *Palm and Oak* (1950), and significant portions of the manuscript that would become *The Orchid House*. Her first collection of poems, *In Circles*, evidences the fusion of the personal, the political, and the nostalgia for the ephemeral and fleeting that characterizes the best of her poetry. Her second collection, *Palm and Oak*, addressed her experiences with migrants, the withering away of the West Indian in England, and a growing impatience with the empire and its consequences stemming from her work with the Committee on West Indian Affairs of the Fabian Society. One of the poems included in *Palm and Oak*, "While the Young Sleep," won a poetry competition judged by Vita Sackville-West, bringing her work a measure of attention it had never received before. The encouragement, and a resulting inquiry into whether she had ever written a novel, would lead to the writing of *The Orchid House*. A third collection of poems, *Contrasts*, was published in 1955, after Allfrey had returned to Dominica, and captured the delight of her reencounter with her home island.

In 1941 Allfrey established a connection with *Tribune*, the newspaper of the left wing of the British Labour Party, where from 1941 to 1944 her reviews, poems, and short stories appeared regularly alongside those of regular contributors like Naomi Mitchison, Stevie Smith, Julian Symons, Elizabeth Taylor, Inez Holden, and George Orwell, who became its literary editor in 1943. The contacts she developed as a result helped her place her short stories in some of the best London magazines and journals of the period: *The Windmill* published "A Talk on China," an autobiographical tale chronicling her work on the Aid-to-China campaign, and "The Tunnel," a lightly somber satire of the "ravens and vultures" who controlled British industry; "Breeze," a tale of her childhood in Dominica, appeared in *Pan Africa*, as did "The Objective," the story behind her sister Marion's marriage to Dominica's Administrator. "The Raincoat" was published in the prestigious literary pages of *The Manchester Guardian.* Her most successful fiction, if judged from the point of view of publication, was that firmly centered on her West Indianness and hence marked by what was otherwise her marginality. In the mid-1940s, when West Indian fiction was not well known—and fashionable only to the extent that it was regarded as exotic—her choice of subjects, the literary themes that were so closely dependent on her childhood in Dominica and her peculiarly colonial sensibilities, gave her some literary visibility while still marking her as an outsider, a writer on the periphery. The manuscript of her second novel, *Dashing Away*—which chronicled her life of political activism in Fulham and her romantic liaison with A. E. Coppard, the well-known English short-story writer—would be rejected by Constable in early 1954 on the strength of its not having a West Indian setting. The impact of that disappointment would be revealed immediately as she threw herself wholeheartedly into her political work and social activism. Politics, not literature, she felt to be her true calling—"Politics ruined me for writing,"[8] she would wistfully write in her poverty-stricken old age—and she allowed the ill fortune of *Dashing Away* to thwart her as a

---

* Many of the short stories written during this period, particularly those with a London setting, remained unpublished or did not appear until many years later, when Allfrey printed them in the literary pages of the *Herald* or the *Star*, the two newspapers she edited in Dominica. Among them are "Babes in the Woods," a poignant tale about Phyllis's separation from her children during the war; "Scraps of Paper," the story of a young man returning to England from the United States after the war to trace information about his dead mother (Allfrey's children had been evacuated to the United States during the Blitz); "Sitting Around in London," about the Popular Front's efforts to prevent the fall of Barcelona; "Dancing With George," a story of misunderstandings and conflicting cultural and gender values concerning a young American soldier and a married but lonely young English woman; "The Spirit Portrait," a light-hearted tale (subtitled "A Wartime Anecdote") about a psychic friend who tried to make a living by painting portraits of the dead at seances; "At the House of the Countess," the story of two little girls forced to leave their stately home, which is being converted into a nursing home; and perhaps the best among them, "Tea With the Bishop," the richly nuanced, heart-rending portrait of an aging and frustrated social worker and her problematic charge.

writer. The book would never be sent to another publisher, and except for her autobiographical work about her experiences as a minister in the West Indies Federation, *In the Cabinet*, and a handful of short stories and poems, her writing would never again rise to the level of her best work in the 1940s and early 1950s. What she opted for, instead, was to live the life she had invented for Joan, the political activist daughter in *The Orchid House*.

The publication of *The Orchid House*—or rather the advance she received for the novel—made possible Allfrey's return to Dominica on holiday after an absence of twenty-one years. While there, her husband Robert secured an engineering job with the L. Rose Lime Company, which allowed them to remain on the island indefinitely. Allfrey returned to her home island at a critical juncture in its political history. A new constitution had granted universal adult suffrage in 1951, but there were no political parties in place, no effort had been made to organize the electorate, and elections continued to be dominated by the mulatto gros bourg. Immediately after her return—and feeling certain that the party system offered the surest path to socialism in the newly opened electoral process—Allfrey gravitated to the Dominica Trade Union (DTU) as the ideal vehicle from which a political party—Dominica's first—could emerge. She found in DTU president Christopher Loblack, a local mason she had met in London in 1949, a political soulmate. Together they began traveling to near and remote villages, explaining to gatherings of DTU members and supporters the manifest advantages of allying themselves to a party committed to furthering the worker's socioeconomic agenda.

The Dominica Labour Party was officially launched on May 24, 1955. Its socialist platform, which would guide a new era in Dominican politics, promised to "secure for the workers by hand or by brain the full fruits of their industry and the best obtainable system of popular administration and control of each industry and/or service."[9] The DLP was to dominate political life on the island until 1980, when a second party Allfrey had helped found, the Dominica Freedom Party, came to power. From 1955 to 1957 (when the party participated in its first general election), Allfrey dedicated all her time, resources, and strength to increasing its membership. This required exhausting treks across muddy paths and impassable roads to reach small villages where she would tirelessly explain the rudiments of democratic, parliamentary politics, and would encourage the peasantry, in speeches peppered with patois, to join the party's struggle to change Dominican politics. She is credited by political friends and foes alike with having almost single-handedly educated the Dominican peasantry in the principles of democracy.

Allfrey, a committed Federalist, eagerly welcomed the inauguration of the West Indies Federation in 1958. She believed wholeheartedly in the benefits it would bring to the "smiders," the small islanders who could benefit the most from a closer association with the more prosperous and economically developed islands like Jamaica and Trinidad. In the first Federal elections, she was elected by an overwhelming 77 percent of the vote as one of the two Dominican representatives to the Federal Parliament, and became Minister of Social and Labour Affairs, the only woman and the only white in the Cabinet.

Her years in the Federation led to the sacrifice of her literary career. Her journals and appointment diaries show tireless activity on behalf of the Federation—speeches to women's groups (a favorite activity where she would promote her feminist ideals); and schemes to improve health, employment, and housing; a keen interest in the welfare of children; and travels to the independence celebrations in Nigeria and to an International Labour Organisation conference in Geneva where she joined the first walkout in opposition to the racist policies of the South African government. The collapse of the Federation in 1962 was a blow that she felt with bitterness to the end of her life.

Thus in 1962 the Allfreys and the two children they had adopted during her tenure as Federal Minister—an Afro-Dominican girl named Sonia and a Carib boy named David— left Trinidad, the federal capital, and returned to Dominica, where she became editor of the *Dominica Herald*, and where they soon adopted a second Carib boy, Robbie. With elections forthcoming in late 1962 and the party's victory assured, it was expected that Allfrey, as founder, president, and political leader of the party, would become the island's next Chief Minister. But an editorial in the *Herald* critical of the Labour government's tax on banana exports led to her controversial expulsion from the party, an expulsion widely believed to have been racially motivated.

In 1965, Allfrey and her husband began publication of an opposition paper, the *Star*, which was to become the government's severest critic. Allfrey created a poetic persona, Rose O (a pun on Roseau, the island's capital), through which she would echo the people's anger and impatience with the Labour government's growing disregard for democracy and the law. As Rose O, Allfrey published often hilarious, clever satires on Dominican politics, frequently recreating local speech, and sometimes writing in the local French patois. In 1968, in an effort to silence her and the other two local newspaper editors, the government passed the Seditious Publications Act, which opened the way for criminal prosecution of newspaper editors who printed articles critical of government policies. Allfrey helped channel public outrage against the Act into the foundation of the Freedom Party, which eventually elected Eugenia Charles as Chief Minister in 1980.

Allfrey's journalistic and political work—coupled with the responsibility of three young children and the economic difficulties that would plague her to the end of her life—left little time for writing. She would occasionally publish a new story in the *Star* or would try her hand at a new chapter of her autobiographical work about the Federation years, *In the Cabinet*, but these efforts were never sustained. Her fourth volume of poetry, *Palm and Oak II*, appeared in 1973, but except for a handful of new poems (notably "Trio by Lamplight," written for her son David, and "The Child's Return," dedicated to Jean Rhys, with whom she had renewed a correspondence during the 1970s and to whom she assiduously sent the *Star*), it chiefly included work reprinted from earlier books or poems scattered in journals and newspapers and not previously collected. In the early 1970s, in an effort to reestablish her literary career, Allfrey resumed work on *In the Cabinet*, but at her death it remained unfinished and unpublished. Its completion was delayed by constant and tireless work on the *Star*, which provided the Allfreys a meager income, and by repeated personal tragedies which

included the death of their daughter Phina in a car accident in
Botswana, her son Philip's mental illness and continued con-
finement in a psychiatric hospital, their own worsening poverty, and the destruction of their modest home by hurricane
David in 1979.

Allfrey died in 1986, destitute and virtually ignored by her
countrymen.

▓ Phyllis Allfrey wrote very little that could not be directly
linked to her own life, and this is particularly true of *The Orchid House*, where she came closer to her own autobiography
than in any other work. In the story of three daughters of
an impoverished white Creole family she interweaves her
own family's history with that of the island of Dominica in the
twentieth century. "The idea of *The Orchid House* had been
simmering in my heart for several years," she wrote shortly after the novel's publication. "The big leap was transferring it from
my heart to the mind, and then to paper, without damaging
the simple emotional language of the narrator, a 'book-taught
English-speaking negress.' Every time I began a new day's work
I had to vault the Atlantic Ocean and land in the Caribbean
Sea, and I had to jump out of my own skin and into the hero-
ine, Lally's."[10]

The Orchid House stems directly from Allfrey's personal
and political experiences of the 1940s and 1950s, during which
she had been a member of the Fabian Colonial Committee, established to aid the territories of the British Empire on their
slow quest for independence. After more than a decade of work
as the committee's liaison to the House of Commons, Allfrey
had a detailed grasp of the forces that were transforming Caribbean politics: the shifting of power towards the working class;
the key role played by labor unions in the development of political parties in the region; the efforts to establish a West Indian Federation; the difficulties awaiting the colonial territories
in establishing independent economies after attaining domin-
ion status; and the increasingly resonant calls for full independence. Allfrey's political work had been aimed at securing for
the islands of the West Indies a meaningful independence which
guaranteed the working classes a central role in the new au-

tonomous governments ready to take over the reins of power from the colonial bureaucracy.

Yet Allfrey, an inveterate romantic, held to a sentimental vision of the world of her childhood, which in her eyes still retained a rare beauty and provided the links to West Indian history so important to her identity. Part of her had clung with tenacity to the sights, sounds, and smells of her birthplace. She once claimed that while writing *The Orchid House* she had only to close her eyes to be home in an instant; "and the rich, oily scent of a squeezed lime would evoke a whole trail of images and possibilities."[11] Her political education, however, had taught her the evils harbored within that idyllic natural world, and she knew full well that it must give way to the politically just society she and her fellow West Indian socialists envisioned. This apparent contradiction she resolved in a Janus-like work which looked back with nostalgia at a world about to disappear, while depicting the process through which its death could be expedited. *The Orchid House*, its lyrical celebration of Dominica's magnificent natural beauty notwithstanding, is a forward-looking text. The solution it proposes is not a perpetuation of a romantic attachment to the landscape and the past but an alliance between labor and the sympathetic remnants of the white upper class as the means towards social justice.

The novel, as narrated by the old nurse Lally, revolves around the return of three Creole sisters to their native island after years abroad: Stella, drawn to the lush tropical landscape by an impassioned yearning; Joan, a grass-roots political activist in London; and Natalie, a wealthy old man's hedonistic young widow. Lally reminisces upon their carefree childhood, shattered by their father's return from service in World War I suffering from a severe case of shell shock. His consequent addiction to drug-laced cigarettes has depleted the family's resources, and the once-wealthy family had tottered on the brink of financial disaster until Natalie's money restored to them their old estate, L'Aromatique.

Stella, in rebellion against the apathy with which her mother and her old French tutor Mademoiselle Bosquet accept her father's drug-induced listlessness, orchestrates the death of the drug supplier; consequently, fearful of growing suspicions of her role in the murder, she returns to the United States, defeated in her purpose to bring about change and leaving behind the prospect of despair when her father's current supply of cigarettes runs out. Joan arrives in her turn, bent on assisting Baptiste, the son of the family's long-time cook, in organizing a labor reform movement in the island. Her pragmatic political vision contrasts sharply with Stella's overly sentimental view of the island as a wondrous garden of beauty and decay. Where her elder sister sees only the astounding resplendence of vegetation in profusion, Joan sees poverty, corruption, exploitation, the mere shifting of power from white to colored elites. Her efforts to organize the peasantry into a union soon draw the wrath of the Catholic authorities, and she is blackmailed into relinquishing her work under threat of disclosure of evidence linking her sister Stella to the drug dealer's murder. Natalie, the youngest of the sisters, brings her nonchalant vivacity and the money to expedite change. "Ah, it's essential to be rich," she argues. "All these drippings and dronings and reformations, they don't get you anywhere without good solid cash!" Her money pays Joan's husband's passage to Dominica, making possible the continuation of her sister's dream of political reform.

In *The Orchid House*, Allfrey attempted a sweeping exposition of her own understanding of the Caribbean historical process. Everything in her experiences in the early 1950s, personal and political, pointed to a crossroads: her own as she severs her emotional ties to England and prepares to return home and the West Indies' as the region moves from colonialism to independence. *The Orchid House* is set at this crossroads and is built upon Allfrey's recognition that both she and her novel stand at the intersection of West Indian political history where former colonies assume control of their political and economic destinies and where, through their fledgling union-based parties, the black masses take over the reins of political control. *The Orchid House* is thus the chronicle of a society at a turning point, an exploration of the past that aims at unveiling options for its political redirection. It is thus that its narrator, Lally, the symbolic repository of a past the island is rapidly leaving behind, becomes a seminal part of Allfrey's exploration of Dominican history, a living reminder of the path that society has trod. In choosing her old black nurse, "the linchpin of her life," as the narrator of her novel, she opted for a spokesperson solidly bound to the status quo, one who serves both as a sounding board against which Allfrey plays several fictional recreations of herself and as a standard against which the characters' and the society's evolution can be measured. Lally can recall the various fictional versions of Allfrey's self to their roots, while she witnesses, at times in bewildered acceptance, what their society has become.

The nature of the exploration of the past we find in *The Orchid House* owes much to the influence of Alain-Fournier's 1913 novel *Le Grand Meaulnes*, a neoromantic work Allfrey had been encouraged to read by Martin Turnell, the young Anglican rector who had tutored her in religion and mathematics. *Le Grand Meaulnes* chronicles the adventures of three young friends as they search for lost love and lost time in a style reminiscent of medieval quest narratives and fairy tales. It is characterized by "a sort of poetry of regret for lost innocence and vanished enchantment."[12] Its influence on *The Orchid House* is felt as much on the structure as on the style. Fournier, like Allfrey a deeply autobiographical writer, had sought to come "as close as he [could] to his own personal life" in his work, creating characters to embody various aspects of himself. Many critics have seen his protagonist, Seurel, as "only one aspect of an ideal protagonist formed by three persons: the memory-haunted narrator Seurel, the Quixotic Augustin Meaulnes, and the enigmatic Frantz de Galais."* *Le Grand Meaulnes*, like *The Orchid House*, is a novel dominated "by

---

* Martin Turnell would in time publish an extensive critical article on *Le Grand Meaulnes*, usually included among the definitive studies of the novel, in which he examines Alain-Fournier's use of "doubles" and the curious mixture of romantic evocation and down-to-earth realism of the novel, a study that points to the tantalizing speculation that he may have discussed these issues at length with his pupil, aiding young Allfrey towards a deeper understanding of *Le Grand Meaulnes* that even a perceptive young reader would have reached on her own. His assessment of the novel underscores aspects of form and style that Allfrey would replicate in *The Orchid House*. "We find in the novel what the French call *dédoublement*," Turnell wrote, "which means we are looking at life simultaneously under two different and usually conflicting aspects. It is the story of a great adventure in which we move at times in an enchanted world, but we are conscious all the time of a sense of fragility and underlaying menace. Once a

memory, and the continuance of sensations which were most deeply held in childhood" but have to give way to the realities of adulthood and history. It is also a book dominated, as Allfrey's would be, by the persona of the storyteller, by the unifying voice of a narrator attempting to explain things beyond his understanding and clinging to the past as the only comforting and safe space.

Like Alain-Fournier in *Le Grand Meaulnes*, Allfrey constructs her novel around two characters modeled on seemingly contradictory aspects of her own personality. Stella, to whom Allfrey apportions her own experiences in the United States, reflects the prepolitical Allfrey, the one firmly entrenched in the Dominica of the past, thoroughly one with the landscape, passionately connected to its nature, but oblivious to the sociopolitical changes taking place around her. Joan, the English Allfrey, transformed by politics, sees a return to the past as both immoral and intolerable and believes that a legitimate role in their home society is only possible for the family if it embraces the people's efforts to take charge of their own political and economic destinies. She underscores what had become a central tenet of Allfrey's political thoughts about the Caribbean: that profound changes must take place in the power structures of Caribbean societies to bring social justice to bear, and that those who persevere in seeking to revive the past are doomed. Lally, a politically unschooled observer, gave Allfrey the perfect foil for the presentation of the world she was attempting to depict in the novel—that of the struggle between a nostalgic yearning for a world gone by and the pressing need to do away with the old.

Allfrey's choice of Lally as a narrator would become the focus of critical controversy. Early reviewers would argue that it resulted in some awkward technical difficulties as she tried to maintain the narrative within Lally's limited scope. West Indian reviewers would take her to task for appropriating the voice of

---

peak has been passed the atmosphere becomes more and more threatening as the magic is gradually dissipated by the sense of disenchantment, the fading of dreams and hopes, the sudden plunge from an earthly paradise into something like an earthly hell" (Martin Turnell, "Alain-Fournier and *Le Grand Meaulnes*," *Southern Review* 2:3 [Summer 1966]: 477–498).

a black woman for her narrative. "Lally's character," Anthony Boxill once wrote, "is . . . embarrassing. She is too slavishly faithful to her employers, and too sentimentally portrayed to be quite credible."[13] *The Orchid House*, given the politics of identity that dominated Caribbean criticism in the 1950s and 1960s, was read "racially," that is, its author's whiteness guided its reading and determined its early fortunes. Hence Stella's passionate romanticism and Lally's obdurate resistance to join the wave of political change are seen as emblematic of Allfrey's "conservatism"; the solution to the political impasse proposed by Joan, the core of which was the growing movement towards unionization and labor-controlled political development in the region, gets lost in early (and even in recent) readings. And Lally—whose perspective as "the last of the slaves" in a novel about the empowerment of the black population is that of the quintessential outsider—becomes "a representative of the black race" who "on occasion sound[s] a bit like a colonial lackey longing for the good old days of the Empire."[14]

However, Lally, because she represents those notions which Joan must help dispel if working-class Dominicans are to transcend their present state, was central to Allfrey's story. As Joan struggles for a relationship of equality with those who, like Lally and Baptiste, had grown too accustomed to treating whites as their social superiors, she must contend with the privilege of whiteness that Lally still holds dear and which prompts Natalie to refer to her in jest as "an early Victorian white spinster." It is through striving to understand Joan's political perspective that Lally begins to question the truth of her own social and political assumptions. Joan's political activism brings to the fore aspects of the society to which Lally had been oblivious: the corruption that rules the economy and political life of the island, the hypocrisy of the press, the repression of the estate workers, and the unyieldingness of the Catholic church. The impact of her calls for a labor union and political participation by the masses is shown in their power to crack, however slightly, Lally's conservatism: "Sooner or later those words would come through to me. . . . All the same, the meaning behind the talk would never come into my possession—nor would their intention. It was no good my craving to be beside them as they strolled away. The things they so often spoke about were outside my understanding. Only later, when their words had turned into acts and results, would I feel the full thunderclap of my ignorance."

Kenneth Ramchand, writing about *The Orchid House* and Jean Rhys's *Wide Sargasso Sea*, speaks of the novels as examples of the "terrified consciousness" that is the "natural stance" of the white West Indian—"the White minority's sensation of shock and disorientation as a massive and smouldering Black population is released into an awareness of its power."[15] Given his prominence as a critic, his commentary has provided the most influential guide to a reading of *The Orchid House*. But to read it so is to misread it, particularly in the light of Allfrey's life and political convictions. The "terrified consciousness" Ramchand describes is the product of alienation, of a failure to belong, and the Shands and Nichollses were always certain they belonged. Allfrey's uncle Ralph Nicholls certainly was, which is why Rufus, his fictional counterpart, is so important to our understanding of the text. Rufus has given himself to the island, and mercenary and unprincipled as he may seem, he has renounced the privileges of whiteness for himself and his children, bridging the racial gap and giving up some of the prerogatives in the island's racial hierarchy that would naturally have been his as a white man. As Joan insists, the whites are no longer the enemy. They have no money and consequently no power—some of them are not even interested in remaining white. Their social world has slowly given way under the siege of the aspirations of the colored elite, but that has not meant an improvement in the peasantry's lot: " . . . the coloured merchants, the educated people," Joan tells Cornélie, "are taking the responsibility over from us—we are now the poor whites, we no longer have any power. But I don't notice any greater tenderness in their attitudes towards those landless, shoeless devils."

Rufus would be a particularly sympathetic character were he not so willing to serve the unlikely villain of the piece, Father Toussaint, a character modeled quite realistically on Bishop James Moris, the Roseau prelate who, in fifty years spent in Dominica, had accumulated a remarkable measure of secular power. Allfrey was never shy about attributing Dominica's ills to the tyranny of "300 years of Catholic morality,"[16] and in *The Orchid House* the church emerges as the most conservative and powerful force in Dominica. "The gentlemen over in Whitehall believed that they were governing our island," Lally observes. "That was not the case. Father Toussaint and Master Rufus were the real rulers. People challenged them now and again, but those people always lost." Father Toussaint is a character remarkable in his Jesuitical awareness of his power to control lives and societies. The pivotal confrontation in the novel between him and Joan—"the two cleverest people in the island"— reveals in a masterly way Allfrey's awareness of the true nature of Dominica's power structure. The bargain struck in the priest's shadow-filled room—where Joan "promised not to engage personally in political activity in the island . . . and to devote [herself] to [her] husband and child," a promise she means to fulfill "to the letter" by having her husband assume her political work—is defended by Joan as politically expedient: "Lally, can't you see that unless people like Father Toussaint and Baptiste and me come to some sort of rough understanding, there's no hope for the world?"

When examined in the light of its author's biography, *The Orchid House* seems like an extraordinary work of prophecy, a blueprint for Allfrey's own fledgling political career. Within two years of its publication, when Allfrey was busily engaged in a political campaign in Dominica, a friend will remark in astonishment that she seemed to have fallen into the plot of her own novel. That it would seem so attests not to any gift for divination, but to the clearsightedness of the novel's analysis of the Dominican historical crossroads. If *The Orchid House* establishes anything with great clarity it is that by 1952, while still in exile in England, Allfrey had her finger firmly placed on the pulse of her island's political and social ills.

Lizabeth Paravisini-Gebert

Notes

1. Kenneth Ramchand, "Terrified Consciousness," *Journal of Commonwealth Literature* 7 (1969): 8–19.
2. Gordon K. Lewis, *The Growth of the Modern West Indies* (New York: Monthly Review Press, 1968), 159.
3. Alexander Hoyos, "The Valiant Woman," *The Vincentian*, 21 February 1986.
4. Graham Stroude, "W.I. Woman Dedicated to Politics: Pen Portrait of Phyllis Allfrey," *The West Indian*, 21 March 1961, 2.
5. Interview with Arnold Active, 6 July 1991.
6. Interview with Lorna Robinson, 10 August 1993.
7. Phyllis Shand Allfrey to Elaine Campbell, undated.
8. Polly Pattullo, "Phyllis Shand Allfrey Talking With Polly Pattullo," in *Writing Lives: Conversations Between Women Writers*, ed. Mary Chamberlain (London: Virago, 1988), 230.
9. Constitution of the Dominica Labour Party (1955).
10. "The Author's Name Is . . . Phyllis Shand Allfrey," unidentified clipping in the Allfrey Archives (Roseau, Dominica).
11. Ibid.
12. David Paul, "The Mysterious Landscape: A Study of Alain-Fournier," *Cornhill Magazine* 162: 972 (Autumn 1947): 449.
13. Anthony Boxill, "The Novel in English in the West Indies 1900–1962" (Ph.D. diss., University of New Brunswick, 1966), 265.
14. Ibid.
15. Ramchand, 225.
16. Phyllis Shand Allfrey to Robert Edward Allfrey, undated.

The Orchid House

The island exists, but all the characters with whom I have populated it are creatures of my imagination.

For permission to quote from a poem by Daniel Thaly, I am indebted to the courtesy of M. Léon Bocquet of Editions "Le Beffroi".

The Days  Before

Madame and ❋ CHAPTER 1
the Master

Madam came to see me this afternoon, bringing the news with her and my few shillings which she has always been faithful to give me, even when there was hardly any money in the house. For a long time now there has hardly been enough money to pay Christophine her wages with, hardly enough to set aside for Mr. Lilipoulala when the mail boat comes in. But now that Miss Natalie's husband is dead and she is rich, Madam and the Master have sold the town house and paid their bills. Miss Natalie has bought Old Master's estate and given it to her parents, but she has done all that in a letter, she has not yet come to see them. And the other children are far away: Miss Stella is in America and Miss Joan is in England.

This is the first time that Madam has come downhill since they moved to L'Aromatique, and this is the first time that I have seen the look of happiness on her face since Miss Natalie's wedding. I would not say that Madam's was ever a sad face, for sadness is not in her nature. She has lived most of her life in the sun here, and her face is just a little brown and not lined, like the faces of visitors from cities, and her hair is that black-brown with only about six white hairs. It is hard for us all to believe that Madam is a grandmother. It was hard enough for me to believe, twenty-eight years ago, that Madam was a mother.

They told me that the young lady at Maison Rose was looking for a nurse for her first baby, but I had some trouble finding my way there. I had come fresh from Montserrat in my middle years, and being an English Negress and proud of my skin, not Frenchy and Catholic and boasting of a drop of white blood, like Christophine, I could not understand the talk of this island very well. At last I found the Maison Rose, and when I pulled the garden gate open a big bell clanged and a young lady in plaits came out on the balcony and smiled. So I went up the stone steps into her drawing-room, for this was not a proud lady at all, who would keep you downstairs in the hall as if you were a beggar. Then I asked to see the Madam, and she said to me, "I am the Madam here". But I still didn't believe her, so she went into another room and came back with a basket in her arms, and in the basket was a little baby—that was Miss Stella. I looked into the basket: I could see that it had come from abroad and wasn't made by the Caribs, and there lying on a little cushion was the prettiest girl child I had ever seen. Then this young lady lifted her baby out of the basket in a very awkward way, so that I couldn't help taking the baby from her and showing her how to do it properly. From that moment I loved Madam and I loved Miss Stella and I knew that I would not leave them until they did not need me any longer.

Christophine and I used to have words at first. Christophine had been cook at Maison Rose since the wedding day, and she favored the Master, but right from the start I could see that the Master would be difficult and bring trouble, I could have told them all about this long before the war took him away and long before he came back as he did.

※ Madam sat down in my one-room house and told me why she was happy. "Lally, the children are coming home to visit us," she said. "Imagine, Lally, after all this while we shall see the children again. For many weeks we have been making plans, and letters have been passing between us. And now it seems to be coming true."

"It's a long while," I said.

"But you know the reasons," Madam said. "You know the reasons, Lally."

Madam was right. I knew all the reasons; for she had never kept anything from me. I knew that Miss Stella and Miss Joan had married poor men and had babies, and Miss Natalie had married rich old Sir Godfrey, but before she could even have a baby the awful thing had happened, the car had gone over the cliff and Sir Godfrey had died.

"And how are you feeling, Lally?" asked Madam. "A little stronger?"

"I never felt better," I told her. For I guessed what she was going to ask of me, and joy took away the ache in my stomach and the stiffness in my legs. I would nurse Madam's grandchildren before I died. I would see Miss Stella and Miss Joan and Miss Natalie again.

"I have brought a little bottle of wine," said Madam. "Have you got two glasses?" I was delighted to show Madam how many glasses I had in my cupboard, even the china cockatoo Miss Joan had given me was still there, and every empty medicine bottle that the Old Master had prescribed for me. Madam looked up and saw Old Master's picture, cut out of the newspaper and pasted above the cupboard, and she said: "Christophine has stuck him between the Virgin Mary and St. Joseph, but I'm not sure that he doesn't look better by himself."

"He was always a one to be by himself," said I.

"Lally," said Madam, after we had sipped our wine and sat thinking for a few moments about old things, "the girls want you to come up to L'Aromatique and nurse their children while they are there. They say that they would not trust the little boys to anyone but you. Do you feel that you can manage this? It's a long time, remember, since you and I have had little children to care for. Please do not be sad, Lally, if you don't feel strong enough to do it."

"I could do it, and easily, Madam," I said, "if Baptiste would help me." (Baptiste is Christophine's son: a gawky sullen boy, but handy. It is he who brings me the few shillings every week, and news of the family.)

Madam was glad that I felt able to come. She went away after a short while, leaving me the half-bottle of wine to hearten me up against seeing the children. I put the bottle into my sewing-bag that I used to carry their torn underclothes in, and I latched my little one-room house door and walked out slowly by the hibiscus hedge and through the gates of the botanical gardens. And there I sat under the big shack-shack tree, on the same bench which was there all those years ago. Mimi Zacariah and I used to sit there and watch our children at play while we chatted and sewed, for Mimi Zacariah was nurse to Master Andrew. Now I sat there under the shack-shack tree, thinking about a great many things that I had kept out of my mind for many a month, and every now and again I drank a little out of the bottle.

Mimi Zacariah is dead, and many others have married strangers and gone away, but Master Andrew is still in the island, living at Petit Cul-de-Sac, or all that's left of him is. Mimi and I used to have some great fights and rivalries over our children. She would say that Master Andrew was the most beautiful child in the Islands, with his brown eyes and dark curls, and I would say that it was not so exceptional to have curls and brown eyes in a place where brown eyes and curls were too ordinary for beauty, and I would call Miss Stella to me and stroke her hair; I would say that thank goodness there was no danger of any curlyheads in Madam and the Master's family. But Mimi and I both agreed that it would be nice for Master Andrew to marry one of my children some day, perhaps Miss Stella, who was exactly his age, or little Miss Natalie, who followed him around like a puppy. Miss Joan and Master Andrew would hit and kick and scratch each other to rags whenever they got the chance. Before Mimi died last year I went to see her and I told her as she lay dying that there never was such a beautiful boy in the whole world as Master Andrew. I told her that he would get better of his sickness and marry a nice young lady, but I do not think that she heard me, for she lay with shut eyes and never spoke again.

The children used to call the Botanical Gardens "the Station". That was because the only trains they had ever seen were toy trains, and as they had never seen a railway station they thought it must be the best and most exciting place in the world. They would say that Mimi Zacariah and I were the trains which brought the children to the Station and took them away again just when they were beginning to enjoy themselves. I don't expect that I shall ever see a train or a station in this life, but still I think that no station could be as beautiful as these gardens spread out under the hill, with the mountains blue behind that, and the nurseries of young plants and vanilla and cocoa trees running all the way up the hollow to the middle of the hill. At this very moment Miss Stella and Miss Joan will be walking in snow and fog, but in these gardens there are only two trees which drop their leaves, and though sometimes in the drought season the grass is yellow and brown, mostly this is a green, green place splashed over with jewel flower colours.

I can see how beautiful it is, now that I am old and have a tumour inside me that Old Master would greatly have enjoyed lifting out in that brand-new operating-room. But there's nobody going to get me to cross that threshold modern or not. I would have gone to him in those early days, when they do say that he amputated legs with a kitchen knife until the equipment started coming: and only one case of blood-poisoning and one case of gangrene against him, in spite of all. But Old Master is gone, and I'll be nursing my complaint to the grave sooner than be looked over by one of these young whipper-snappers. When I was nurse to the little girls, I had no time to fall ill or to see how beautiful everything was. And anyhow, when you are working for white people whom you love, you can only think of those people and their wants, you hardly notice anything else. I did not even pay any attention to my own people, the black people, in those days, but now I am observing them and seeing what is happening to them. I am seeing how poor they are, and how the little babies have stomachs swollen with arrowroot and arms and legs spotted with disease. That was something which Old Master saw and fought against right from the moment that he stepped onto the jetty in his panama hat for the first time. He never forgot. When he brought his English and American friends who dropped in from their yachts or pleasure cruises to look at his orchids and these gardens, Old Master would say to them seriously, "Come and see the other side of the picture. Come into the back alleys." I do not think the visitors cared to see the back alleys, especially when they had ladies with them who were all dressed up in beautiful clothes.

No lady ever had more beautiful dresses than the American lady who took Miss Stella away to America. Oh, what a lovely face she had too, better and kinder than the face on Christophine's Virgin from Lourdes! It all happened in such an easy, quick way. Old Master showed them the gardens: Old Master walked with his man-friend, and Miss Stella walked beside the man-friend's daughter, as she was the eldest grandchild, and the American lady was quite young. So while Miss Stella walked beside the strange young lady, an understanding came up between them, and they sat on the grass, and the American lady asked Miss Stella about her life, and Miss Stella said: "I am very unhappy, I would like to go away, please help me to get away soon." Then Miss Stella told the American lady about Mr. Lilipoulala.

I remember the first day that the children were frightened of anything. We passed the carpenter's workshop, and the one-eyed carpenter who was paralysed sat in the doorway. Miss Joan was skipping along in front of me and the other two were following behind us, like little ducks, all dressed in white muslin with white muslin hats on, lined with red silk to keep off the sunstroke. Suddenly Miss Joan saw the one-eyed carpenter; she stopped and screamed. She sat down in the dust of the road outside that shop, staring at him and screaming. The other two came up and stood there looking afraid. "Don't you cry, Miss Joan," I said. "It's only Papa Poulet, the carpenter. He can't help looking that way." "He looks like that because he's wicked," cried Miss Joan. "Oh, no, he doesn't," said Miss Stella—but she was frightened too. Miss Natalie was too young to do anything but cry. "Get up, Joan; Grandfather will fix Papa Poulet up," said Miss Stella. But Miss Joan said that her grandfather could never fix anyone who was so wicked, who had such a terrible look in his one eye.

With Mr. Lilipoulala it was different: he seemed like a funny man at first. He made the children think of a banana which had been picked and left in the sun, and was covered with black mole-spots. His face was long and yellow and secret, but not ugly, and nobody knew what he was, except that he came from

Port-au-Prince. He was a little short man and wore a black alpaca coat and black trousers, like a lawyer's clerk, and he carried a small black leather bag. The first time he called to see the Master he handed in a little printed card at the door which said: Lilipoulala, Cigarette Merchant. That was many a year ago, and though I have seen Mr. Lilipoulala too often since then for my liking, I don't know any more about him than what it says on the card; I don't even know what the H. stands for.

I only know that I hope with all my heart that he won't be travelling down to see the Master in the same ship as Miss Stella and her little boy. For I think that if Miss Stella saw Mr. Lilipoulala walking the deck in a dim light she would faint clean away and fall through the rails and her little boy would be motherless. But perhaps Miss Stella has grown into someone brave, like her mother. Perhaps she has grown out of the days when she would come sobbing and shuddering into my bed and cry all over my flannel nightgown, telling me that she saw Mr. Lilipoulala coming through the keyhole, that he wasn't a man at all but just an evil spirit wrapped in a banana-skin. I do indeed hope that she has grown as brave as Madam.

Not that it always made me happy to see Madam so brave. I used to think, "Now if Madam for once would be the weak one, and throw a fit, and need to be cherished; if Madam had been the weak one right from the start—right from the moment when I saw her standing there in plaits with Miss Stella in her arms—all of her life and the children's lives would have been different. It may well be that we would never have known Mr. Lilipoulala, and then Miss Stella would never have been frightened."

But there you are, you might as well try to empty the boiling lake or split Rodney's rock in two as to make Madam the weak one. For she has always stood there so staunch and firm that it was natural for weak and selfish people to lean on her; you might indeed say that she invited the leaners. I have been thinking that it is Madam's way not to have mentioned whether Miss Stella and Miss Joan would be coming with their husbands or alone. Alone or together—what would be the difference to Madam? She would not have it thought that her daughters could not stand alone at any time, just as she stood alone all those years when the Master was fighting in the war, and afterwards. She would not have it thought that they needed *men* to be supporting them and caring for them. Without men they would never be, as it was naked to the eye right from their early days. But with or without men they were Madam's daughters, and that means to say that they could be sufficient unto themselves.

I am thinking back to the time when the telegrams used to come in those war days, and when I took upon myself to open them first, so that if the worst one came I could read it out to Madam. "It's only Master Kenneth," I'd say to Madam. Or I'd say: "Master Rufus is wounded. Nothing serious." Or I'd say: "Master David is killed." The three little girls would be hanging at my skirts. But Madam would only give me a stubborn brave look as the envelope was torn open, daring me to tell her everything that she couldn't bear.

When the Master Came Home CHAPTER 2

I remember well enough the day that the Master came home. Miss Stella and Miss Joan were sitting on the flagstones at Maison Rose, playing with their puppy. Miss Joan had bought the puppy the day before, for three shillings and sixpence. Madam had always told them that they could not keep a dog at Maison Rose. "It would be different," Madam would say, "if we lived at L'Aromatique with Grandfather. This garden is too small, too full of flowers and other people's cats and chickens." But the children thought that their mother would not notice the puppy, because of all the excitement.

It was a lovely time of year. The garden walls were covered with white jasmine flowers, thinner and spikier, the tourists said, than the kind which grew in the North. And sweeter to smell. I was busy that morning tidying up the old stables, which were always empty of horses now and were filled instead with old cribs, wine-bottles, a clothes horse and a perambulator. Miss Natalie was asleep under her mosquito net upstairs. The two big ones sat on the baking cobble-stones and played with the puppy, which up to now I had pretended not to see. Mimi Zacariah's sister had sold them the dog. I heard her say to Miss Joan, at the back gate: "Nobody know who he father be, dey say it a dawg got left behind by de mail boat and pick up again next trip. But he mudder me own sometimeish longtail bitch." Madam always used to say that she was glad I was a book-taught English-speaking Negress, who wouldn't let bad words fall like the Zacariah family did, or even Christophine. Christophine was helping out by ironing Madam's underwear while the sweet potatoes were cooking. I could smell the hot flat-irons on the hot coals, and I could hear Christophine groan every now and again: "Jesus! The heat!" And Christophine would wipe the sweat off her forehead with the dampening rag, and she would say: "Holy Christ! The heat!" Baptiste, Christophine's son, crouched by her bare feet pounding green almonds for the dessert.

I saw Miss Stella take advantage of this and steal into the empty kitchen, which she called the black hole of Calcutta, to snatch a little milk for the puppy. She brought the milk out in a sardine tin and put it on the flagstone path. The little dog began to lick at the milk like a clumsy suckling. I stood there leaning on my broom and watching the children and the puppy, knowing that everything would be changed for them in a few hours' time, and wondering how much difference the return of their father would make to them. That was what they were wondering too, for as I stood there watching and listening I heard Miss Stella ask:

"Joan, do you remember Daddy?"

"No," said Miss Joan, tipping up the sardine tin to help the puppy. She looked over to where I stood, but she did not see me. But I could see her square little head, shaped like Madam's, and her green eyes which were smaller than Miss Stella's. She blinked and then she peeled away a scab on her knee. That was Miss Joan: always falling down, and liking it, and trying to make the scars last a long while.

"Did you ever *dream* about him?" asked Miss Stella.

"Lots of times," said Miss Joan. "But in my dreams he is as old as Grandfather."

"I dream, too," said Miss Stella softly.

"But your dreams are always horrible," said Miss Joan.

"If I were to tell you some of my dreams about Daddy," said Miss Stella, "they'd put you off him for ever."

"I wonder why," said Miss Joan, "Daddy didn't come home before? The war has been over for two years, but Daddy just hangs around on the continent and in England, and all of a sudden he remembers that he has a family . . . "

"He may have been mixed up in another fight, a rather private sort of fight that we don't know about," said Miss Stella.

"I suppose," said Miss Joan. And then she said, taking the puppy by its front paws: "Now what shall we call this lovely little dog that I bought for three and sixpence?"

Miss Stella said: "I've thought of two names for him. One is Flanders and the other is Flounders. If Daddy wants to talk about the war, and seems proud of how he rushed around shooting down Germans and Turks, we'll call him Flanders. But if he is rather smashed up—you remember those telegrams, don't you, Joan, about being invalided home and all that?—well, if he is rather a wreck, we'll call the puppy Flounders."

It didn't seem natural to me that the girls should talk this way. So I put down my broom and drove them indoors, saying that I would tell their mother about the puppy if they didn't get tidy for lunch. Just the same, I could not scold them when I remembered that Miss Stella was four years old when she saw her father last, Miss Joan was two and a half, and Miss Natalie was not yet weaned.

▨ I brought Miss Natalie downstairs and helped her into her chair. She was looking very pale, and I was afraid that she would have a sudden attack of malaria and spoil the home-coming. There she sat, like a doll, with her yellow hair dancing round her little white face, begging her sisters to let her play with the puppy after lunch.

Through the green jalousie-blinds of the downstairs dining-room we could see slits of sunlight and we could hear all the sounds and smell all the smells of the island. When the wind came from the bay we could smell the newly-landed cargo at the customs, or the strong fresh perfume of lime-oil and crated oranges waiting to be shipped to New York. The children gobbled up their fish and yam and sliced avocado pear, behaving as if they would like to gobble up the day whole. "Your mother's lying down," I told them. "She's not eating anything yet."

"I never liked this room," said Miss Stella, "since we used it as a schoolroom."

"Thank goodness Mother has given up teaching us," said Miss Joan, swatting a fly and putting it under her glass. "I wish we were coloured and could go to the convent with all the coloured children, instead of having lessons from Mamselle Bosquet and Dr. Caron."

"It's afternoon now," said Miss Natalie's little voice. Miss Natalie couldn't say her r's. The other two made great sport of this. She would say *l* for *r*: she would say, "I'll have some more lice-pudding," and the other two would shout and giggle. As they would not keep still that day, I let them romp around until they got hot and tired, and then I sent them up for their afternoon rest. The two younger ones lay down obediently in their cool bedrooms, but Miss Stella took the puppy in her arms and sat among the ferns on the bottomless well.

Once long ago when the French owned the island they had sunk this well, and it was Miss Stella's fancy to say that it was magic. It was firmly planked over and covered with plants, but Miss Stella said that she could see the black water through a crack and that one day a waterspirit would burst the planks and enchant the whole household. Whenever she wanted to make a wish she would walk around this well seven times and eat some fern-seed. I took my needlework outside and sat near to Miss Stella so that she couldn't get into mischief. We sat perfectly still, and suddenly I heard a soft swishing sound through the hot stillness: it was Madam brushing her hair, at her dressing-table under the window.

"Dear me," said Miss Stella, "I thought that she had brushed her hair and done it up already."

"It's because your father thinks Madam's hair is very beautiful," I said, not knowing how much I could say to Miss Stella.

"Oh, I know about *that*," said Miss Stella. "Christophine says she heard him say that it was the mane of a proud black racehorse."

"Christophine's tongue is as long as the hangman's rope," I said.

"Well, don't get angry, Lally," said Miss Stella. "I expect he meant it as a compliment."

All this while the neighbours and people from all over the island had been coming to Madam with flowers and other little presents to show her their gladness that she would not be without her man any longer. Early in the morning I had to tie some rags over the bell-clapper at the back gate, because it was making a noise like Easter Sunday. When Coralita-bigmouth brought the *fraises* from Laudat wrapped in a dashine leaf, she said to Christophine, who liked to talk low talk with her: "Tisn't fittin' for a young madam to be only taken up with her children, and contrariwise it's a good time for makin' boys after a war." But now there was a hush in the streets, the people were resting from the heat. Christophine was snoring in the kitchen, lying on the broad shelf under the dresser, her head among the pots and pans, her feet on a sack of potatoes.

"Of course, I've read lots of stories," said Miss Stella, "about a princely bridegroom who had been to battle, and a princess waiting on a rock or in a turret, combing out her hair . . . "

"Don't jump to hard on the well-planks," I said. "One of these days there'll be a rotten board, and you'll go through the hole, and what will happen then to your adventures in foreign lands that you are always planning to have when you grow up, Miss Stella?"

Miss Stella would not listen to me; she kept on jumping. But soon we heard a voice from above, and saw Madam looking out from the balcony, and she was all too much like the same young Madam I saw when Miss Stella was newly-born. Only she was cross. "Lally," she said irritably, "as soon as the little ones wake, get all the children dressed and take them out. Take them to the library. Anywhere. Stella! Stop jumping up and down on that dangerous thing." Then Madam saw the puppy. "Wherever did you get that little dog from, my dear?" she asked Miss Stella in a different voice.

I could tell that Miss Stella was struggling with herself.

She couldn't trust her own disposition yet. It sometimes came to me that Miss Stella did not think so much of loyalty.

"Joan bought it," said Miss Stella.

"Joan shouldn't have done that," said Madam. "You know I said that we had to choose between flowers and creatures."

"We thought you just meant chickens," said Miss Stella.

"Well, don't let him wander among the new slips I have just laid out. Put him into the big chicken-coop until we decide what to do about it. I don't want him in the newly-cleaned house."

Miss Stella set the puppy down on a pile of straw in the chicken-house which was now only used to keep turkeys in for the Christmas fattening. "Mother will come round when she sees how sweet he is and how few fleas he has," she said to me. She latched the wire door and went upstairs, hanging on to the rails which were covered with glossy vines. I went after her and tied on her hair-ribbon which she had dropped in the ferns. We were in the drawing-room, and I noticed that the slats in the walls needed dusting. The way those French builders had made the walls was peculiar enough. They had cut bits out in patterns so that the breeze could filter through and so that everybody could hear everybody talk in the next room, and goodness knows it was not designed for a stout woman as I was even then, and a feather duster.

"Lally, shall I tell you what I plan to be when I grow up?" asked Miss Stella. But this was nothing out of the ordinary; for every day she had some new idea or the other about her future. And if I didn't listen to her it would hurt her feelings. "Perhaps, after all," said Miss Stella, "I'll be a saintly sort of missionary and run a mission for seamen in Malta, leading poor sailors like the ones in H.M.S. *Resolution* (you remember that poor terrible one under the palm tree, Lally?)—away from drunkenness into grace. Let's see, I'd need a large hall full of tables and chairs, a piano (Joan could play the piano), lots of glasses and gallons of milk and lemonade. And some cheese straws. The rest would be easy. I'd change my name to Eve Darcy. And always wear white. But later on, after I'd reformed thousands of sailors and Malta had grown very dull, I'd have a chance to be wicked. By then I'd be very old, and people would call me an old witch, and I'd slink past to work my spells . . . "

I was not paying much attention to this silly wild talk of Miss Stella's, because I could see that one of Madam's Crown Derby vases was over-full of flowers, and would crash over in another moment. I took out a large spray of coralita to lighten it, and then I saw that the wedding picture still stood behind the vase. There was Madam, a gipsy in white satin, and the Master, good-looking and blond and haughty, a little bored, holding his top hat in a small frail hand. I took the picture and slipped it under my apron, and afterwards I put it away in my own tin trunk.

✻ That was the longest day of my life, I do honestly believe. The children took ages over changing into their afternoon dresses. Miss Natalie was fretful. You just had to look at her and she would cry a little, and then her face had to be washed again. I put the thermometer into her mouth as she stood there waiting for me to button up her frock behind and tie her sash. Now that I think of it, it always came natural to Miss Natalie to stand still and have things done for her. But her temperature was normal. So I tightened the elastic which kept Miss Joan's straw hat in place, and I let the puppy out and we started off, and it always seemed that we were some sort of procession, like the Corpus Christi when Olivet is a Child of Mary. Miss Stella walked first with her head in the air, and after her Miss Joan, leading the puppy on a string, and after that I came along, short of breath even in those days, and holding on to my white pique skirt came little Miss Natalie.

On that day, as he sometimes did, young Baptiste clanged the gate behind him and followed slowly after us. He had a book in his hand. Miss Joan was forever lending him her books against my wishes, for the dirt of that kitchen was not fit for *Little Arthur's History* or the *Red Fairy Book* or *Sylvie and Bruno*. I was tired of scolding her about this, so I let it pass now and again. But I always took the books from him when I caught him at it, and breathed on them and rubbed them with my apron. "You'll put him outside himself," I used to tell Miss Joan. "Encouraging a black boy to read so much."

"He reads better than I do," Miss Joan would answer. "He doesn't even like all our books. He says they're silly."

"The insolence of him, complaining about your English godmother's birthday presents," I'd say. But Miss Joan would reply: "I think they're silly too, sometimes."

She always seemed to know when he was coming up alongside, though his bare feet made no noise, and she would wait for him and slip another book into his hand: he would pass his over to her and run off. But once he thought I was far enough away for him to linger, and I heard him say in a disrespectful manner, "Haven't you got anything *real*?"

"No, but I'll borrow something good from Miss Rebecca and sneak it into the kitchen," Miss Joan said. I made a big disturbance that time, and reported Baptiste to his mother, who gave him a proper flogging.

It was natural for the people in the streets to speak their mind aloud as we passed, and to say that Miss Stella's legs were like matchsticks, and how she favoured her father and the little one favoured St. Agnes in the holy pictures, but the middle one, that was Miss Joan, she was Madam's own daughter except for her hair. They were all observing us hard that day because they all knew that the Master was coming home, and they had plenty to say, and there were some words I hoped the children would not understand. Well, we were heading for that library which the American millionaire had given to the islanders, and filled up with books of his own choice, but after a while Miss Rebecca who was put there to manage it, she took out a lot of the books and had them burnt or thrown in the sea, beginning with a gentleman called Tolstoy and running through all the German-sounding books during the war, and so on. But we never went there to bother about books. We went there because the library was built almost on the edge of the cliff, and from the library grounds you could see ships coming in, you could see horizonwards almost as far as Martinique on the left. And there we met Mimi Zacariah and Master Andrew, but Miss Rosamund was sick in bed with the fever. So Mimi and I talked about temperatures for a little while, and got out our embroidery, for we made a little money on the side selling drawn-thread nightgown tops to the tourists.

Miss Stella, Miss Joan and Master Andrew swung on the lianas of the banyan tree until they felt sick and giddy and their hands were raw with gripping those long strands as they whizzed through the air. But Miss Natalie sat quietly beside Mimi and me. "Go and play," I said to Miss Natalie, giving her a little bit of a push. "You are all right. You haven't got a fever today."

"I'm aflaid," said Miss Natalie. "The others are too lough. I'm aflaid because Daddy is coming home. I don't want a stlange man in our house."

"Now, look out on the horizon," said Mimi Zacariah. "There's a ship coming in. Did you ever hear of a ship, Miss Natalie, which didn't bring luck to someone? That may even be your father's ship, coming home to bring him back to your mother. Think how long she has been lonely."

But Miss Natalie hid her face in my embroidery, so that she couldn't see the ship, which was only a tramp cargo boat after all. "I'm aflaid," said Miss Natalie.

"Well," said Mimi Zacariah, getting sour in the voice and showing the yellows of her eyes, "being afraid is as catching as the kaffir-pox, to my mind." Now this put anger into me, for I would not have it said that we were afraid of receiving our Master, who had gone out to fight while some hearty gentlemen in the island had stayed at home. I looked at the other children, who were now playing hide-and-seek in the guinea-grass almost on the edge of the cliff. There was no use in telling them to keep out of the guinea-grass. Mimi and I had given them into God's hands as far as that cliff was concerned; only my God saw things in a Methodist way and Mimi's saw things in a Catholic way. But so far they had not tumbled over. "It's a curious thing," I said to Mimi, "with Mr. MacArthur having that Scotch name and that red complexion and the parrot on his shoulder and all, that he should have a little boy like Master Andrew who is as light and dark as those Spanish pictures of Madam's!"

"Oh, I wouldn't bring the parrot into it," said Mimi. And though she pursed her mouth we did not argufy any more, but did a lot of good silent work on our embroidery until the sun began to drop and it was time to go home.

When I got back with the children Madam was all beautifully dressed up in her eyelet-muslin with the red and green twisted girdle, and her hair done up in those wonderful snaky top-coils. She was standing by the piano, propping a sonata on the rack and then exchanging it for another. She told me to bundle the children to bed. "The Master's ship will drop anchor at dinner-time," Madam said. "I want you to be free to help Christophine." But the children did not want to go to bed. They were angry with Madam. "It would have been more truthful if she had stuck out my Stephen Heller's exercises, or Stella's dull minuet," said Miss Joan crossly. But they all plunged under their mosquito nets the minute I promised to carry the puppy up to them to say goodnight. And in about ten minutes all three of them were sleeping soundly. So I didn't have to bring the puppy up after all; but I gave the poor little thing a dish of breadcrumbs and gravy.

※ Old Master came to see Madam before dinner, and when I brought in the cocktails he stood there with an arm over Madam's shoulders. He was saying to her that it had been a long time, yes, a very long time, and she had been pretty patient, but she mustn't worry. "Time and war change people," said Old Master seriously. "But I think you are both young enough, oh yes, I think you are both young enough." He did not stay very long. I let him out of the gate myself, and I untied the muffler on the bellclapper so that we could all hear the bell loud and clear when the messenger from the bay reported Master's ship on the horizon. I stood there at the gate watching the thin little moon struggling through the clouds. It had grown to be a heavy night, the breeze had died. I was feeling heavy, too, and tired. I thought of the house, which had been a house only of women for six years. I thought that I must be different from the others of my dark skin, for I had small love for men. They made everything of a different quality and sound and smell. They would bring into a house deep voices and smoke and a feeling in the air. I suddenly thought of Christophine and the dinner, and looked round to see what was going on, for I could hear faint grunts and snores from the kitchen. I found her lying under the dresser, dead drunk. Someone had given her an extra chopée of black rum to celebrate with, and she had celebrated already. Her fourth child, Olivet, was sitting on a mat at her feet, fanning her in silence. When Olivet was born Madam dismissed Christophine, as she always did when a new baby came by a new father. "I don't mind your not being married," said Madam, "but I do think it is rather unfair to the children to have these incessant fights over the various fathers, and Father Toussaint has asked me to co-operate with him in disciplining you." But Madam could not keep from smiling when she made these speeches, for in all Madam disciplined Christophine six times, and always when the new baby was old enough to crawl it used to crawl in our kitchen, and the children (my little white ones) would recover from their stomachaches and bad appetites and everything would be the same again.

I took and poured a calabash of cold water over Christophine's face to bring her together again, and I told Olivet to roll the crapauds' legs in a little flour and chop up the red pepper and beat up the special English marshmallow sauce that came from the Pharmacerie to be poured over the special fruit salad. For the island cows wouldn't squeeze out a pint of cream not to please anyone, not even the Prince of Wales when he stepped ashore in his plus fours. The milk that came from the hills, and that started out thin enough God only knows, reached Maison Rose coloured a lovely pale blue, because of all the streams the carriers passed on the way. It was never a wonder to me that my three little ones could not hide their bones decently under some fat, in spite of the Allenbury's food I had boiled up for hours and months when they were babies.

I went again to the front gate while the water took effect on Christophine. There I saw Bill Buffon the boatman with his gold earring hanging on one ear and his silly smile. He was sitting with his feet in the open gutter, which was still sweet with the remains of Madam's bath water. "Boat's only half-hour away," said Buffon to me. "I'll be the one," he said, "to row Madam out to meet Master." And he grinned again, stupid. But Buffon has a good heart, for all his rags and foolishness. I never saw such a man for smelling out a hurricane, or keeping his boat right side up in rough sea. And he truly loves the family. The family is everything to a man like Buffon and to a woman like me. I suppose that in coming years poor people won't take such stock of families, royal families and ordinary high families like Madam and the Master's. But it's a comfort to have a family to tend and admire, at least I have always found it so.

"Did you smell the rum off Christophine?" I asked Buffon angrily. You must remember that by this time I was tired and sick of everything. But Buffon said that he had come to tell Madam that he had mended the leak in *Sainte Ursule* and bought a new oar from the master of a Guadeloupe schooner, all for the Master's sake. "La pluie ka vini," said Buffon; and indeed it was beginning to drizzle. So we went and sat in the downstairs hall, and I leaned against the wall and fell asleep. I only woke up when I heard the loud rattle of anchor dropping, and then I heard Christophine singing O *Vierge* in her feast-day voice, and I saw that Buffon had gone, and with him Madam.

✳ Afterwards Buffon told me how it went at the meeting. The drizzle was still falling, like spun glass beads between the boat and the ship. Madam wore her Maltese shawl over the eyelet-hole muslin, and she took the rudder. I saw in my mind the picture of Madam steering that boat, with her eyes and the little moon and the light rain shining. I saw the picture, not because of what Buffon said, but because of what he did with his hands when he told me. As the boat drew alongside, the passengers crowded near the head of the gangway; but there was one who hung behind and still leaned over the rail as if in a dream, and that one was the Master. Buffon says that the Master took Madam's hand and held it as if he was seeing her for the first time. Then Buffon got bashful and looked at the sea, so he couldn't see whether they kissed or not.

I looked the Master over for wound-marks when he came into the house, and there was nothing that you could see on the outside. But he was very pale and thin, with hollow cheeks, and he looked as if he had forgotten all about us, although he was polite enough. Goodness knows what had guided him back to Maison Rose to be a husband and a father, for he had the look of a wanderer without direction. Anyhow he ate up his dinner right enough, and went into the kitchen afterwards to compliment Christophine on her cooking, and then he went upstairs with Madam to see the children again. The sight of the three children, so large in their beds compared with the little creatures he had left, seemed to amaze him, for he had little to say.

In the meantime Buffon had gone back to the bay-front and carted the Master's luggage to Maison Rose on an iron barrow. The luggage he brought back was not exactly what he took away; even the trunk had changed, and instead of his suitcases there were two chests with bands round them, weighing the devil and all. Madam asked him where his clothes were and he picked up a little leather case fit to lay by a christening-robe in. "I don't know," said the Master. "It's been a long time: but I brought back some exciting trophies." So Buffon sweated up the stairs with the boxes, and the Master opened them, and then he nailed some of the stuff up on the walls of the hall and drawing-room—outlandish Arab helmets studded with imitation jewels, daggers and great clumsy pistols you never would imagine capable of shooting anyone, a tin German hat and a grand smoking pipe with a long tube, a fine brassy shield and arm-pieces to match, and some more fancy nonsense bits with the old bloodstains long dry on them. Buffon thought these things were wonderful, and stood by twisting his cap and saying, "Lawd, that's something!" But Madam and I could not endure the noise of hammering in the night and we were afraid that the children would wake up. After a long while, when I was rocking in the chair in my own room, everything was quiet, quiet without even the sound of voices. I went out to see if the puppy was all right and I saw a light still in the drawing-room, so I took the puppy in my arms and carried him up to show the Master.

He was sitting alone. Madam had gone to bed. He was reading a book and smoking, and the whole room was full of the sick faint smell of flowers and cigarette smoke, for after the rain the air was heavy again.

I said to myself, Lally, you must show friendliness. You must help to bring the Master out of himself and the bad war days and back to his family. I spoke to him kindly and respectfully and I laid the little dog at his feet. I told him that the children had bought it for him. "*Flanders* they called it, sir," I said.

The Master put down his book and looked at the little dog. He looked at it queerly. I did not feel comfortable. "An extraordinary name for a dog," said the Master.

There was his book on the table where he had put it down. His finger, thin and white, pressed on the page to keep the place. Because he was staring at me and then at the little dog, I shifted from one foot to the other and I fixed my eyes on the book. It was French, and I cannot read French, being an English Negress, though Christophine can. I saw the title, *A La Recherche du*

Temps Perdu, but it meant nothing to me. I saw the words where his finger pressed, and though I could not understand them, the whole look of the print, the whole feeling of something foreign on the page, in the air, made me very unhappy.

The little dog lay down beside the Master and shut its eyes. I turned to go, and the Master said:

"Tell me, Lally, does the mail-boat leave tonight or is there much cargo to load? I have an important letter to post."

"I can't be sure, sir," I said. "But if you give me the letter I'll find Buffon and he will take it off in his boat."

The Master gave me a letter, and I said goodnight. I left the puppy with him. I had the feeling that I could do nothing useful in that drawing-room then. There's English words, I thought, which might be said tonight, and the Master sits reading a French book like a guest in the Bellevue Hotel. I read the address on the letter as I went out to find Buffon. It was then that I saw the name for the first time: H. Lilipoulala, Port-au-Prince.

※ Downstairs in the playroom, wood-ants had eaten away a hole in the wall. The wood-ants had been at work all over the house, and we fought them as we fought the little milky insects on Madam's roses and the two-inch cockroaches which flew in and frightened us when there was a gale from the sea. We fought the centipedes too, but they came more rarely, although I never failed to knock the children's shoes out of the window before they dressed in the morning, since Miss Natalie got stung on the big toe when she was three.

Miss Stella called the hole in the playroom "posterity hole". She used to write poetry and stuff her papers into it. In the evening I would come and remove her writings, and next morning she would say that they had been claimed by posterity. Posterity was a zombie, a magic shape which lived on words and pictures, said Miss Stella. She even got Miss Joan and Miss Natalie to stuff their scribblings into that hole. I had a large biscuit tin full of the children's work, and I used to read the better pieces aloud to myself when I sat in my rocking-chair at the end of the day, with the kerosene lamp lit, for the electricity did not reach as far as my room. There was a time when Miss

Stella wrote a lot of verses about Jesus and the Virgin Mary, but she had grown out of that lately. On the night when the Master came home there was nothing in the posterity hole from Miss Stella. There was a picture of a bird, drawn by Miss Natalie with printing underneath:

A COMMON SISIZEB

Beneath that, in Miss Joan's handwriting, there was an article:

HOW TO REAR SISIZEBS. I have never tried, but they look tough and hardy. They probably feed on flies and ants with wings and legs carefully picked off. HOW TO HATCH SISIZEB EGGS HUMANLY. The human should tie the egg in a little flannel bag and keep warm in the hollow underarm, knotting string on shoulder. The arm must be kept stiff for several days. Tennis is not advised, nor is fighting. When bird is hatched, keep cosy in cottonwool and feed on sugar-and-water until feathers are grown.

It was something new for Miss Joan to be writing about birds. She generally wrote stories about life in England. She would often shut her eyes when she was alone with me, and say: "I can see England. It is grey and green. The trees are different. The people talk so fast—chirp, chirp! I can see my English godmother. She looks quite different from her picture. She looks very noble, and lives in an enormous house. She smiles at me, and invites me to live with her for ever and ever. I climb all the trees on her estate, and in the winter I put out my tongue and the snow falls on it . . . Oh, it is delicious! It tastes like vanilla ice-cream."

The English godmother was a great comfort to Miss Joan. Whenever she fell out with the others and they made her cry, she would shriek: "I'll write and tell my English godmother how *hateful* you are! I will go and live in England for ever and ever, and I will never invite you to my godmother's enormous house. My cheeks will get nice and rosy, and I will be an English school-girl and wear gloves!"

I saw on that night that Miss Joan had written another story:

CEDRIC'S CHARGE

Long, long ago, that part of England called the "fens"—the swampy, marshy part of our British country—was divided between two princes of great wealth.

Strange to say, they were brothers, and both of them felt equally proud that the noble house of Turmot should have had such honour conferred upon it by King Ethelred the Unready, who was reigning at that time. They were Saxons, and Prince Halbred Turmot the younger and taller of the two princes, had married a princess of Normoandy and had one baby daughter named Roxana.

Prince Edmund Turmot was unmarried though brave, he was also cruel and cunning, and planned how he could contrive to sieze his brother's dominions.

So he took advantages of the time when his brother Halbred was away on a tour, to capture the richer soil and finer jewels and to kidnapp the little Roxana. But here he was mistaken; for Halbred had left Roxana under the care of a brave, though rough, celt named Cedric.

Here Miss Joan's story ended at the bottom of page one, like most of her writing. I tore it up, and put HOW TO REAR SISIZEBS in my biscuit tin. It was late, and I turned the lamp low, intending to undress. But just at that moment I heard something fall with a thump outside my window, and at the same moment—or perhaps a second before or after—I heard a little soft scream like a hurt baby, and when I peeped out there was something white-and-black on the pavement. I quickly put on my flannel cape and ran outside.

It was the puppy, Flanders . . . it was Flanders lying on his back on the pavement in the darkness. I could just see the four little spread paws and the fat exposed body of a male baby-dog. I lifted a paw, but it fell back limp, and then I saw that his back was broken. So rather than make a to-do about something that was finished, I wrapped him in my cape and afterwards in newspaper, and I walked quietly to the bay-front and dropped him in the sea.

In the morning the children carried in the Master's coffee and orange, and there was a lot of talk and laughing, the Master pretending to get their names mixed up and calling them changelings, and all being very jolly together while Madam stood by. I called Miss Stella down to have her hair washed, and when she sat in the yard with it all spread out like golden coconut fibre in the sunshine, I asked her:

"Well, do you like your father now he's come?"

Miss Stella said: "I don't mind his face—its rather fine and ghostly—but to tell you the truth, Lally, it's his own voice I don't like."

"You'll get used to that in time," I said. And I went on brushing out her hair and tugging at tangles.

"Where is Flanders?" asked Miss Stella suddenly.

"Flanders is dead: he died in the night," I said.

"What killed him?" cried Miss Stella loudly and in grief.

"Well, it was partly the sardines," I said. "Remember I told you children that sardines were not good for dogs of that age. Flanders was sick in the night. I got up and let him out of the chicken-coop, and the queerest fit came over him. He ran around in circles, like a mad dog. He climbed up on the well, like a cat."

"On the *wishing-well*?" Miss Stella cried, drawing in her breath.

"Now, let it be a lesson to you," I said. "Flanders climbed up on the well, a plank gave way, and he fell into the well. If a little dog, weighing only a few ounces, can disappear like that, imagine how easy it would be for you to drown yourself that way."

"It was the water spirit," whispered Miss Stella. "Show me the place. Is there a hole?"

"There's no hole," I said. "Come here and see."

We pushed the ferns aside. "No hole," said Miss Stella, her eyes very large and dark and her hair getting full of fernseed. "That proves it. It was the water spirit. I *knew*—I knew that the water spirit would appear one day." She began to dance and call to her sisters. "Flanders was bewitched by the water spirit!" she cried. But I hushed her, and when the other children came downstairs they hardly made a row at all. Miss Natalie only said, "I would have wheeled him in my doll's pram, as we have no little brother." But Miss Joan said: "Poof! He'd have grown out of that in no time. Tell me, Lally, when a dog dies, what happens to the fleas on it? Do they die too, or do they just hop off and find another dog?"

"Flanders had only a few fleas," said Miss Stella gloomily.

※ And there was the Master's head at the window, his face smiling and kind, his hands on the sill. "Where's Buffon?" called the Master gaily. "Heah, Master!" answered Buffon from the kitchen, where he had spent the night with Christophine.

"I've got a present for you," said the Master. "Catch!" And he threw down a small packet wrapped in tissue paper, which burst when it hit the cobble-stones.

A shining of ribbons and metals was what we saw first, and then Buffon picked up the Master's war medals and pinned them onto his rags above the heart.

"T'ank-you, t'ank-you, Master, may the Lord bless you," said Buffon.

Marse Rufus and ✸ CHAPTER 3
Mamselle Bosquet

That day, as I remember it, Marse Rufus came to see the Master and drink a before-lunch cocktail with him. Now Marse Rufus was Madam's brother who had been invalided home early in the war and had gone back to this woman and that and this and that collection of many-coloured young, some in the hills and some in the valleys. It was an understood thing that as long as Old Master was alive the family should not notice Marse Rufus overmuch and should not act as if they knew about the women and the children. This was to protect Old Master from scandal, for since Queen Victoria had caused him to be called Sir Oliver and had made him a fit companion for St. Michael and St. George, all the decent people in the Island made a conspiracy to keep scandal away from him. Old Master himself seemed to be in the conspiracy, for he would not see what was under his nose, and for a long while he let Marse Rufus manage L'Aromatique and another small estate which he owned in those days. So Marse Rufus had one or two families every ten acres, and the goings-on were tremendous.

One of Marse Rufus' women was quite a property-owner and she was working hard to make him respectable: it was a pity that she was the plainest of the lot, for she owned a grape-fruit plantation and a rum shop, and they already had three children.

It was always very difficult for me to keep up the conspiracy and keep off the scandal, for when I walked my children in the botanical gardens I often came upon an elegant imported pram with Marse Rufus' babies sitting inside, and another child hanging onto the handle, all dressed up in the best muslin and lace, and the nurse (a sly gaudy Capresse) flouncing about the place as if the children had been born in wedlock and pure white. I used to say to my little girls, "Look the other way", but they never did: they stared and stared. And once Miss Joan said: "Lally, I want to play with my cousins." But Miss Stella said quickly, "Oh, Joan—you *can't*. We mustn't encourage *these* children; think how awful it would be if Uncle Rufus married their mother and not Cornélie's mother."

You see, Marse Rufus had a daughter by a very gentle, lovely dressmaking Martiniquan. She was his first-born of all, and after her birth the mother went back to her dressmaking and gave up Marse Rufus entirely, although she settled down to work in our Island so that she could keep an eye on him. Her child Cornélie went to the convent, and the convent rails adjoined the botanical gardens, and my little girls used to creep under croton bushes and talk to Cornélie through the rails while I sat at my embroidery. I did not find out about this for a long time, but then it was too late to break the friendship, and besides I grew fond of Cornélie too. White and fine as my own children were, I had to admit that Cornélie was the most beautiful of all Old Master's grandchildren. She had the same small wrists and ankles and thin long neck as Miss Stella, but her eyes were very dark and seemed to float in her face, and her mouth was full and sad, even in those days. It seemed to me that she was very silent, perhaps a little stupid, and the nuns kept her reddish-brown hair, which curled at the ends a little, short and plain. Marse Rufus never behaved as if he knew of her existence. "I hope Cornélie marries a Governor or becomes a famous actress or a Mother Superior," said Miss Stella to me one day.

I do not know how well aware the Master was of these happenings, but he never cared much for Marse Rufus, although I believe that this dislike was more a matter of looks and talk than bastard children. "Rufus revolts me," the Master said to Madam once. (And that was even before the war.) "He is getting fat. He never reads a book. His clothes are spotty. He is disgustingly healthy, and doesn't deserve to be. In fact he is a bore."

Anyhow, up came Marse Rufus, the day after the Master arrived home, with a grin on his face and his collar flying open and his yellowing panama-hat stuck on the back of his head. One lucky thing about Marse Rufus was that he did not guess when people didn't like him. He was so used to being liked by the foolish women that he was quite confident about everyone else. Not that we saw much of him: he was seldom in town.

"Welcome home and greetings," said Marse Rufus to the Master. He always had a hearty way of speaking, even at funerals. He enjoyed attending funerals, and when the corpse was being lowered he usually said something hearty to the relatives which made them cry. "Well, John, I'm glad to see that you came through unscathed too, but you're a bit haggard," said Marse Rufus, picking up a cocktail and swallowing it down.

"And you have put on a considerable amount of weight," said the Master, pulling a chair into the shade for Madam, for they were out on the porch and the midday sun was beating down.

Madam spoke then for the first time in my hearing that day. "Rufus hasn't come here just to welcome you, John," she said. "He wants your advice. He's got something on his mind."

"What is it?" said the Master, not invitingly.

"I want literary advice," said Marse Rufus, making a silly bashful face and wiping his forehead on his sleeve. The white linen was frayed and neglected-looking. Cornélie's mother would at least have looked after his clothes!

"Out with it, then," said the Master.

"Well . . . I have more or less taken on . . . I have become an editor of our local paper," said Marse Rufus.

"What, the *Caribbean Tribune*?" said the Master.

"Oh no, that died in 1918," said Marse Rufus. "But I have been the sub-editor of the *Island Bugle* for the last three weeks—you know, the one run by the committee, the respectable one. It is a temporary arrangement, unless the circulation goes up. Father Toussaint does the foreign news and the leading article and I do the lay-out and arrange the advertising and the other news items."

"I see," said the Master. "But how did you get into this?"

"Business and family connections," said Marse Rufus. "And they needed a people's man. The paper was getting too secular. They needed"—Marse Rufus heaved himself into condition to make a speech—"a *liaison* man with wide interests in the Island."

"But you aren't a Catholic," said the Master.

"My connections are," said Marse Rufus, scratching his neck.

"Of course," said the Master. "Of course. I see. But if you are already the sub-editor, why come to me for advice?"

Marse Rufus coughed and poured himself another cocktail from the frosted glass jug. "John, I'm no scholar, as you know," he said. "I wish you would tell me what to read to get myself into condition for editing the whole paper some day."

"Let me have a look at the latest copy," said the Master.

Marse Rufus took a folded newspaper out of his pocket and pointed to a column. The Master began to read it out aloud to Madam.

"HYGIENE AND SANITATION. Hygiene is taught in the Schools but the parsimony observed when making provisions for education forbids its intelligent practice . . . "

"What's the matter with that?" asked the Master.

"I thought that as you had travelled so much and read so much," said Marse Rufus, "you could help me to work out a more attractive journalistic line."

"Quite impossible," said the Master. "I couldn't do better than that."

"But is it up to the standard of the London Press?" asked Marse Rufus anxiously.

"Absolutely up to the standard of the London Press," said the Master. He looked wearily at Marse Rufus, but Marse Rufus did not get up to go.

"There's another matter," said Marse Rufus, drawing an envelope out of another pocket. "A matter of an agreement with Father Toussaint—and . . . someone else."

"Let me see," said the Master. He looked across at Madam to see if she was curious, and when she gave him a sign he read the document out in a low voice.

"I, Rufus Oliver Mowbray of L'Aromatique, do hereby promise to continue the Catholic instruction which I have voluntarily begun, and I do promise that when merciful death shall release my beloved father Sir Oliver Mowbray from the toils of this earthly life, I will voluntarily and of my own free will and desire take unto myself the woman Marie-Louise Coralita Dubonnet to be my lawful wife according to the rites of the Catholic Church.

"I fully realise that this agreement is in no way legal or binding, and as a pledge of good faith I offer to relinquish my editorial office in the *Island Bugle* if the above promises are not carried out within a month of the date of the demise of my aforesaid beloved father."

"And have you got to go on being the sub-editor until this agreement is carried out?" asked the Master.

"Well—that depends," said Marse Rufus. "That is why I came to you. I thought that if I could make the circulation go up tremendously . . . "

"Any advice I might give you would tend to keep down the circulation," said the Master, pushing his chair back. "See here, Rufus, your father is coming. I can hear his carriage at the door."

I could hear the pony-trap myself, for I had been sitting on the stone step below the porch as they talked. Old Master didn't exactly disapprove of the nine motorcars in the Island, but he stuck to his pony-carriage just the same, with its neat canvas hood and well-shone brass and leather trappings.

"I'll let you out the back way while he ties it up," I said to Marse Rufus, and without a word he stuck on his panama hat and followed me out.

※ Old Master did not stay very long that day. Hardly a moment it seemed; just long enough to shake the Master's hand and wish him well. There was an epidemic in the Island, I forget if it was dysentery or the kaffir-pox, and he had to hurry on. In my view he wasn't just hurrying to the sick-beds but hastening to get back to his orchid house at L'Aromatique, for that was where he spent his rest time pottering. He would stand there under that roof of palms plaited with bamboos, unhanging wire baskets to dip his plants into a tank swarming with tiny fish: the fish were there to eat mosquito grubs. Very often he got paid for his attention with rare flowering things; the poor patients knew his hobby. He would scoop out bits of log and fill the hollows with charcoal, then bind these queer roots with coconut fibre. Hours and hours he would spend there making beautiful labels, and goodness the number of names one spray might have, written in his small script: *Cattaleya crispa purpurea—Bee orchis or golden shower—Madonna or Eucharist or Holy Ghost orchid* . . .

Even then he was looking very old and tired, though it was not until many months later that he got a groom to drive him around. Old Master was not a great talker, and he did not show how he felt about his son-in-law's return.

So we had a family lunch, with the children sitting around their parents, and only Miss Natalie fidgeting as usual in the corner seat. There was a funny feeling about that lunch, as if some strange people had met in a hotel and were being purposely well-behaved. The children had missed their morning lesson, but that afternoon Mamselle Bosquet was coming to teach them geography in French.

As the Master laid down his knife and fork he said:

"It's very hot indoors. I remember a spot where we used to go when we wanted to get cool. I remember it very well: the nutmeg grove. I used to think of it when I was abroad. The tree trunks were like white pillars; a cathedral in mourning. Arches of dark green leaves throwing shadows . . . and the dried nutmeg kernels dropping softly . . . there was a wild rat's nest high up in the branches."

"I haven't been there since you went away," said Madam.

"Then let us go there this afternoon," said the Master.

I could see that Madam was very pleased. The Master said to Miss Stella: "Run upstairs and get me my hat and the book of plays on my dressing-table."

I brought down Madam's green-and-white sunshade myself, and when they had gone I realised that Madam had not told the Master that Mamselle Bosquet was coming that afternoon.

※ The children liked Mamselle Bosquet, although they made fun of her and called her Mamselle Bossy, and sang a funny song at her which began:

Poussez, poussez les lèvres
Tout en haut, Micheline . . .

For that was Mamselle Bosquet's name: Micheline, though I never heard anyone call her by it. Even Madam didn't, and they had been girls together in the Island. At about the time that Madam met the Master, Mamselle Bosquet had gone to Paris to finish her education, and she came back with beautiful clothes and many fine Frenchy ideas and she ordered several bookcases from Papa Poulet the carpenter. But it seemed that she had no money left after being educated, for she wore the Paris clothes even when they became shabby, and after some time she gave French lessons.

Everyone knew that Mamselle Bosquet was in love with the Master. She had never made a secret of it. She loved my little girls because they were his daughters, and while he was away in foreign lands she used to ask before every lesson: "What news of your father?" Then Miss Stella would run up to Madam and borrow one of the close-written sheets in the Master's handwriting, and Mamselle Bosquet would read it greedily, her eyes determined to see wonderful hidden meanings between the lines. She would come to the end of the page and she would shut her mouth very tight with a look of envy and resignation, because there were other pages which she could not see.

I thought then: the Master used to write a lot to Madam, but now that he is back he can hardly talk to her! Are there people who write more easily than they talk, is that what education does? I could not help wanting to know what Mamselle Bosquet would say to the children on this day. She always had the excited eyes of a bird when she first came in through our gate, and then the excitement would die down and she would look just like a teacher. But this time it was the children who burst out with news, who told her that their father's hair was a little grey, that they were shy of him, and that he liked to read and sit silent.

"*Faites attention!*" said Mamselle Bosquet, beginning the

class without her usual chat and kindness. It was a bad lesson, for Miss Natalie was hopeless on account of her *r*'s being *l*'s, and Mamselle Bosquet pounced on all her mistakes. Miss Natalie began to cry, so I said to Mamselle Bosquet that the children were upset and tired and that I wanted to ask her something. I took her upstairs into the drawing-room and I picked up the book which the Master had been reading. I had a reason for doing this. It was not only that I was inquisitive; but Mamselle Bosquet looked so unhappy, I wanted to comfort her. I knew that it had always been very important to Mamselle Bosquet to know what the Master was thinking and doing. And what was the harm? As far as I was aware, the Master had only met her at Government House parties in the old days, and lent her a few books. Mamselle Bosquet was not in those early days the kind who took to the Church. She had to have a hero who breathed and was a booklover like herself.

"This was the page," I said: "forty-six. Please tell me what it means. Please read it out."

When she spoke her own language, Mamselle Bosquet made music. As I listened to her, the words and Mamselle Bosquet and the Master's mind became more and more mysterious.

I hesitated to ask Mamselle Bosquet what the words meant. She spoke at last.

"Lally," she said, "I doubt if you would understand." Then her eyes filled with strange hot tears and she twisted the book in her hands. "In search of the past, that's it, Lally," she said, choking a little. "In search of lost days . . . but the effort is nearly always useless. . . . "

✉ That is in the past now. The day of the Master's homecoming is in the past, and the day after that. It is in the past how Madam came down to my room that second night, very late, and sat in my rocking chair as I lay in bed. I tried to get up, but she would not let me. "Lie still Lally," she said. "Oh, Lally, it's no good. It's all broken. He is taken away from me."

"Did you know that from the first moment, like me, Madam?" I dared to say.

"I wouldn't believe it. I fought. I'll go on fighting. But it's all broken, it's hopeless," said my dear Madam, while I lay there aching with love and pain for her. She did not cry, but sat cold and stubborn.

"Madam," I said, "I'll find you a good obeah-woman who could bring him back—perhaps. I'm only a Methodist, so it's not mortal sin to me."

"Oh, no," said Madam. "Oh, no."

"Miss Stella believes in magic," I said foolishly.

Madam said, speaking low to herself: "Once I did too. What is it that he brings from the old world? A feeling of unrest and evil.—No, no, he is not wicked, he is only hurt and spoiled; our whole lives are hurt and spoiled by something we could not control. Lally," said Madam, "it is dreadful that we never guessed what this war would mean."

"Ah, Madam," I said, so full of sorrow and helplessness that I bowed my head. "Ah, Madam."

"We must take the greatest care of him," said Madam slowly. "After all, I have always wanted a fourth child—a son."

It was not the time then for me to comfort her with this saying: "Madam, you'll have a son one day, you've as good as got one already! Master Andrew—for all that he's only a little boy—is in deep love with all our girls, and with one of them in particular." Oh! I could have told her that the three girls loved him too, and that a kiss between children, a first kiss in the sunlight of innocence, is something never forgotten: how it was Miss Stella who lifted her flying hair to welcome that kiss.

Mimi saw it too and would have separated them. She saw her little boy catch and hold my first girl so tight and long that it wasn't seemly to her, for Mimi used to sit beneath Father Toussaint's sermons when he said that the coming together of flesh was sin except under marriage. But I jabbed her with my embroidery needle. Children are children, I said to Mimi: turning her attention to the other two and Miss Rosamund who stood by watching, Miss Rosamund disdainful, the sisters envious. "Shoo!" called Mimi, flapping her skirts. "Shoo!" Then sudden rude laughter changed the kiss into a game.

But the sound of the words *kissing* and *loving* would have struck at Madam's heart sharper than any needle; so I kept my silence.

It was this way: at first only Madam and myself knew that everything was wrong with the Master. Only at intervals, and mostly at night, would the dreadful despair come over him, so that he sat silent in a haze of smoke, his cheek resting on his hand, and his eyes shut. We came to know soon why he hung and depended on Mr. Lilipoulala, who brought the precious and fearful cigarettes which changed the Master again into someone reasonable, and without which he was so ill and wretched that we were afraid for his life and his mind. Why, sometimes even the sound of a car starting up in the street—and now there were nine cars in the island—would cause him to tremble and shudder for hours. It was a strange thing: while he trembled so he would go to the window and look up into the sky.

I do not think that the children knew for a long while. They had expected the coming of someone strange, difficult and uncomfortable anyhow; they had looked for the coming of a man to a house of women. And besides, there was something so love-worthy about the Master, there was such a fineness of feature and speech, a gentleness in him when he was not sick and desperate, and over all the feeling that he was someone who had been hurt, that sometimes it was as easy for us to forget his frightful moods as it was for *him* to forget them.

But I have never really forgotten anything that happened to Madam and the Master and my children. I may have put certain happenings out of my thoughts, but they wander in again now that I am old and idle. For me it is not impossible or hopeless to go in search of lost days. My days were not my own, and I lived my life through other people. Today I am still so much a part of those people whom I love, that who can tell whether it is the child Miss Stella living the days again through me . . . or the grownup Miss Joan, sitting by an English fire with her boy in her arms, who cries to me through space: "Lally, Lally, do you remember?"

Miss Stella �֍ Comes Home

L'Aromatique ※ CHAPTER 4
and Stella

Miss Stella was the first to come home, as was fitting for the first child of Madam's body and of my love.

Marse Rufus had made me an offer of a lift in his Ford car, but I chose to walk up the little mountain a few days beforehand, Buffon carrying the waterproof carib-basket packed tight with my belongings, and me carrying my cup and saucer and the china cockatoo. Buffon had moved up to L'Aromatique with the family. He had given up the sea for the land. He was always a bad labourer, hoeing and planting with his eyes shaded to the blue water in the bay, and not much thought for the little lime-plants or the sweet-potato roots. There was an eternal fight in his thought between the Master and the sea. As we walked up, I measured the road with my eye and I was thankful that I had not taken up Marse Rufus' offer, for there were only a few inches to spare over and between the old tyre-marks and the cliff. It would have been foolish to die in a car accident like Sir Godfrey after enduring my complaint all these years.

Christophine's son, Baptiste, carried my mattress with the flannel sheets rolled up inside, and I will say this for Baptiste, although he was once a primary-school teacher (until people complained to the Government that he was a radical and he got dismissed for being unpunctual), he is not above carrying a good load on his head. But Christophine says that he got ruined when she put him in boots instead of letting him go barefoot like his brothers and sisters.

I was not surprised that Madam and the Master had hidden themselves away here and given up all their old life in the town, for after all Madam was never one to spend the year waiting for a Government House *at home* or a bridge-party, and the Master built his life around his books and his queer memories of foreign lands, thoughts that hung about his head like the smoke of Mr. Lilipoulala's cigarettes.

Baptiste's boots still squeaked like new leather and Buffon hummed as he turned the last bend, while I wondered to myself whether Miss Stella might have grown up to look like the Master. She would be coming in the cool of the afternoon, and I'd see her ship anchor from my look-out beside the cows and the pea-hens. The pea-hens were always fussing and making their screech-cries, but the peacock folded up the glory of his feathers at a certain time each day, taking solitary walks when it pleased his dignity. The lime-trees were glittering, the hibiscus flaring in the hedges, and indoors Madam had spread the linen coverlet and put roses in a guest-room. The little crib that Miss Natalie broke all to pieces had been mended by Papa Poulet and it stood ready for little Hel. I'm ashamed that a child should have such a terrible name, but it is part of his father's baptismal name, Helmut: Miss Stella had to go all the way to the United States to marry a man whose parents were bone-German, after all the warnings Miss Rebecca gave her when she borrowed library books.

Mamselle Bosquet was there at L'Aromatique too, for the years had brought a strange accommodation between Madam and Mamselle: they had become the closest of friends. Mamselle spoke hardly a word to the Master from day to day, but she came first of all every week-end, and then for ever; she did the shopping for Madam and chose the special books from the library for the Master. She brought bits and pieces of town life up to the doorstep, and altered Madam's clothes when they got too old-fashioned, and turned the collars on the Master's shirts. I have noticed that time does this to two people who both love the same thing. At first they are jealous and unhappy and fight each other quietly, but if they can outlast the struggle, then they are good company, for what they both want is the welfare of whom they love. But I wondered just the same what Miss Stella would say to this . . .

※ At last she arrived and I had her to myself. She lay one afternoon under the flamboyant tree, drawing breath deeply and stretching her bare legs out in thick grass. Little Hel was picking the baby jumbie-beads off a long trail of vine and dropping them one by one into a calabash. He wasn't talking, the funny sandy boy, but whenever he did speak his voice was a sweet little whine, not like our creole whine when we are small, just a little bit more from the back of the throat and from the nose. Of course he was spoiled, but I liked children spoiled anyway, I liked them to feel that everything belonged to them, time enough for them to find out that it didn't. Miss Stella turned over and looked at him, slowly, then she looked at me with her grey eyes and said:

"Lally, I came back because I couldn't bear not knowing *exactly* how you all were. I was so afraid one of you might die before I got here! I want to ask you a thousand questions, and the most important—"

She stopped, closed her eyes against the sun, and said very softly: "Lally, is everything just the same, does Mr. Lilipoulala still come?"

I said yes to this, I said yes but I also said that it didn't matter any more, we were so used to him, we were so used to the Master and his ways now that Mr. Lilipoulala's comings and goings meant nothing more than that he took our money and made us poorer and poorer.

She was pale and silent for a while. Then she sighed: "Father" (she called him father, as if she saw him from a distance), "sits in his cane-chair like a ghost with clenched fists. Mother is the same kind true person, but doesn't it sometimes strike you that there's something a little complaisant in her kindness? And as to Mamselle Bossy! Poor soul! Fancy loving a man all these years and watching him become a ghost! Do you know, Lally, I don't believe that she has ever gone to bed with him?"

"Miss Stella!" I was obliged to say sharply. "That's a bad American way of talking."

"But who can hear my bad words if not you, Lally?" she pleaded, wrinkling her nose. "Oh! You are really angry! I'm sorry."

I had to be severe with her, even though she was grown-up, for Madam and the Master were my sacred people, and Miss Stella had forgotten that I was a servant. But secretly I was glad. My first child, my heart's child, had come back from the North and would tell me everything. She asked more and more questions, hungry and breathless. She asked about the past: she wanted to know what her father and mother were like when they were young. She asked if I thought that they would have been happy in their marriage, if the war had not come. We talked and talked for a long while, and sometimes she did not wait for an answer, for she said that she was reading my face.

"And Andrew," she said, low. "Is it possible to see the house at Petit Cul-de-Sac from this point?"

Yes, we could just see the beginning of the bridle-path in the valley woods and the tip of a shingled roof through banana trees. I pointed.

"So he lives with Cornélie now," said Miss Stella thoughtfully. Someone, perhaps Madam, must have written to tell how Old Master left the little wooden house and the forty acres of land to his coloured grandchild, when no one even knew that he was aware of her; and of how Master Andrew began to be sick and spit blood, and of how Cornélie took him to be her lover, and cared for him; and of how they had a child three years past.

"Just before I left home . . . " began Miss Stella—but her voice faded clear away. She put her arms round the trunk of the flamboyant tree and drew herself into a sitting position against it. "This marvellous roughness!" she said in excitement. "All the while, when I lived in New York City, I noticed the awful smoothness of things. I would touch walls with my hands in gloves, and I would feel so sad, so sad! I longed to have a cocoa-pod in my bare hands and turn it over and throw it far into the roughness of dead leaves and broken branches!" She put her cheek against the tree. Little Hel came up and sat in her

lap, his calabash half-full of jumbie-beads already. I looked over
to the west and I saw that Buffon was at it again—he had left
his job of stamping on the dried cocoa-beans and he was hack-
ing away at the shell-boat he was making out of a gomier tree.
For Buffon was certain that one day Madam and the Master
would be rich enough to give him two or three days off a week,
so that he could take this boat out fishing. It was now three
years since he had started to scoop out his boat. He was in no
hurry about it, and once in a while the Master came out and
called to him that he must go back to the cocoa-treading or
the lime-picking or the cutlassing, and he covered the boat up
with an old piece of tarpaulin, and went back to work.

"But Miss Stella, surely you had trees on your farm?"

"Only useful trees," she said. "Don't you know, Lally, that
in America everything has to be useful? Our trees were for cutting down. After breakfast, in the winter, there was always the
wood to get in for the next year. The hired men hauled out
four-foot lengths and sawed it with an old machine built up out
of a Model T. engine. You never would believe what a contraption it was! And the noise it made, too! They'd pile up the wood
outdoors to season; for green wood caused creosote in the
chimney."

"A chimney," I said, dreaming of it, for I'd never seen one.

"Yes, a chimney," said Miss Stella. "Let me tell you Lally,
it's a mistake to live in a country where chimneys are necessary. Death to chimneys, is my motto! Oh Lally," she said mer-
rily, "I was a perfect scream as a farmer's wife!"

"Now don't you make too much fun of chimneys and the
like," I told her. "Remember you've got to go back there."

"Maybe," she said. "Maybe, Lally. Shall I tell you about my
bridal room? I've never told anybody else. It was a warm room,
heated by a large iron stove. It was once the living-room, and
on the sideboard was a huge book called *Die Ganze Kochkunst*,
supported by marble bookends. My mother-in-law had set out
a plate of cole slaw salad, some liver-sausage and a large iced
cake. She was in the kitchen, making coffee. Helmut and I stood
at the window and looked out. Oh Lally, it was a fair white world
we looked out on! Everything was frosted over with feathery
crystals. It was very lovely. And my life had changed colour

three times: the green world of this island, the straight grey world of New York, and now the white world of Maine in winter."

"And you in white, like the snow," said I.

"And me dressed like a snow-maiden, but with a burning heart, Lally darling. And the awful thing was that I could hear Helmut's mother singing in her bass voice 'Kennst Du das Land?'—and all at once I imagined that I smelled real orange-blossom, and I got so dizzy with the smell of orange-blossom and coffee that I nearly smashed the windowglass frosted with snow-flowers, to escape. . . . Then, Lally, right then and there I knew that I must come back for a little while, before too many winters smothered me."

"Tell me more," I begged. But she had danced away from the snow and the farm and the bridal room.

"You've had hard times since the last hurricane took the crops," she said. "But in the sunshine it is easy to forget how hard the times have been, when you only feel the heat, and the beauty . . . Father and Mother stay indoors so much, with the blinds drawn half-way, as if they want to shade the whole of life! Oh Lally, even if the sparkle of the sea hurts my eyes, I want to see it, I don't mind being hurt! I want to lie in the sun until I'm so hot that I crackle."

"Little Hel would get sunstroke," I told her. "He's a North-baby."

She stood up, lifting Hel high in those thin arms, the little hands like spiders, as Christophine used to say in the old days. "Take him into the cool for a rest," she said. But Hel screeched: "Don't wanna. Don't wanna." So we all settled down again, and I was regarding them the way people look at mother-and-child pictures. Miss Stella wasn't shaped for a mother yet, she hadn't gathered any fat on the ribs at all, and above and below the ribs she was only round in a girl's way. This, I knew, was a danger. When the body doesn't seem changed, who is to know how changed the heart is? For all her light talk, Miss Stella had a wild and serious heart. Was it possible that long plain years, with winter seasons, and home-making in the American way, which is so different from our way, had no power over Miss Stella, to change her? "Tell me again about the winter, Miss Stella, and the snow," I said.

"Snow . . . " said Miss Stella, and how she laughed! Little Hel rolled over and spilled his jumbie-beads, so had to pick them up in his very small fingers, two or three at a time. Then Miss Stella stopped laughing; she took my arm in her hands and leaned her smiling face to me, and she said: "Snow is the most beautiful thing in the world. It is so beautiful that I was frightened of it. I used to think: *if snow can do this to the land* . . . So I put on two or three jackets before I went outdoors: I was afraid that a small piece of ice, just a few crystals, would sink right into my heart and that I would love the snow-country better than anywhere in the world—that I would forget you and Andrew . . . and of course Father and Mother and the island . . . "

"But the jackets protected you better than Christophine's scapular, and kept you warm for us," I said.

"Not only the jackets. The thaws, and the summers which were never so glorious as our whole year of summer, and the people . . . Sometimes I forgot you, yes, for I was so busy growing up and learning new ways. But after months and months of not quite remembering you, one day it was spring again."

Miss Stella sighed. "Snow has such blue shadows! It is as blue as our moonlight between the trees. When you see whole fields of it, time stands still. But when you touch it, it is smooth and cold—like cities. That's something else I learned in America: never try to touch what you can never enjoy."

Her voice was as bitter as the Master's. She laid her head in my lap, in my blue percale skirt that had so many gathers and was stained with guava juice, and she murmured, with her eyes shut, "Why do you plague me so, Lally? I came here to forget the lost years. I came here to grab the past and feel how rough and real it is."

"But if you came here to forget your husband," I said to Miss Stella, looking away to the sea and hearing Buffon's chop-chop between my words, "you made a mistake in bringing little Hel along, with the face he has on him, like a German Christmas card."

Hearing his name, little Hel came up and leaned on me from the other side. He was beginning to trust me. "Do you like it here?" I said to him. "Blue and yellow," he said, casting his eyes around. "Blue and yellow, and no red trucks. No airplanes. No fire-engines. Nice grass. But the ants sting." I tipped his starched cloth hat well over his eyes and brushed the sandflies away from his neck.

"You are wrong in thinking that I want to forget Helmut and little Hel," Miss Stella said. "I love them both very much, but in America people love a little differently, or that's what I came to think. They are more sensible. Goodness, how hard I tried to be sensible! But it was utterly useless. I'd be sensible in their way for a few weeks, and then I'd be in an agony of loving and hating, the way *we* hate and love. From the moment I stepped on board that American ship I felt how unlike them I was in this matter. I was so dreadfully happy to be free, to be going somewhere. I skipped around the decks like a squirrel—oh Lally, I wish that one day you could see a squirrel—I love squirrels dearly—yes, I skipped with pleasure as we raced out into the ocean and left all the islands behind. And yet I felt so dreadfully sad to be leaving you all . . . I could have cried myself away and dissolved into the waves. Then I searched the faces on that ship, and they were closed in, with shutters over their eyes. It seemed that they only knew how to like and dislike; they were the kindest people I had ever met, yet that did not comfort me. You see they were tamed city-living people."

"Little Hel is asleep," I said to her. It was so sweet to be a nurse again, to be caring for my first boy-child. When I gave him his bath that morning, I thought: *now here's the little thing that makes all the difference*—and I was happy that he was a boy.

I covered his legs with the linen cloth I was embroidering, to keep off the flies. I rested his head against me more comfortably. Just then Baptiste came out of the house, with a blue envelope on a tray. He walked towards us between the cows Belle-mère and Doudoux, and smiling shyly at Miss Stella, he said: "A letter sent by your mother. A letter from Miss Joan. Madam and the Master read it first, and now it's your turn." But he did not go away, and waited, as I did, for Miss Stella to read it aloud.

"Gracious, she says she hopes I have lots of cotton dresses, as she will have to borrow some!" cried Miss Stella. "Does she still think, as so many others do, that I've married a rich American? . . . Edward is learning to write with his left hand . . . What does that mean?"

"Because of the four fingers he lost on the Aragon front," said Baptiste solemnly.

"Now what war was that?" asked Miss Stella vaguely.

"The war in Spain," said Baptiste.

"Baptiste studies Miss Joan's letters—he got into trouble with Father Toussaint over that war," I said.

"He was throwing a hand-grenade," said Baptiste. "He didn't throw it quickly enough. Father Toussaint calls him a murderer."

"So Edward lost four fingers and Joan hasn't a cotton dress to her name—what a lot of poor whites we are becoming!" But I could see that Miss Stella was troubled.

"I wanted to go there too," said Baptiste. "But there was no way for a black boy to get to Spain. So now I wait for Miss Joan; but I think it's all over now, it's in the past."

"But Edward is an engineer—how can he work with his fingers gone?"

"He has no work, like me," said Baptiste.

Miss Stella got up in silence. She stood looking out to sea. "I'll leave Hel with you, Lally," she said. "I'm going for a walk. What an old romantic Grandfather must have been, after all! Calling this the place of sweet smells . . . I must say, it's a lot more aromatic since they took away the old privy which hung over the cliff. How beautifully the vanilla pods are filling out! Lally," she said softly as Baptiste went away, sadly swinging his tray, "if I don't tell you enough about the between-years, it's not that I don't want to or that I'm ashamed. It's because so much of it was feelings and not happenings . . . "

I watched her as she swung over the rise of the hill, past the pea-hens and the bamboo clump, over to the bridle-path: and then her bright hair disappeared in the sinking valley. She was on her way to visit Master Andrew at Petit Cul-de-Sac.

Petit ✽ CHAPTER 5
Cul-de-Sac

S he was escaping from me, and I sat there anchored on the grass, Hel clinging to my skirt like a piece of yellow seaweed. There's nothing to stop a nurse feeling like God towards her children, even when they are grown. She is constantly brooding over them, watching and listening, planning for them. But a nurse can't hear and see everything, like God: she strains forward to follow, and her old flesh restrains her. This helpless interval is sad misery to a character like mine.

"Your mother thinks she's getting away from me—escaping," I said to little Hel.

"Huh, Lally?" He was half-asleep.

"Yet somehow or other I'll find it all out afterwards. Everything they've been up to. I'll find it all out, and I might as well have been alongside them all the while. See that cloud? I'm as good as rolled up in it. See that ramier? He's a tattle-tale bird. Not to mention Fifine's aunt who goes to chapel with me, old Majolie's visits to the kitchen, and the words which will pass from Cornélie to Marse Rufus and the priests."

He was not listening: his head lolled.

"I might as well be going with her every step of the way like her own black quick shadow," I told him as I gathered him up for indoors.

✖ In Stella's sick dreams of home the island had been a vision so exquisite that she was now almost afraid to open her eyes wide, lest she might be undeceived and cast down or lest confirmation would stab through her like a shock. Treading the black damp earth of the bridle-path, brushed by ferns and wild begonias, experiencing the fleet glimpse of a ramier flying from the forest floor through branches into the Prussian blue sky, it was impossible not to look and look and drink it in like one who had long been thirsty. *It is more beautiful than a dream, for in dreams you cannot smell this divine spiciness, you can't stand in a mist of aromatic warmth and stare through jungle twigs to a spread of distant town, so distant that people seem to have no significance; you cannot drown your eyes in a cobalt sea, a sea with the blinding gold of the sun for a boundary!*

Stella put her arms round the trunk of a laurier cypre and rubbed her cheek softly against the bark. *I've come back*, she said to the tree. A little yellow lizard jumped out of a hole at the trunk-base, sliding across her path, and above her there was the sweet frightened fuss of hummingbirds' wings. *I've come back*, said Stella, squeezing the laurier cypre as if she would strangle it for joy.

Her sandals made a noise in the rutted narrow way which was simply a river bed in the rainy season. She descended into the valley, crossed a stream by stepping stones, bending to cool her hands in the sparkling water, and began the ascent towards Petit Cul-de-Sac. The way was not very familiar to her for she had only ridden there on a donkey once or twice during her grandfather's lifetime, yet she felt so strong (had she not learned to be a farm-hand and braved the rigours of zero weather?), that the sharpness of the incline meant nothing to her, and she was surprised to find beads of sweat on her forehead when she arrived at the clearing.

Cornélie's house was very small, a wooden shingled shack with a verandah and outhouses covered with palm-leaf roofs— it was so small that it looked like an old dolls' house, dwarfed by the immense trees which leant towards it lovingly. On the verandah stood a child's wicker cot on wheels, covered with mosquito-netting. In the middle of the clearing, stretched out in a canvas deck-chair of purple and green stripes, lay Andrew.

He did not see her at once for she had come up from behind, and his head was in the shade. His bare brown legs
emerged from shorts into the blazing sun. He was holding an
old violin and picking at the strings, and on the grass beside
him lay a box of violin strings, a sheet or two of music weighted
with a rock and one or two queer-looking gadgets.

Stella brushed the damp hair off her forehead and called
to him as she did in the old days: "Coo-ee!" shyly as a child.
He looked up, a sign passed over his face, his eyes brightened
in the old mocking way. But he was very thin. "Coo-ee, Stella—
hullo!" he said, laying down the violin and waiting, not rising.

Stella called to Cornélie: "Coo-ee, Cornélie," thinking of
how she used to call through the bars of the convent.

"Hush," said Andrew. "You'll wake the child. Cornélie will
be out in a minute, she is going to church in town almost at
once. It is her name-saint's day."

Someone else stole out of the shadows: a vision in stiff scar-
let creole dress gaudy with flowers, shoulders sleekly covered
with a grey silk foulard, her copper head balanced with a stiff
yellow and black turban: "That's Fifine, our servant," said Andrew carelessly. Fifine, deathly shy, gave a quick bird glance
at the visitor and retreated into the outhouse on her bare horny
feet; a rosary tinkling in her fingers. When she disappeared, it
was as though a whole flower-bed had been removed. Stella sat
on the grass and pressed her hands into its wiry tufts to make
sure that everything was real.

There was a faint sound on the verandah and she caught
in a confused glance the whiteness of embroidery . . . it might
well have been an angel who had appeared so quietly, for Cornélie
was dressed in snowy material and on her black hair perched
a hat of gauzy silverish lace. In one hand she carried an ivory
prayer-book and crystal rosary, and in the other hand she carried
her white kid shoes pinched together with the stockings stuffed
into the toes. Her legs were bare and she was wearing alpagatas—
brief leather soles strung together over toes and heels.

She also was very shy, wary. Stella approached her silently, for fear of awakening the child, and put an arm round
her waist. "Well, cousin Cornélie," she said, gazing and gazing
at the white naiveté of the apparition, "I came to call on you

and Andrew, and to see your daughter. Must you really go to town?"

Cornélie glanced in vexation at her feet. "I go down the mountain like this," she said, thrusting out an innocent ankle. "And when I get to the road-turning by the river, someone picks me up in a car, and I put on my shoes and stockings for church . . . otherwise they might be ruined." The sweet convent sing-song of her voice filled Stella with childhood memories.

"Don't worry," said Stella. "You look lovely." There was no envy in her voice, no mockery—only wonder. Surely the island was enchanted, to contain so many beautiful things? Fifine emerged soundlessly with a large paper bag, into which Cornélie put her halo hat, so that it would not be whipped off by thorny tentacles on the route downwards.

Of all the beautiful things, Cornélie was nearest to perfection. She was as frail and supple as bamboo, her gazelle eyes were limpid with ignorance and the tranquil life, her mouth as fresh and unpainted as a child's. Her body filled the simple lines of the embroidered dress with a gentle narrow fullness.

Far down in the valley a bell sounded, slow, dirge-like: the Catholic church calling its faithful. "Where's Fifine?" asked Cornélie, petulantly. Gorgeous Fifine darted out from behind a hibiscus bush to stand beside her white angel. Seeing Stella's eyes on her, Cornélie said: "I made this dress myself. Do you like the eyelet-hole pattern? I made the hat too, out of some lace from Martinique and a piece of wire. What is the material of your dress? It's very nice, I like American summer plaids. Did you make it yourself?"

Stella shook her head, and Cornélie picked up the hem of her cousin's dress and said regretfully: "Ah, machine-sewn. I thought so."

"You'll be late and the car won't wait," said Andrew restively.

"Stay till I come back," cried Cornélie to Stella in her clear child's voice. "I will show you the house, and by then baby will be awake. Will you bring your son the next time you come . . . ?" She leapt from sentence to sentence without a pause, airily; she ran to Andrew and kissed him on the head, equally lightly. Then she called to Fifine to hurry up, waved goodbye, and disappeared with her hand-maiden into the hollow of the bridle-path. Soon from the shadowed valley a sound of low singing, religious but filled with dancing rhythm, came back to Andrew and Stella, who sat silent.

After a while, Andrew spoke. "I got this violin from a tourist."

"And can you play it?"

"I play things out of my head, island things, and one or two respectable pieces. When I play the birds get angry and they seem to fly away, though that's not because I play so badly but because they are jealous. The minute I stop, they come back and raise a row. Listen!"

There was a busy burst of song and a general twitter all around in the thick shrubbery. A grave distant bell sounded like a note of censure. They could still hear voices faintly in the valley. "Cornélie sings," said Andrew. "That's why the church fathers forgive her for living in sin with me, and have her in the choir. It is your Uncle Rufus who is driving her in to Mass."

"What, Uncle Rufus!" exclaimed Stella.

"Our esteemed editor," said Andrew. "He takes his wife and three eldest children and Cornélie, whom he never thought fit to notice until she became a property-owner, all in the car at once."

"That's a good violin," said Stella.

Andrew smiled, his face delicately malicious: "God, the old boy was drunk when I bought it from him! He was a concert violinist from Philadelphia. He hadn't a nickel left on him when he got here—had spent it all on drink. I gave him enough for this instrument to see him safely away to Barbados, but I didn't give him my name because I was afraid he'd come back for the violin when he was sober . . . poor old fool!" Andrew laughed heartily at the recollection of how he cheated the stupid old drunk violinist, just as the boatmen and guides laughed when they cheated the well-to-do tourists; but his laughter sounded hollow and came from the back of his chest, ending in bubbly coughing. The strong light filtering through the saman tree showed up the hollows in his cheeks and neck.

"I'm very weak, you know, Stella," he said. "That's why I didn't get up to welcome you . . . I'm sick with consumption. They expect me to die within a year or so."

He spoke casually, almost in a taunting vein. Sitting in lavish sunshine, Stella felt her body as cold as marble. True she had known all that before. The servants had told her, mother had warned her . . . something secret and lively in her had refused to accept it.

"Can nothing save you?" she asked.

"They keep telling me to go to Switzerland, to a cure-place. But where's the money? Besides, I'm not always sure that I want to be saved. When I see the old people and even the middle-aged people, I think: what is life, anyway, with bodies like that and half-blind eyes?"

She could not speak, but stretched herself out hopelessly on the grass and touched the violin.

"And besides," Andrew went on, "when I read the papers and hear the news of all the blood that is being spilt or is just going to be spilt over the world, can you blame me for preferring to cough my own blood out privately and without too much fuss, in a scene of beauty?"

"There are beautiful things outside," said Stella desolately. "Pictures . . . and music. And the sharpness of change, which makes you see so clearly what you have left behind and what you are coming back to—oh, Andrew, you are giving up a lot if you give up your life without a struggle."

"Rich men and museums own the pictures," said Andrew stubbornly. "And after a few echoes, the music is gone, it is nothing real. But here I have the birds, and my violin. My pictures are alive and I make my own music or nature makes it for me."

"But when the rains come," she cried, "when you are stuck in that little wooden house, very ill, without the books which could build you another world, getting tired of the same voices day after day, longing for change—surely then you wish you had grown strong and seen other lands?"

"When the rains come," said Andrew solemnly, "I cough so much and have such a fever that I can't think of anything, and I don't hear anyone . . . "

"Didn't you ever think," whispered Stella, "that it might have been good to do some work, something interesting?"

"Work . . . !" exclaimed Andrew in disgust. "They forced me

behind the bars of a cashier's desk. That's when all my troubles began. It was dusty there, I was always stooping over ledgers and handling filthy notes. One of the other clerks had a bad cough all the time. After work I would feel so terribly cramped that I would dash out and change for tennis, and I would play set after set, wild to stretch my limbs and forget about my job. One day I fell on the grass court after a set. That was the end of clerking and the end of tennis, and the beginning of my life with Cornélie. You know how it happens here. Men who can't work live on the women who love them."

"How she must love you," said Stella gently, averting her face.

"She loves me—yes. But she wouldn't bind me to being alive, as you would," he said with puckish shrewdness. "You see, you've picked up strange ideas in the North about usefulness and purpose and that kind of stuff. Cornélie is wiser and simpler. She would rather see me dead, young as I am, than taken away from her to be made strong and well. Cornélie is a Child of Mary still, although she was expelled from that organization for adultery. She relies on the Virgin to keep me faithful, and she relies on masses for the soul after death . . . "

"Shall I tell you about some of the beautiful things in the outside world?" tempted Stella. Andrew smiled a little ironically at the ruse. "Go ahead," he said.

"You are in a concert hall" (she spoke dreamily). "The orchestra has become so much a whole thing that it sings with one voice, the sound is a delicious madness. It sings to you of thoughts that can never be expressed in words! You listen, and you learn to know the different spirits of the men who made great music, and you feel that they would have been your friends, for they understand everything. You see paintings. Some of them annoy you, but when you come out into the city streets again you find that the whole scene has been sharpened up, and the colours are more fantastic than before, yes, even the grey tones. Other pictures hurt you with their loveliness. There is a painter called Goya, whose men have skins like yours and just such a look of darkness and wilfulness, and whose women have eyes like Cornélie's. You can get all the poetry books you want, even in the country. Sometimes I would read to Helmut (he's my husband), and once I read to him the Nightingale poem, where it says, 'thou wert not born for death, immortal bird, no hungry generations tread thee down' . . . And Helmut asked me, laughing, 'Now why did you say *thou wert not born for death immortal boy*?' For it always happened that when I heard the best music and saw paintings which wrung the heart and heard poetry of youth and immortality, I thought of you."

"No, it's too late, you can't drag me back to life, I'm content to go the way I'm going," said Andrew. He studied her with pity. "Are you thirsty? Are you hungry? I'll call old Majolie, and she will get us something. We don't have afternoon tea here, but we might have something cool." He clapped his hands, and how lightly the long bones came together, like a brushing of twigs. Old Majolie stumped out of the outhouses, a dirty ancient Negress whose rags hardly clothed her meagre frame; a wisp of greyish cloth tied round her head. She stood there unsmiling, awaiting orders, and Andrew told her to open two fresh green coconuts and bring the water poured out, and to bring some fresh bread and some honey. She stumped out of sight again, and they heard the hack-hack of her cutlass on the young coconuts, and the clink of glasses on a tin tray. Stella realised then that she had not eaten for a long while.

Majolie put the tray between them, and offered Stella half a loaf of fresh-baked bread which stood hacked off on her plate, resembling the hard breast of a mountain girl. The nectarine coconut milk flowed coolly from a ruby glass between Stella's lips and into her parched throat.

"Get the child up—bring Roxelane out to us," said Andrew to the old woman, who stood with folded hands watching them eat and drink. Stella turned to watch old Majolie lift the baby out of its cot in her ragged dirty arms, heard a tender dialogue between the bass croak and the young pipe, and soon a small girl of about three came slowly down the wooden steps and sat on the grass a few feet away from them, covering her eyes with a small round arm, heavy with silver bracelets.

"Take your arm away from your face—the lady won't eat you," said Andrew, mockingly. "Now, Stella, you may keep your museums and your orchestras and all that sort of thing, as long as I've got my Roxelane. Come here, we won't touch you and we won't tease you, the lady here will give you a little bit of her bread and honey . . . " But the child, clothed only in a cambric petticoat and sandals, kept her distance. (And well she might, thought Stella, for I would like to seize her and keep her always.) The little girl had drawn from both parents a languor, a Spanish-seeming olive charm, a subdued fire. Stella's head began to swim as if the beauty and grief of the afternoon were evilly affecting her. The frightening insouciance of Andrew's attitude and the child's contemplative gaze took away her self-assurance. She laid down the last uneaten mouthful of bread-and-honey.

"Do you know why she is named 'Roxelane'?" asked Andrew. "Because of a river in Martinique. You know Cornélie's mother was a dressmaker there? Well, this river, Rivière Roxelane, was there before the volcano destroyed the town of St. Pierre, and it was still there afterwards. It kept right on sparkling and dashing into the sea. Cornélie thinks that when we are destroyed by death there will still be Roxelane, and afterwards Roxelane's children." His voice was boastful. "Don't you think she is a strong little thing, almost fat?"

"If she were mine, I would wish to live for her."

He ignored this. "I don't even let her sit on my knee," he said. "I never kiss her. I kissed you once, though, didn't I!"

"You kissed me now and again. And you kissed me goodbye," said Stella.

"I told Cornélie, but I didn't quite tell her," said Andrew. "I said, 'once I kissed one of those girls'. She always calls you and your sisters *those girls*. She is frantic to find out *which one*? But I don't tell her. Why should I? I like to see her jealous."

"You are tired," said Stella, feeling the situation suddenly unbearable, longing to escape. She got up to leave. But Andrew had lost his sweet malicious mirth and was instantly serious, slumped in the deck-chair, bored. "Don't go," he begged. "We have so few visitors . . . "

Stella blew a kiss to Roxelane and threw a frangipanni flower, milky and scented, into Andrew's lap before she turned her back on the enclosure and went down into the valley, prey to vague antagonisms and desire, thoughts darker than the

velvet-falling dusk. On the way home she met her mother and
Mamselle Bosquet, arm in arm, talking together like two friendly
women who have but one problem—the problem of how to keep
the thing they love best in the world alive—alive and sane.

Coming up to them, she perceived that they were in the
middle of a domestic conspiracy.

"Oh, the drought!" exclaimed her mother. "It is drying up
everything, ruining everything. Poor Buffon has so much extra
watering to do."

"And it's bad for your father, too," said Mamselle Bosquet,
addressing Stella evasively. "All this waiting. Waiting for the
rain. Waiting for the mail-boat . . . It upsets him."

"Stella," said the mother, "we've fixed up for little Hel to
sleep in the orchid house with Lally—cooler for him in this hot
dry weather . . . "

"But the insects!" Stella cried in surprise. "Will he really
sleep better there? Isn't it an awful lot of trouble? He seems
perfectly content in my room."

"He'll have his mosquito net, and Baptiste is putting up
screens on posts."

The two older women stood still for a moment.

"He will sleep better. Your father is restless," said Mamselle,
who had quite given herself over to speaking English to the
mother, and who when she spoke French nowadays lapsed into
patois with the servants.

"It is because of father," said Stella stubbornly.

"Well . . . mostly." Her mother's voice was pained. "Mostly.
He's sometimes almost well. But then he has a crisis."

"He's no better—he is the same as ever!"

"No, sometimes he is worse," said Mamselle Bosquet with
unexpected honesty. "He . . . *raves*."

Beauty and disease, beauty and sickness, beauty and horror: that was the island. A quartering breeze hurried eastward,
over cotton tufts of clouds; the air was soft and hot; colour
drenched everything, liquid turquoise melted into sapphire and
then into emerald.

A bird like a ramier or a wild duck made a long floating
swerve into a grove of coconuts.

"Those poems you used to read aloud when we were little,

when you spoke your old language—I never forgot some of the lines," Stella said, "I never forgot them entirely. Something would remind me—a bird floating like that . . . I would hear you saying, *Les captifs . . . agissent en vain leurs ailes impuis-santes*—Baudelaire, you remember?"

"Guy de Maupassant," said Mamselle promptly and shortly, glancing sideways at Madam. "I don't recollect reading you children any Baudelaire."

"But you didn't read them to *us*, you read them to yourself, really, Mamselle! We just sneaked up and listened. And there was some Baudelaire, too, for how could I ever think of the words—

> *Une île paresseuse où la nature donne*
> *Des arbres singuliers et des fruits savoureux;*
> *Des hommes dont le corps est mince et vigoureux,*
> *Et des femmes dont l'oeil par sa franchise étonne.*

Ah! How often that came into my head, *des hommes dont le corps est mince et vigoureux*—without thinking of this place! Oh, don't you ever read those wonderful poems, ever again, these days?

"I haven't the temperament for poetry now. Before I retire I recite my prayers and my rosary," said Mamselle.

Conversations CHAPTER 6

"It was a tourist in Queen Victoria's time brought the spitting blood to this island."

That's what I heard Baptiste say to Olivet as I drew up to the orchid house next morning, me thinking of my old friend Mimi Zacariah and Master Andrew, and straight from the kitchen where Christophine had been telling of Miss Stella's first visit to Petit Cul-de-Sac.

It was Old Majolie who had whispered the gossip last night, her twig hands snapping and the smoke from her clay pipe rising up to mix with steam from the mountain cabbage. In this island we have a habit of calling rare things by common names: mountain cabbage was nothing less than the white heart of a palm-tree, sacrificed for the Master's dinner. If old Majolie called Miss Stella by a common name, Christophine didn't translate it to me: and I've always been above patois-speaking. Now, hearing Baptiste, I knew that the report had not reached me alone. As he spoke he drenched the large clump of orchid-lilies outside the hut, managing not to smash their large petals and wide-apart antlers. Olivet was mending little Hel's sunsuits while the boy stood waiting naked. Every now and then Baptiste would throw a few drops of water on him, and he would shriek with pleasure. "Don't throw your water into my little flower-house," he would dare Baptiste.

"But we had our own diseases long before that," said Olivet disdainfully.

"I don't think it was an American tourist," said Miss Stella, coming around the corner with the *Island Bugle* in her hand. "They're too hygienic, don't you agree, Lally?"

She sat down beside Olivet, opened up the paper, and after announcing that she would treat us to the news of the town below and the big outside world, began to pick out items. "Ma'am Cassile is getting married. Good heavens, is she still alive? What happened to Mr. Cassile?"

"He got drowned, fishing for tarpon," I told her.

"Beautiful, marvellous, orchid-lily!" Miss Stella touched an antler. "Hel, you will have to become a poet. Sleeping with aenides and calanthas and madonna orchids hanging like lanterns above your bed!"

"And I don't touch them—Lally told me not to," said Hel piously.

Olivet got up, biting the thread off with her teeth: she had grown so tall and stark that she looked like a black tree leafing out into green cotton. "Got to give the hen a bath. Seeing watering reminds me."

"White hen Félice," said Hel. He knew all the animals by name.

"But *should* hens have baths?" Miss Stella was surprised. "I'm sure we don't wash hens on *our* farm."

"Only white ones. She's not for eating," said Olivet.

"The *Bugle* hasn't changed much since Uncle Rufus started running it. Religion, agriculture and gossip; complaints and birthday greetings. 'Those who place cords of wood and heaps of bagasse along the road, obstructing the motoring population from going about its business . . . ' 'I, a mere layman, consider the gully and swing bridge most unsafe during the rainy season . . . ' A new consignment of canvas and leather shoes is expected, Lally."

"Bad hard shoes—machine-made," grumbled Baptiste, flogging away at weeds with Buffon's cutlass. Nearby, we could hear Buffon hack-hacking at his long canoe.

"Baptiste, don't you ever want to get yourself a real job—you with all your education?" Miss Stella asked him mildly.

"I'm waiting for Miss Joan to advise me, Miss Stella," said Baptiste, smiling.

"He thinks Miss Joan will start him up in politics. He thinks she will help him start a trade union," I told her.

"Miss Joan," Baptiste proclaimed proudly, stretching himself, "is something big in the English Labour Party."

"Oh! Is she?"

"But you know Marse Rufus has already started up a trade union. There's not room for two in this little place."

"That's not a proper union—Marse Rufus is in everyone's pocket," said Baptiste, turning sullen. "Besides, he's a white man."

"And Miss Joan's a white woman," said I severely.

"Well, listen to what Father de Vriet has to say. It's a piece out of his sermon last Sunday. What enormous capitals the headline is in! L—U—S—T. Dear Lally, please put up with it. It doesn't apply to you, or to Baptiste either, I'm sure. Who's he getting at?—Ma'am Cassile perhaps—but then, she's being married tomorrow. 'You wouldn't expect to wander through a sewer without soiling yourself. Sexual sin is such a vulgar thing that even a discussion of it is fraught with real danger. In St. Paul's time he strictly forbade the faithful to talk about it at all . . . ' Lally! Maybe St. Paul was right."

Baptiste had sauntered away; he was quick to be disgusted. Little Hel ran after him screeching: "Bucket, Baptiste! Gimme bucket!" they disappeared towards the hydrant where Olivet was crouched over the meek white hen, gently sponging its feathers with a damp rag.

"See, a yacht!" I told Miss Stella; and her long-sighted grey eyes watched the beautiful white thing, as small in the waters of the bay as hen-Félice, curve and seem to settle. Even the Master came out on the verandah with his spy-glass and leaned over the rail, watching, watching. He did not turn when his own daughter waved to him and called. His clothes hung on him baggy, and he stooped a great deal; all his movements were nervous and restless.

"Nothing changes here, except that the coloured merchants grow richer and the white people poorer," murmured Miss Stella.

"Are you sorry?" I asked. "Did you want to find change?"

"I came here to change things myself," said she. "In America, if we don't like something, we change it. If we don't like goods, we exchange them or throw them away. And cars. Everything."

"And people?" I asked her.

"And people—especially people," she said. "Why, why" (and there she was, flinging herself flat at my feet) "didn't Mother and Mamselle try to change *him*? Why must we all live in the shadow of a sinister mood? Something that comes like a hurricane, only oftener? Why didn't Mother and Mamselle get rid of that monster Lilipoulala long ago, and why, instead of ministering to Father and keeping him dependent on that evil creature, didn't they help him to free himself and disentangle his mind and body. Oh Lally!" she wept, "when I think of Father and Andrew, I feel that my heart is breaking . . . but how can a heart break in these glades of loveliness?"

"Hearts do not easily break, not here. And people die in their proper time," I said, to comfort her.

"But we should not die inside while we are still alive and on earth," sobbed Miss Stella.

"Sometimes it is too late to change things."

"No, Lally, no!" she insisted, strong and hard. "It is never too late."

"There's a hopelessness when people are old," I said. "There's a hopelessness in the fixed flesh. It's dangerous to try and change things against people's will."

"But if people have no will—if they are just drugged and made weak by something wrong, or because they can't see anything positive to be aware and alive for . . . "

I laid my hand on her hot head. "Be a good little girl, Miss Stella, and let things alone. Now here's a letter from your sister Joan in my pocket—an old letter. She's another one who keeps wanting to change things, and see how she finds herself. No clothes to her back and her husband has to write left-handed."

Do make Stella stay with you for ages long, won't you, Lally. Ned is quite a hardy little boy. When Edward was in Spain and I had a job, he learned to be very independent, because he

was at nursery school so much. I hope Natalie at least has some
dresses to spare—maybe I can rob her! Will they let me rum-
mage around in the town, talking to everyone, I wonder? Do
you think Uncle Rufus would print some of my articles in his
paper? I will hear all the answers when I get home. I want to
warn you that I look rather thin, for I've been so worried . . . Oh
but I'll be my old self again as soon as I'm with my sisters,
and with Andrew . . .

"Does she know," asked Miss Stella, drying her eyes, "that
Andrew and Cornélie live together?"

"She knows. But she pays no more attention than you do.
In the old days it used to be that poor coloured girls like
Cornélie were no-account girls. But, Miss Stella, I'd like to
impress you that all that is different now. If you or Miss Joan
treat Cornélie like a no-account, you will be making a bad mistake."

"I've never treated her that way," said Miss Stella.

"No—but how you think of her—as someone whom Master Andrew might leave . . . "

"Lally, you're an old zombie," Miss Stella laughed in concern. "You know too much." She walked over to the hydrant
and picked up wet kicking Hel in her arms. Bringing him back
to the orchid house, she dabbed at him with her pocket handkerchief and stuck his fat legs into the sunsuit. "Hel, we're going walking, we're going visiting—to see a little girl named after
a river," she said to her boy.

❁ She had one way of talking, with me: we had the same
tongue, for wasn't it from me that she learned her first words?
Her other way of talking she kept for the rest of the world, and
I could only guess at it; but it always seemed to me that when
she left me even her manner of moving changed. She would
become restless, not so dreamy, and sometimes energetic like
an American woman. Yet I imagined that when she was with
Master Andrew she spoke in our special way.

To little Hel she had another tone entirely, but even this
was variable: sometimes more thoughtful, and sometimes a bit
sharp. I watched her half-dragging that boy along until pity

seemed to seize her at the turn in the path where all the valley lay exposed. She knelt down and let him climb on her shoulders. Oh she was away, away off again, with only that boy as a witness! And he so small that all the learning I'd ever do from him would be by guessing.

※ Ragged labourers could be seen like ants below, oiling the town road, as Stella knelt down to let Hel drape his legs round her throat like a necklace. Throwing an angry look backwards at the road-labourers and nearly spilling him into a thicket she said aloud:

"I wish they wouldn't make any more roads in this island." It was a thought she had often nursed. The great glory of the island was its beautiful secrecy. The further into the interior that the "good" roads crawled, the less safe the secret would be. Tourists would mount the hills then, cars would splutter along, and the town would become just another commercial harbour.

"You like this bad road, ma-ma?" asked Hel placatingly.

"This isn't a road, it's a private track," she told him. "I'm taking off your sandals, Hel, they're bruising me." She slipped them into her pocket. Not for nothing had she practised in childhood carrying basket-loads of fruit on her head like Baptiste and Olivet; fat little Hel sat as lightly on her shoulders as a grasshopper, and she balanced her way across the swing bridge without the slightest shudder of hesitation.

"Will there be anything to eat, where we are going?"

"Don't be a silly boy. There's always something to eat, everywhere. If there's nothing cooked, Uncle Andrew will pick you some fruit." Stella was determinedly erasing all those planned Germanic farm meals. She was feeding little Hel as she loved to feed herself, like a bird of the air, settling to pluck something delicious now and then. "After all," she'd say to Lally, "I grew up that way, didn't I?"

"No, Miss Stella, you had your regular sitting meals."

But Hel was perfectly agreeable. He was an imaginative boy, and had risen to the prolonged adventure. New darker faces, new voices, pale mauve potatoes called dashine, the legs of chicken-tasting frogs—he'd try them all, and ask for a little more. Tiptoeing up to the child Roxelane, as she sat plaiting straw in Andrew's clearing, he wet his finger and touched her bare arm. She lifted her white petticoat and wiped away the spot. He sat beside her and took hold of the other end of her straw plait. Regarding him with moody beautiful eyes, she gave him the whole of it. He hastily gave it back to her.

Old Majolie, who had been crouching beside Roxelane, stretched her twig limbs and gave Hel a few strands of straw. She was teaching the baby girl to weave a basket. Knotting Hel's straws together she tried to explain to him in patois and with deft gestures, how to start the bottom circle. Hel put the straws against his nose: they smelled good, like dry perfume. Old Majolie, barely greeting Stella, attended only to the two children, muttering in a hostile undertone:

"Trop pressé pas ka fait jou ouvé."

"Is Mr. Andrew at home?" asked Stella.

Old Majolie shrugged. "Pas sav. Ca c'est pas s'affaire-moi, Mamselle Stella." But Stella knew from her uneasy looks that Andrew was at hand, just as she had known in advance that Cornélie and Fifine were in town, practising with the Children of Mary for Corpus Christi celebrations.

"S'enfant-moi ni faim. Bai-li kaishoi pou' manger, souplé," she told the suspicious old woman, who said nothing, but rambled off to the cook-hut and brought out a little bowl of saltfish and a cup of milk, which Hel consumed.

"Andrew!" called Stella. Only her own echo floated back to her. Old Majolie looked cynically pleased. Stella turned away and parted the riotous bougainvillea hedge. He would be down by the spring—certainly down by the spring; the coolest spot for a day of drought and endless leisure. She remembered, too, his delight in rushing water. So she pushed her way through a bank of lordly staghorns. And there she found him, fishing for crayfish like a young boy, with a net on the end of a bamboo. She took off her sandals and sat on the rock beside him. Their four long, undulating feet appeared and retreated as the gushes of water eddied in and out. Mosses and lichen of tender purplish green made a cushion for their heads. Along the damp banks of the spring, selanginellas and rare begonias danced between the tree-ferns.

"I came back for this," murmured Stella, savouring paradise, feeling for a few moments divinely happy, craving nothing more. Then she saw through the glassy water that Andrew's feet looked chilled and blue, and she begged him to dry them in the sun. "I will if *you* will," he said (just as he used to say in the old days), and they moved out of the cavernous shade, stretching out together on a large warm slab of rock. There they lay with clasped hands, while Andrew stung her with questions. He seemed to enjoy plying her with pin-pricks of affectionate malice, and this day he was possessed by a demon of curiosity. He was most curious in his probings about Helmut, puzzling over what had caused her to marry him, what had caused her to leave him. "Why didn't you marry a rich American? There are plenty of those, aren't there? I thought you went away with some of the richest people in the United States?"

"Ah, yes," she mused. "They were rich indeed. But they didn't ask me to marry them. You don't realise! They thought of me as an impoverished *child*."

"Well, you're still an impoverished child, and I'm one too," said Andrew. "And we've reproduced ourselves in two other impoverished children. Did you bring your boy with you today?"

"I brought him, yes. He's playing with Roxelane. Old Majolie is minding them. She hates me, you know, on Cornélie's behalf. She muttered in patois when I came up, 'too great hurry won't bring the daybreak'. Pretending she didn't think I'd hear."

"Oh, she's a snarly old bitch, never let that worry you," Andrew said. "We all have our watchdogs here. You've got Lally. And I had Mimi, though she has stayed in the town with my sister Rosamund, and last year, as Lally may have told you, she died. Cornélie has Majolie. And Roxelane will have Fifine, later. They are probably the last of the guardians. For things are changing, as you would notice if you lived in town yourself. That sort of devotion is ending. Yes, they're the last of the slaves, and out of fashion . . . Let's get back to New York. Tell me how the rich people live! Tell me how you met Helmut!"

"It all circles around opera and orchestras, and the background is brocade and velvet and satin. Can you imagine taking an elevator to your bedroom, in a private house? That's how I lived for a while. I lived with a royal family of finance. They were good people; more honest than we are; *they* would never have cheated a poor tourist, like you—"

"Or come secretly to capture another woman's man, like you," said Andrew, hitting back in his time-honoured manner. "Don't feed me that line about how good and honest they were. They must have been robber barons behind all their church-going."

"Whenever I think back to them, I hear the music of Wagner, I think of my friend Margaret's father as Wotan, that supreme god of Northern mythology. I see Wotan lying asleep in a flowery meadow, and I hear a solemn chorus expressing splendour and dignity. Did you ever hear about the palace built for Wotan by the giants Fafner and Fasolt? It was the symbol of his power. Margaret, too, lived in that Hall of the Gods. And so did I. But privately, Andrew, though I luxuriated in it—I was never really comfortable there, in my mind. I felt like a modest little govern-ess, somehow or other. Yes, I felt like someone by Jane Austen who had strayed into Wagnerian heights, into Valhalla—"

"Oh I don't read books, don't pester me with those stuck-up allusions," Andrew cried pettishly.

"Andrew, darling, don't get angry, it only makes you cough," said Stella in an anxious voice, for he had wrenched his hand from hers and lay face averted, heaving tormentedly. After a pause he rolled on his back again and commanded her:

"Go on."

"The kinder they were, the more the brocade and velvet began to smother me, the worse I began to feel. I had beautiful days, brilliant evenings, and terrible nightmares. In my night-mares, there was always Mr. Lilipoulala."

"Well, he's still alive, sucking the blood of his victims," said Andrew cruelly.

"During the daytime I determined to make myself strong in the north so that I could destroy him in some way, even if only in my dreams, but perhaps by killing him. After a long, long while, a feeling grew that he was not actual, that I must have imagined him . . . Once, turning a corner suddenly in New York City, I saw him. It was on a day when I felt homesick and tense. I took fright and hurried into Grand Central Station. But it couldn't have been *him*. It was just a man in a Homburg hat, perhaps just another man making money out of human misery."

"Dear little Stella," Andrew exclaimed tenderly, "I like this kind of bookish talk, honestly I do. It's so grandly *impossible*."

"It was a wonderful thing to have an older woman of great elegance for a friend. She linked up with the operas. All the dirt of the struggling world was shut out of that gorgeous house with seven floors. If they were really robber barons, Andrew, they were surely the most upright and moral robbers in the universe! And meanwhile, I was becoming mad about music. Whenever Margaret could not go to a concert, she would give me her ticket, sometimes half a dozen tickets. I would sit in the most expensive seats and sometimes I would have a whole box of the Diamond Horseshoe to myself, for I had no other friends, and knew no one to invite. On one such evening—Oh, you're not listening, you're asleep!" she said sharply.

"No, I'm not asleep, I'm just joining in your dream story," he protested. "But didn't you ever dream of *me*?"

"You're too conceited, I won't answer that. Anyhow sometimes I used to remember Lally saying, 'We ought to be grateful for the boiling lake, simmering and spouting, we should be very glad the lake is there, it's a safety-valve, remember what happened to Martinique which had no boiling lake at all. Your grandfather went there after the terrible volcano, and he saw nothing but charred bones and a silver slipper and the river carrying on as usual'. You see, the utter comfort of my wealthy friends was like a cool evening cloud over the boiling lake, and in the cloud there were angels of music and food and talk and pictures and polite society ways."

"I'm waiting for the tale of how you met Helmut."

"And I was getting to it when you nearly fell asleep . . . One evening, I had two tickets for a concert at Carnegie Hall. I went there early, and watched the crowds around the box-office trying to buy last-minute returns. I had the impulse to give away Margaret's second ticket to a total stranger. But they all looked so smart, and so hustling. Then I saw an extremely shabby young man with a fair sad face turn away in disappointment and put his money back in his pocket. I touched his arm and

said, 'You may have this one, if you like. My friend can't come.'
And he gave me three dollars for it. That was Helmut."

"A funny way to meet a husband," Andrew commented.
"Did he fall in love right away?"

"I don't know. But we sat alone in a regal box, and the music swept over us like a storm! When Helmut saw how expensive
the ticket was, he invited me to a little German coffee-house
afterwards, trying to repay me with hospitality. We both felt confused, after the Brahms Concerto in D major. Of course we met
again, and again. Always to music. We measured our acquain-
tance by recitals. I used to give away the spare tickets to him,
and he always insisted on paying me two dollars and fifty cents
or something like that for them."

"But why did you marry him?" asked Andrew brutally.

"Come to think of it, why did you give yourself to
Cornélie?"

"I needed her," he said simply.

"Well, I needed Helmut even more. I needed *someone*!"

Andrew did not retaliate. He closed his eyes again, and
Stella hoped he was reflecting on her isolation in that city of
long box-buildings pressing skywards, a beggar-maid among
millionaires, without a contemporary friend even until Helmut
had appeared; a footloose child among the moral robber-barons.
A pleasant wave of retrospective self-pity and remembered opu-
lence washed over her.

He opened his eyes. "I'm hungry."

"Come back to your house, then. We'll eat something."

"No, no. I'm too tired. Go and bring me some sandwiches.
Chicken ones—get old Majolie to fix them. We killed a fowl yesterday. And bring some rum punch too."

Stella parted her lips to declare, "Why should I run errands
for you?"—it was what she would have said all those years ago.
But she gazed at him, and repented; he seemed so ill, so unut-
terably weary. And what was even more compelling, he was as
beautiful as Narcissus.

"Don't you even want to see my boy?"

"Later, later." A faintly jealous shade overlaid his airiness.
This inspired her with loyal anxiety towards little Hel, whom
she found outstretched beside baby Roxelane, both children fast

asleep, almost in the exact spot where they had played with basket-straws. Old Majolie had slipped coloured cushions under their heads and covered their feet with mosquito netting. Now she sat beside them, smoking a clay pipe and fanning those small babes in the wood with an enormous palm-leaf fan. The children's lips were stained red with the juice of berries ("fwaises," said Majolie, in answer to unspoken interrogation). She reluctantly handed the fan to Stella while she wandered off to do Andrew's bidding. Stella sat beside the sleeping pair, softly brushing aside flies and mosquitoes, cooling their stained cheeks. As she sat there she could feel her love for Andrew and her passionate desire to draw him back to life and health surging like spring water, oh no—like the boiling lake—in her body, in the hot brooding air, in the smoke which escaped from Majolie's cook-hut.

✿ She resisted the impulse to waken him with a kiss, and setting down the copper tray on flat moss, dipped her finger in weak rum punch and touched his lips with it. "A strange diet for an invalid," she said as he sat up.

"I shan't be an invalid much longer. I'm either getting well— or dying. At any rate, something's happening to me . . . "

The pounding of the spring dissembled her pounding heart. "Since I came?"

"*Now* who's conceited?" He laughed. "Of course, since you came. And your sisters will complete the cure. But don't you and Joan imagine that you're going to reform me. That's what I like about Natalie, the doll-beauty. She takes me as I am. But she's like Cornélie, she hasn't any conversation. Oh I've been missing your conversation, and Joan's, my dear preachy little Stella!"

"I wish you wouldn't speak of us in that plural way," she burst out.

"But that's how I've so often thought of you—each of you having something which I couldn't help loving—couldn't help needing . . . " He munched, and she poured him out a ruby flagon of rum punch, in which fruit juices swirled. "Weren't we talking about *needing* people?"

"I don't remember." She sulked.

"Yes, we were. We were discussing Cornélie and Helmut. Tell me—do you love him?"

"You seem capable of loving four women, so why shouldn't I be capable of loving two men? The answer is, of course."

"That's no answer," said Andrew. "Tell me about your life with Helmut."

She gave him one of her old-time grimaces, and narrated, firmly and reasonably: "At seven-thirty we water the animals. At eight we begin the real day's work: like getting in wood for the winter, picking fruit, tending the vegetables. In the winter it is dark at four-thirty. Can you *see* that, Andrew? The thick wall of early darkness? We haven't got refrigeration yet, we've been too poor, so after a big freeze we go down to the pond and saw the ice. There's a special ice-saw with very long teeth and a cross handle, and we walk backwards as we saw. I must admit that I don't do much of *that*! Helmut and the hired man do it. We pack it in the ice-house with saw-dust for insulation, right up to the roof. Helmut churns the butter, and my mother-in-law and I stamp it, in a lovely stamp that holds just a pound. Once a week we women go to market. We get top prices there without the middleman. Machines and furniture are always needing repairing. Bits of the house have to be reshingled every summer. My mother in law—"

"Oh, don't kill me," said Andrew in an infinitely languid voice. "What do you do in the evening? Sleep?"

"Mostly. But if we have any energy left, I read and Helmut plays the piano, rather well. His mother studies the mail-order catalogue. She can only just about make it out. She's very German, you know—thinks all the English are decadent."

"Well, are we?" he asked. "And are we even to be considered English?"

"Decadent? We are I suppose. Father certainly is. You are, in your way. And Uncle Rufus. But Mother isn't. Joan doesn't seem to be. Natalie may be. And I"—she held out her hands in triumph—"could you call hands like these decadent? They're as hard as nails from sheer hard work."

"But still beautiful," he said, snatching one and scrutinising it.

"She didn't like them—Helmut's mother. Once, when we

were stamping the butter, she lifted that hand which you are now—which you are now . . . "

"Kissing," he concluded, and promptly released it, as if the narrative was more important.

"She lifted that hand and said: 'Take a look! This hand came from folks who quit working a coupla-hundred years ago! It's a mercy Helmut has good thrifty Bavarian blood on both sides of his family, or your Bubi would have been born with fins!'"

"Horrible old hag," remarked Andrew.

"No, Andrew, don't speak against her. She's failing now—quite worn out, you see, with all that terrifying work. They didn't start with money in the bank, like so many American farmers. Oh, you ought to hear her speak against the rich farmers who just farm for a hobby and carry on other businesses! Anyhow, I'm grateful to her. It was she who gave me the money to come home on."

"And did she buy you a return ticket?"

She ignored the mockery in his tone. "Yes, she did."

"I wonder if you will use it—Stella, darling Stella," he said, heartier now that he had eaten and since he had kissed her hand; somehow assuaged.

Stella was contemplating in memory the farm living-room: dim, solid, decorated with a greenish carpet and overcarved upright piano, a place with many doors, one of which was propped open to the kitchen by an oak figure bearing a faint resemblance to the statue of liberty, bearing in her uplifted hands brass petals, gangrenous with age, which in turn supported ten-cent electric bulbs shaped like pineapples.

"Ravishing Stella, come away from the farm and be a water-sprite again. Take the pins out of your lovely hair that you've screwed up so unkindly, and let it float out as it did when you were a little girl," he pleaded.

"Oh, you're as bad as Lally, wanting me to slide back into childhood."

"No, I'm worse than Lally." His eyes made her flinch, and she turned away to watch an army of large black ants heave up her unfinished half-sandwich on their backs and stagger in formation down the bank of moss.

"Anyhow, it's an innocent request." She pulled out several

bronze pins and dropped them on the marching ants, who scattered in confusion, reassembling like guildsmen when her hands were empty.

"No, Stella, my adorable hoaxer, you know it's not innocent." But he did not touch her; she could see him staring at her through the long veil of hair under which she hid her face. It was so thick that it muffled the spring's sound.

"Your marvellous hair—Joan's nose and throat—Natalie's mouth and feet! God, what a tantalising lot you are!"

"*Detestable* Andrew!" she cried in a thick voice. Love-hatred and the warmth of her falling locks nearly suffocated her. Yet she seemed to hear in the mazy distance the sound of a child crying. She threw back the long unravelled coils and exclaimed: "It's Hel. Hel is screaming. Do you hear him?"

"Might be Roxelane," he said casually, seizing a large streaming bunch to hold her prisoner. But she tore away from him, and his weak hands slipped regretfully through the vulnerable stuff. The screams were those of a boy in pain or desolation: she knew them well. When complacent little Hel was unhappy, he was loudly miserable.

"Stay with me," begged Andrew, watching with resentment her bundling-up operations.

"No, we've both been here long enough—I must take him away. You're too *dispersed*," Stella told him sombrely. "And too callous."

"It's only that I like to plague you."

"Well, I can't bear it. Come with me if you want to see my poor little darling. Listen to him!" She rose lightly and anxiously, poised for flight. He did not at first attempt to catch up with her, but before she parted the bougainvillaea hedge she could hear him coughing wildly behind her, pausing as if to cling to a tree for strength, and calling hoarsely: "Stella! Wait! I'm coming."

A Storm ✼ CHAPTER 7

I took little Hel right away from her when I saw her coming back like that, the poor boy hanging loose in her arms, for he was too limp to balance on her shoulders and hang on. Anyone could see that he had been sick, and crying too; he smelled of sickness and tears and when I laid him on his cot in the orchid house he fell in a fainting drowse until I sponged him off, when he began to fret weakly.

It was a great grave pity, for I had so much to tell Miss Stella, but that had to wait. "Whatever have they been giving this poor boy to eat?" I asked her quite sharply.

"Majolie gave him some fish and milk—and I don't know how many fraises," she told me, tired, stretching out her aching arms.

"Oh, Miss Stella—you didn't trust that old woman to feed him? That dirty old Obeah woman?"

"Poor old Majolie, I know she's a rude old thing, but she's no dirtier than Christophine, is she?"

"She's a lot, lot worse than Christophine and you should call to mind that she has no cause to love you."

"I know that." She looked at me sadly, touching Hel's damp hand. "I've been with Andrew."

"You're not enough of a mother, Miss Stella. Not enough of a mother yet. And you've been missing an important time to be a daughter, too—wait till you hear what happened this afternoon! Please, I do beg of you, leave Master Andrew alone. Let him die in peace. Look after the living."

"He will not die," she said, angry and proud.

"Ssh! You'll make him cry again." I put a wet cool handkerchief on little Hel's forehead, took off his sandals and covered him only with a linen sheet. He did not wriggle, but seemed to be comfortable. Then I led Miss Stella outside and we sat near the water pump while I told her the strange thing which had happened: that a gentleman from the yacht had hired a police horse and ridden uphill to see the Master.

"The yacht!" she sang out, gazing to see if it was still there. And it was, but only just; the beautiful white sails were as full as pegged washing, and its prow dipped as if ducking to run.

The answers she wanted to have from me, such as what was his name and where and when did he ever know the Master, I could not give her; for Madam and Mamselle Bosquet had been the ones who replied to *his* questions. All he had told the ladies was that he had been a dear close friend of the Master, and having heard he was in trouble, ill, hidden away (so to speak) . . .

"Hidden away," repeated Mamselle Bosquet. She knew the Master's secret hiding-place, where he went to escape from the household, from Madam, from herself, even. And every time the Doctor came to have a look at him; and the messengers with bills; and anything which his poor wild mind considered troublesome. That's where he had gone the minute he heard the hoof-clops.

The stranger had reined in, but had not dismounted; and the barefoot runner-boy who had come as a guide had now caught up with the horse and stood there hanging on to its tail. Madam and Mamselle Bosquet leaned frightened over the verandah rails. Perhaps there was just a little look of hope in Madam's eyes; but nothing like it in Mamselle's.

"I came to ask him if he would like to sail with me. Clear out. Get clean away. In other words, make an attempt to recover," said the stranger in a rush of effort.

"Oh, if he would . . . " Madam spoke in such a small voice

that it was almost crossed out by Mamselle's frown. Every year Madam was growing more gentle, more timid, and Mamselle more bold.

"Will you ask him to speak to me?" the stranger said. And Madam, overcome by shame and hopelessness, went indoors: but she knew he would not be there. She simply retired to her bedroom and sat in a rocking-chair, rocking with her head in her hands.

"Don't you think he would accept?" the stranger asked of Mamselle Bosquet, politely.

"No. It is too late," replied Mamselle Bosquet; and just then Olivet came up with a tray, carrying whisky and soda for the visitor. Mamselle Bosquet poured for him, and he accepted the glass.

"Do you people know—" the stranger began, pausing to swallow, "that he would have been a great man—he *should* have been a great man, or at least a *big* man?"

"Yes, we know," said Mamselle Bosquet stiffly.

("But great at *what*, Lally!" cried out Miss Stella in the middle of my telling. "Great at what! didn't the stranger say?")

The stranger thought we knew all about the Master's lost greatness. He finished his drink and he stayed there for a while longer, watching Mamselle twist coralita tendrils into a plait. The horse was getting restless; and the runner-boy wandered off after Olivet, humble but disdainful. It seems that more than one person had told the stranger not to waste his time.

"Will I see him—is his wife coming back?" the stranger asked.

"She does not know where he is." That's what Mamselle Bosquet told him finally.

"Well, I am sorry," said the stranger, disappointed and proud. He was gingery, like a Scotsman, and all his clothes and even his Panama hat looked fresh and new. But he was not like the Scots overseers. He had a face full of learning and sorrow.

"I am sorry," he said again, lifting his hat and turning the horse's head. He rode away slowly, and the runner-boy trotted alongside sucking an orange.

Oh! Miss Stella was in a wretched rage over the stranger's parting in disappointment. It was as if she had been defeated and disappointed herself. "Mamselle doesn't want him to go away and get better, she wants to hold him here to his fate just as Cornélie wants to hold Andrew!"

"Maybe," I said, thinking I should brew little Hel a good ginger tisane.

"And she's got all this on her side. All this!" Miss Stella threw her arms wide to take in the island. The beauty of the evening cast her into another fury. We both saw that the yacht had grown smaller and paler in the far water, and did not speak of it; but Miss Stella ran down to the turn in the road and stared after it as though she would cast out a line and haul it back, beg of the stranger to try again, detain him somehow until the poor man with lost greatness could be caught, bound, put on a stretcher and somehow rescued against his will. But it was no use—only a weariness. I went into Christophine's kitchen and wheedled some boiling water from her. My poor little boy was rubbing his stomach and moaning. But the birds had never sung so beautifully as on that evening—the tropiales and the mountain doves especially; and the scent of oleander flowers was so strong that long after the stranger went to sea he must have borne it in his nostrils.

※ Whatever it was Majolie had given my darling boy to swallow, it had done him evil and it's my belief that was her intention. I told Miss Stella so when the Doctor had gone and the Master had come out of his hiding-place again, and poor Hel had ceased his panting and choking over the terrible taste of physic. "Not to kill him this time, but to frighten you away—don't ever you take that boy to Cul-de-Sac again," I felt myself bound to say. "No, Lally, I never will," she said—and she was frightened all right. For a time she even managed to keep away herself, weaving in and out of the house with books and sewing, going shopping in town but coming back dusty and depressed, waiting all the while, scanning the sea. "Patience, patience, Miss Joan won't be long now, and then Miss Natalie. But you always used to fight with them so—why can't you do without them?" She'd never make answer to this. Her eyes searched the sea so often that they were turning sea-colour. The Master was waiting too; he peered behind his dark glasses, hanging about in the verandah shadow, speaking little, boiling up for one of his raging crisis times. The scorching drought went on; and at night L'Aromatique was full of distress and shadows. Sometimes Miss Stella made Madam and the Master angry with her careless words. I thought once that Madam would say, when little Hel was at his peak of sickness (and we all knew how a hot dragon could carry off a little child in one quick gulp): "My dear child, why don't you go home—go back to your husband?" If she did not say so, it was because of her long-starved love for this first daughter of hers.

One day when I was unpacking the things from the old chest to air them, as I did once a year, I came upon the white dress which the girls wore, one by one, when they were confirmed. It was not as lacy as a Catholic child's First Communion dress, nor was it made of silk, for we'd had a Low Church man then, I remember, and besides Madam had been so poor—she could only afford fine muslin. The veil was of very fine net like gauze, just a straight long thing which made Miss Joan look like a little hospital nurse and Miss Stella like a nun, and yet seemed to turn Miss Natalie into a fairy princess. Fifteen years old they had each been in their turn, older than the Catholics, old enough to know what they were doing, the Low Churchman said; and all the girls had been almost at their full height.

Miss Stella came up to me and asked if she could try on the dress. Always the same trouble getting the opening over that big head so glistening with hair; but the side fasteners did not burst except for two across the chest which I left undone; the dress fitted her, though she did not look any longer like a holy child; yet as I watched her the sly little nun look crept over her face and she lifted her long white-sleeved arms. The minister had required a modest length, but now the dress fell only just below her knees. "Oh I wish Andrew could see me in it!" Miss Stella said. "It might make him feel better . . . he'd remember funny things like singing in the Anglican choir, and old Sir Twistleton or Grandfather reading the lessons—"

"Listen here, my darling Miss Stella, though you look a lot lovelier in that dress than in your American clothes, it wouldn't be right for you to wear it to amuse anyone. That's a sacrilege, to treat a confirmation dress so."

"And you a Methodist, Lally!" she mocked me.

"Me a Methodist, but we have feelings about sacrilege too. It's the smile on your face that doesn't go with the dress. And your thoughts . . . I'll have it back for putting away, *if* you please."

She let me help her out of it, but pleaded with me not to pack it up again, and I let her take it to her room and hang it in the cedar press.

I had hung and laid the other things out of doors, but I'd chosen my day badly, for the air was heavy with coming damp. Prayers for rain had been going up from the island like steam for a month; it was nearly the first of July. July: *stand by*: the start of the hurricane season.

As I stood with my face upwards taking the feel of the damp and not knowing whether to leave the clothing out or not, Mamselle Bosquet came out of the house leading little Hel by the hand. Hel didn't often go into the house; he was shy of his grandfather. It reminded me of what Miss Stella had said those many years ago: it's his voice I don't like. Every time the Master spoke, mostly to give an order to Buffon or Baptiste or to speak briefly to Madam, little Hel seemed to shrink away. It was as if he was hearing in the distance another voice, his father's young twangy voice perhaps, and feeling a little homesick. Hel was still looking pale and weedy after his illness; in spite of a sleeping net and all my watchfulness, he had a few red insect bites on his neck and chin; his blue eyes were larger than ever. The German in him shone gold and white against Mamselle's black skirt and dark thin person. Today Mamselle was almost merry. Her bird lips were smiling. "The mail-boat, Lally—the mail-boat is due in! I've been telling Hel that the ship may bring him a letter from his father!" But it was not of a treat for the boy that she was thinking. She was thinking of the arrival of Mr. Lilipoulala.

"And will it bring Aunt Joan?" asked the child

"No," I told him, taking his hand from Mamselle's. "She'll be coming from the south. The mail-boat sailed from the north. What have you got in your other hand, Hel?"—his fist was clenched.

"A candy," he said, opening his palm out and showing me a brown lump.

"Old Majolie gave it to him. She brought Madam a basket of fruit from Cornélie," said Mamselle Bosquet.

"Let me have a taste, Hel!" The little boy gave it up trustingly. He was never hungry nowadays anyhow. I smelled the lump and licked it. It was a tamarind ball boiled in syrup. It tasted only like tamarind and syrup. But I was afraid of what it might do to him; I threw it down the slope into the bougainvilleas. Although Hel had not wanted to eat the sweet, he howled when he saw me throw it away. Mamselle Bosquet shrugged in distaste and went indoors again. Miss Stella came running back to comfort her son.

I did not tell her right away why I had done it. But after Hel had been consoled with sugared orange slices and laid down for his nap, I asked her:

"What is it about the father of that boy that you don't want to return to?"

"It's not what I don't want to return to. It's what I don't want to leave! But since you ask, Helmut isn't complicated enough for someone like me. He's too simple . . . "

"Simple, Miss Stella?"

"Do you know, he actually thinks that men are more important, stronger in every way, than women; that women are designed to be happy around the house, to have children, to be taken care of, to work hard and to take orders! His old mother thinks so too! And that from someone who loves music!"

"Never mind, you've told me that he is a good man. Isn't that something? Isn't that safe?"

"Safe!" she cried lightly and bitterly. "Safe! Who wants to be safe! Oh yes, I know I'm a darn fool to leave a country where nice ordinary young men are ten cents a dozen, and come to this glorious inferno to chase after one rare half-extinct specimen!"

"Children should be safe."

"Hel is perfectly safe. You fuss over him too much. Oh Lally, look how the sky darkens! Look at the enormous size of that cloud—and another—and another! The rain is coming. Quick, I'll help you to drag in the clothes."

We went to our work as fast as we could, but I said to her, panting, for I'm in no condition to be a working busybody really:

"Hel is not safe." And I told her about the tamarind ball. I think she would not have believed me but for the menace of the storm, which made our island world dark and frightening, like early night. Every bit of sunlight was blotted out. The land was dirty grey, like those strange fogs Miss Joan wrote about. There was a gleam of lightning, and I saw that Miss Stella's face was as white as her confirmation dress.

"Maybe you're right, Lally. But you always used to discourage me from believing in magic."

"Majolie's magic is real, I never told you I didn't recognise obeah," I said sorrowfully. "Do you know what she puts in those medicine spells of hers? Human dirt. Chopped lizards' tongues. Things like that."

She shuddered. "Lally, you're trying to scare me. Yes, you've frightened me, I admit it. But I've got to be brave . . . because of something else. Yes, I must be brave."

"Don't carry your braveness too far." We went into the orchid house and sat beside sleeping Hel, talking in whispers. But soon he woke up. The wind had begun its violence and was whipping round the house and the sheds like a mad agouti. Large clots of rain began to fall, wide apart at first, and I could see the Master leaning on his stick outside, talking to Buffon. In a short while he disappeared from view and Buffon pegged a hurricane lantern on the verandah like a beacon. It was my fancy that the Master had looked happily impatient. Miss Stella put little Hel's sou'wester on him and prepared to take him into the house for supper. Careless of the boy's listening ears, we continued speaking anxiously.

"What chance of a hurricane?" she asked, her eyes seawards.

"Very little, Miss Stella. It's before season."

"I wish," she said quietly and low, "that his ship would turn turtle and that he would be drowned."

"But you're surely not afraid of him any more!"

"Afraid—no," said Miss Stella. "But so angry, so furious! I've been thinking about the stranger from the yacht—what he said about Father. Only once in all my life have I ever had a good and fine conversation with Father—long years ago, just before I went away. He talked to me of his youth, of schooldays at

Harrow, of how he found himself poor at twenty and had to teach in a basement school . . . He must always have been very proud. He talked to me of books he had read . . . but when it came to the war, he would say no more."

"It's night in the afternoon," said little Hel. He pulled my skirt. "Let's go out in the black rain."

"War is terrible," I said foolishly, bundling up Hel's bedding. He could not sleep in that frail building. It might well be swept away. If within a few hours of such downpour, stone bridges were swirled away, what of a little orchid-house? Funnily enough, I thought of Miss Joan's husband, dropping his fingers under the olive trees in Spain.

"But war is not as terrible as Mr. Lilipoulala!"—she dared the name at last. Now the rain was falling so hard that we could hardly hear each other speak, and when we got across the few yards' distance to the house we had to change most of our clothes.

In the dining-room I met Mamselle Bosquet; she was arranging coralita sprays in a crystal vase. She wrung her hands a little. "Oh, I hope the ship's not late! Oh, I hope he can get up here tonight!"

"Well, as you know, Mamselle," I told her, "he's such a man of darkness and mud that it would take more than a rainstorm to keep him from sucking the blood of a corpse."

Miss Joan �֍ Returns

An Ending CHAPTER 8

There were too many of us sitting in the pantry during dinner that night. Luckily Christophine never put her face in there; nowadays she did not leave her cookhouse at all, having Buffon to wait on her and bring her up the raw goods from town and the bottles of black rum. At meal times Christophine would pass up each course on a tray to Buffon, who would run along the palm thatched passage and pass it through the long window to Olivet, who would carry the food in and wait on table. Tonight, because we were all chased from our special places by the rain, and because the electric plant that Miss Natalie had installed the year before was always turned off and boarded up against lightning and floods in bad weather, we gathered around the brass lamp and the candles on the dresser-shelf, and Olivet fretted that we were sorely in her way.

Baptiste too, though he had no business to be there, not being anything but an idle retainer (though I believe that Buffon used to pay him part of his money to do jobs for him while he hacked at his boat), was there sitting on a stool in a corner reading the *Island Bugle.* He studied with a very serious face the long piece on "will the drains await the next visit of the

Governor". After that he took to reading over and over the list
of properties up for sale for the recovery of taxes.

"One lot, one house, Harbour Alley, property of Eudoxia
Bethalmie; one house, one outhouse, Pious Road, property of
Afrodidy Thompson"—he knew he was provoking us, that we
wanted to hear the talk from the dining-room, difficult enough
through the dropping of rain. I didn't want to engage in argument with him, but when I saw him pick up the peeling knife
and cut the page out, I felt bound to ask him if he had the right
to do that.

"I'm cutting it out for Miss Joan to see how these poor
people lose their homes when they haven't any money," he said.

"And the most part of them pay up at the last moment, it's
annoying the Government they enjoy, you know that well."

"Miss Lally," he had the impertinence to say, "I'm better-up
in knowledge of these matters than you are, and you over-
esteem the pleasure these paupers get out of annoying the Government."

"Don't you ever let Afrodidy Thompson hear you calling
him a pauper!"

Olivet came out of the dining-room and said to her brother:
"Master says, will we kindly keep quiet in here."

Now that was a little thing but I found it good, for seldom
did the Master interest himself in the ways of the house or give
an order. He left it usually to Madam, and of late she had laid
this duty more and more on Mamselle Bosquet. It was true,
though, that if he was going to be pleasant at all, or formal at
all, like in the early days, it was always at dinner-time; that was
the only time when he came out of his shell, wore a tie, and
made a little conversation. While Olivet was dishing up the vegetables, I heard him telling Miss Stella what a pity it was she
had come too late in the year for carnival, that it had been a
very good lively carnival (he understood) with plenty of libel-
lous songs—good tunes the slander-verses had to them, bois-
terous tunes, to match up with their words; he had heard
Christophine bawling them in her kitchen.

I peeped through the door-crack and I could see Madam
half-rise to contradict him and change her intention, I heard
her say in her voice that was growing so much softer and

weaker: "They are organising a committee to improve the carnival and raise its moral tone."

"Who are?" asked Miss Stella.

"Father de Vriet, Father Toussaint, Uncle Rufus and the Society of Christian Ladies."

"Well, they'll wreck the songs—and the music," said the Master.

"But the costumes need a little improving, they've been getting more and more indecent," said Mamselle Bosquet. "And I know Father de Vriet thinks everyone ought to unmask before sunset. Too much revenging and beating up takes place in the dark, as we all know."

"I should have enjoyed a good old carnival brawl, now that the family isn't in the Government," said Miss Stella.

"Rufus is not a disinterested party. Most of the songs in the old days used to be about him—and his many liaisons," the Master said. My! He was in false good spirits. It was eight months since I last heard him laugh. Yet the oil lamps threw differences of shadow on the faces round that table, so that they looked anxious behind their chatter. Olivet was nervous too; when the long loud roar of the mail-boat's double-hoot forced its muffled sound through the rain, she dropped the silver ladle she was spooning out the fruit-salad with. At that moment, too, the Master pushed back his chair with an ugly scraping noise and went over to the harbour window. He stood there until Miss Stella reminded him that his dessert was waiting, though I knew he could not see a thing through that wall of black water. "Send Buffon to me in my study," he told Olivet when she brought the coffee. And out he went, carrying his coffee in a hand that trembled.

Miss Stella went to her room to look at little Hel, who was curled up on one side of her bed, near the foot. Madam and Mamselle went into the drawing-room with their books, which anyone could see they had no mind to read. I thought I might as well make myself useful, so I gave Olivet a hand with the washing-up. Baptiste had gone out to the kitchen, perhaps to read his mother the article on *Rum—our Ruin*. Now and again he used to try to reform her: but she took it very kindly. It generally ended by his having a shot of rum himself—just one.

From the study all we could hear was a low mumble, followed by Buffon's loud sheep-voice: "Yes, Master. I'll take the big one." I knew he was being sent to guide Mr. Lilipoulala up to the house. The thing about Mr. Lilipoulala was that he trusted no one. He would come to the door with his devil's goods, and collect the money: to give him due, he had come through worse weather than that, he was less afraid of the elements than of the law—and I doubt much if he was afraid of the law—he had too many friends.

Miss Stella came back into the pantry. Buffon had hitched down the big old rusty hurricane lantern and was giving it a careless cleaning. He filled it to the brim with kerosene and tested the wick.

"Oh, are you leaving now, Buffon?" asked Miss Stella. Of course she knew: she didn't need to listen to guess his mission.

"You be well asleep, Miss, before I go," grinned Buffon, fingering his gold earring. "Customs takes long-while. Motoring bridge under water by then. I light Mr. Lily the way on swing-bridge. You well asleep, everyone well asleep." The wicked fellow—he knew perfectly that no one in that house except little Hel and Olivet would sleep hard that night. Christophine would be drunk in her outhouse, and Baptiste would be sitting beside his mother despising us all, thinking about the arrival of Miss Joan and the bad conditions he would be happy to unveil to her.

"Mr. Lily gives me a good tip," Buffon said.

"How much?" asked Miss Stella.

"A dollar," Buffon answered, putting a box of matches into his ragged pocket. "Miss Lally, allow that I lie on the floor and take my doze before the journey, please, ma'am."

I said nothing to him, but I unclenched Miss Stella's hand from the dresser-edge and I blew out the candles and dimmed the lamp. "Go in and join your mother and Mamselle, Miss Stella, darling. Or go and lie beside your child. There's nothing you can do to prevent anything. Go, take your book, and keep those poor ladies company."

"Those poor *willing* ghosts," Miss Stella cried in a voice of great bitterness. "Oh, hush!" I begged her. So she went to her bedroom and shut the door.

For a brief half-hour after that the rain ceased; going on

my rounds to try the windows, I saw the lights of the mail-boat bobbing in harbour: the sea must have been rough. Meanwhile the wind had come up, and I thought me of how next day the banana fields would look like a battlefield of wounded soldiers. That would be another thirty pounds lost in the night. The wind was banging and plaguing the shutters and bolts all around the building. The fireflies had put out their lights and hidden for shelter. The trees were stooping under their wet fruit and orchids, and as I opened the front door a chink I smelled the dampness of leaves and knew how ruined and treacherous the road would be after such rain. There were forms that took shape in the darkness on such nights, and it was as well that I did not believe in dread zombies and soucouyants that Christophine sees in delirium. I found human beings bad enough and good enough without having to look around for devils in the shadows and angels in the Methodist chapel.

Presently I heard them all go one by one to their bedrooms, and I went to my little room which was between Miss Stella's and the portico, but I did not hear her undressing. When I tapped and opened the door, there she was sitting on the bed. "Why don't you go to sleep—Hel's perfectly all right," she said to me crossly.

I was offended and went to my bed and settled myself for sleep, but soon it was my fancy that the rain began to fall again and that I heard Miss Stella pass outside my room with a silky sound of her cape raincoat. I fancied too that she went into the pantry, and that I heard whispering, and the clink of teaspoons or silver money: yes, it was silver money, changing hands. I did not open my eyes—I was afraid—but it was my fancy too that I heard her galoshes on the soft mud and in my body I felt the wet branches sting her as she took the narrow way to the bridge.

I myself have only been that way at night once, that was a long time ago when the Master took bad and Buffon was not there to fetch the Doctor. The shadows are much blacker on a rainy night. The torrent of the river made a loud noise like drums against the piping of little frogs in the grasses. The valley was like a long dark pit and the tree-ferns, battered by wetness, were like people watching. Something seemed to follow me step by step, but being sensible I paid no attention. Part of the way was through thick forest, and there I needed a strong hurricane lantern—a little round spot from a torch was no good. I was relieved when I came round the shoulder of the mountain and saw the stars again, for then I was nearly at the bridge. But even in those days the bamboo stakes at the base looked weak and old and easy to chop through. Yet it was a funny thing, the stone bridge would be under water and crumble away each rainfall, and that little frail swing-bridge would go on swaying and being used.

It was darker than a fancy, it was a nightmare thought I had that when Mr. Lilipoulala would come to be greeted by the flashing of the lantern and Buffon's earring and teeth shining in its glow, he would see there on the opposite bank Miss Stella, whose face he had only known when she was a child, standing there looking a little like the Master when he was young and clear-minded. She would be holding the lantern high, and he, that man of darkness, would be so dazzled by this sight that he would balance forward eagerly, holding to his little black bag, not able to hold to anything else, for there was nothing else to clutch.

❋   Next morning very early Buffon went to Christophine in the kitchen for the empty milk bottles. The cows were sheltered in a shed down in the valley. He usually loaded four bottles into a basket and took an extra empty one along, for he was not above making a little profit on milk too, when he reached the fresh spring in the forest: he had a willing customer. We did not generally see him again until noon, when he brought up the fish or meat and provisions, and Marse Rufus' paper.

But barely an hour passed that morning before he was beating at the pantry door, mud on his ragged suit and his mouth falling open, his eyes rolling wildly. "Corpse!" he said hoarsely to Baptiste and Olivet and me. "Corpse of Mr. Lily, cigarette man, head down in river!"

Christophine must have heard for she stuck her head out of the kitchen and shrieked *Holy Blood!* Baptiste and Olivet were solemn, but not much disturbed. There was a rustling, and who should come out to hear it all but Mamselle Bosquet, her bird's eyes blinking. She said to Buffon, "Have some sense, boy. Sa-qui faite?"

"Bridge bust up," said Buffon. "What a commesse! What a kalaloo! Rain and wind broke up bridge. I saw him in the water. I holler, and three women carrying limes came down the road. We hauled carcass out onto bank, and the women went to tell the town. His hat was gone . . . his lovely hat—gone down the river. But I found this between the rocks. Rocks are sharp there. They caught him by his clothes, and this . . . " From under his rags he drew the little valise marked with the letters I well remembered: "H. Lilipoulala, Port-au-Prince." It was still dripping wet, but the leather was thick-grained and good, and it was tightly shut. Then Mamselle Bosquet put out her thin, thin hand and said softly: "Give me the case, Buffon."

He handed it over, and Christophine found breath to ask, "What have you done with the milk?" Buffon said that he had left the bottles on the river bank beside the body. "Go on back about your business, then," said Mamselle Bosquet. "The police may want to talk to you. But wait—wait a minute."

Mamselle left Buffon standing there in the pantry telling his tale over again. It was getting richer and more horrible. She only went around the corner into the dining-room, took a long black hairpin out of her chignon and fiddled with the lock of the valise. "I'll do that, Mamselle," said Baptiste eagerly. And he twisted the hairpin so neatly that the lock sprang back and it was opened without damage. "Did you learn that when you were a primary-school teacher?" asked Mamselle Bosquet, not even forgetting at that moment to be sharp.

She went through the contents of the case. It was neatly divided into little packets, each labelled with someone's name. There was also a long typed list which said "accounts outstanding". Mamselle took out the packet marked with the Master's name, and half a dozen others; her hands hovered as if they would have emptied the case but did not dare. She put the accounts sheet into her pocket and concealed the little packets before clicking the case shut and giving it back to Buffon. "A very well-made case," said Mamselle Bosquet. "Take it quickly back to the river bank for the police to find, and forget about it. It's a bad case—a dead man's case."

"Yes, Mamselle," said Buffon, wiping the sweat and mud off his forehead and starting obediently downhill.

※ It had turned out to be a fair day after all that darkness of rain—a beautiful yellow day, and I went into Miss Stella's room to dress little Hel. He was awake and sitting up, tying a large knot in the sheet. "Hullo, Lally," he said. Miss Stella opened her eyes. Her clothes were in a heap on the floor, and her oilskin cape was thrown into the china basin.

"You look tired, Miss Stella," I said. "Why don't you stay in bed while I give Hel his breakfast?" She shut her eyes and did not answer. So I began to dress little Hel and he talked all the time about ropes and lassoing and wild games. After breakfast I took him for a walk, for the sun was scorching down on the damp ground and had dried it up as if no rain had fallen for a month. The land, except for those ruined bananas and flowers, looked as if no yesterday had ever happened, and that was how I felt, being with little Hel. But soon Miss Stella joined us, swinging her straw hat. In the town below the Catholic dirge bells could be heard, far but distinct.

"Have they told Father yet . . . about the accident?" asked she.

"Madam is with him," I said. "She'll tell him when she thinks the moment is right."

"Now that Mr. Lilipoulala is out of the way," said Miss Stella rather clearly, as if she dared me to contradict her, "the air seems a lot lighter and sweeter."

"That may well be—for the two of us," I said.

"Well—if I can *drive* myself to be brave and strong, surely he can be too!" cried Miss Stella, "even at this stage. He has been a soldier, and he's still a man, after all."

"I've told you before, Miss Stella," I said, "that there's a hopelessness in the fixed flesh, and that it's dangerous to try and change things against people's will . . . or God's will."

"We shall see," said Miss Stella stubbornly. And as she stood there, hard and proud in the morning light, not afraid of anything or anyone alive in the world, it was impossible to discourage her. But I could feel the greatest of trouble on its way, and on its way fast. It didn't surprise me to look back and see Mamselle Bosquet hurrying down past the two cows, who seemed to notice her agitation, for they moved aside to make way for her.

Hel pulled at my hand and said, "Lally, I'm hot. Let's go inside." But I didn't want to leave my Miss Stella alone to face the attack: I told him, "Just a minute, darling. Just a minute."

Mamselle was beside us, and she looked yellow and wretched. "Wonderful weather," she said to Miss Stella. "Lovely clear weather, after last night. The wind was so strong that I couldn't sleep. I sat by my window till the dawn."

"Were you expecting someone?" asked Miss Stella, her voice cold.

"I was waiting for Mr. Lilipoulala," said Mamselle. "We all depended on him. We all hated him, but he had the power to soothe . . . We were always afraid of the day when Mr. Lilipoulala wouldn't come any more, for then the horror and the loneliness and the weakness coming over one who has been in terrible battles . . . " Mamselle stopped to sigh, to gasp. "The horror and the loneliness might get too strong for a body and mind growing old—and death for Mr. Lilipoulala might mean death for another, or madness." Her lips trembled. "I saw you going downhill with the lantern, with the wind tearing at your raincoat, Stella," she ended up in her severe governess manner.

"Well, why didn't you follow me?" asked Miss Stella, trying not to sound impertinent, trying not to sound like a schoolgirl.

"Because . . . " said Mamselle Bosquet, in shame, "it so happens that I am growing old myself . . . my rheumatism is bad; I am afraid of the night damp."

Miss Stella had nothing to say to this—she turned it over and over in her mind. Then she said gently: "Don't you think that Father is brave enough to renounce his old habits and live for other things—perhaps for you and Mother and his grandchildren—particularly his grandchildren?"

"Renunciation," said Mamselle Bosquet mournfully, "is something for the young. The old have so little to renounce. All they ask is to be left in peace, to live out their poor lives in the way they have chosen."

("Lally, I feel hot," said little Hel in a spoilt whining tone. "Hush, darling," I said to him.)

"Oh, dear," said Miss Stella wearily. "It took me so many years to learn to be ruthless, to learn that Mr. Lilipoulala was only a person after all, that he could be destroyed quite simply!"

"You did the wrong thing," said Mamselle. "Now you must go away. Haven't you got a man of your own, all to yourself, up in the North? Whatever made you leave him and come down here to disturb us? Was it love or was it hate that brought you here? Was it love of your father and Andrew and the island, or was it hate of an evil thing, of being frightened in dreams— which was it?" She was very bitter.

"I thought it was love," replied Miss Stella in apology. "I thought, love. But how can one ever be quite sure?"

"You can be quite sure that you love," said Mamselle, "when you will go through the utmost misery to make the one you love happy. You may see this one doing the most foolish and wicked things, but you say to yourself: 'If it makes him happy and keeps him alive, let him do it, let him have it'. All the while you want desperately to be near him. But you feel that you would go away for ever if the going would mean contentment for that one. Yet at the same time you would remain a servant in his house if it would bring him comfort."

"Love doesn't mean just that to me," said Miss Stella. "But then we are different people—different generations."

I saw the bird-eyes of Mamselle sharpen and flare and I could not imagine what the end of this duel would be, for two women fighting at cross purposes might tear each other to pieces before surrender. I touched Miss Stella's arm: "Little Hel is hot, he may be getting a fever, he may be getting sunstroke. Won't you please take him indoors, as I have to speak to Christophine about the vegetables."

Miss Stella's eyes travelled back to Hel as though they had been on a journey, and she said to him, "Hel, would you like to come with me to Roxelane's house, and play with her on the nice cool verandah?" Before the little boy could answer, she swung him up in her arms, and balancing him on her hip, she turned away from Mamselle and walked off in the direction of Petit Cul-de-Sac. Once she looked back at me as if to deny her promise.

Mamselle Bosquet faced me before we made our way back

to the house. "Lally, listen: it's about time that Miss Stella went away. As you are so devoted to her, why don't you see that she goes home soon?"

But I could not answer, for I was worrying about little Hel, my poor baby.

We passed Buffon, hack-hacking at his gomier-tree boat. He looked up and smiled idiotically, well pleased with the morning's scandal and tragedy, for he found life at L'Aromatique dull compared with his old days as a boatman when he had encountered sharks, baracoutas and mean-minded tourists.

A Coming ❋ CHAPTER 9
and a Going

They buried Mr. Lilipoulala that afternoon, because it was too hot to keep him. He had a Catholic funeral of the first class: it was established that he was a very religious man in Port-au-Prince. There was also plenty of money in his pockets to pay for the funeral, so he had the best organ music and plenty of flowers, and afterwards he had a splendid Requiem Mass. The public never heard what happened to his valise, for Buffon could not remember whether it was picked up by Father Toussaint or the Police Inspector: anyhow no more was heard of it by any of us, not even long afterwards when Mr. Lilipoulala's relatives arrived to dig up the coffin and take it back to Haiti, where he was buried again in a much finer coffin with real silver handles. I did hear tell, though, that the ship which carried him to his last earthing was a ship of disasters, nearly running on reefs off the Virgin Islands, and suffering from so much sudden sickness that two other bodies were carried ashore in the end.

Madam and Mamselle took the easy way with the Master. They just did not tell him anything at all, but let him go on living in a false peace for a while. So, except for a look of darkness in everyone's eyes, that look which says *What will hap-*

pen next?, a kind of calm settled over L'Aromatique, and Madam went on laying-out her new rose-beds overlooking the valley and the river.

The only break in that calm was the illness of little Hel. When his mother brought him back to me that night—and mark you it was a night when the moon was like a dinner plate, so that after a short dusk the sky turned blue again—it was easy to see that he suffered from a fever.

Baptiste was reading the *Island Bugle* out to the others. "Death of a Distinguished Merchant", said the front page. He handed it to Olivet when he saw our distress, and volunteered to fetch the Doctor: but first he paused to polish up his boots. Miss Stella was dreadfully anxious, but the Doctor said Hel would be all right in a few days. "A touch of ptomaine, and a touch of malaria—nothing to speak of," he said. Just the same, Miss Stella sat all the while by Hel's cot when she was not at Petit Cul-de-Sac, for she found it difficult to conquer her anguish, and difficult also to be with Madam and the Master and Mamselle Bosquet.

"Talk to me about the farm, and the snow," said little Hel in his peevish voice. Miss Stella put him to sleep with long, long tales of snow-men and haying and the cream souring behind the kitchen stove, and the German grandma driving the old Chevrolet into market. I got to know the name and look of every animal on that farm by the time that Hel could sit up again.

"He's homesick," I said to Miss Stella. "Believe me, he'll come down with the fever again, just because he's homesick."

"Oh, Lally—oh, Lally!" cried Miss Stella. "Do you *genuinely* think so?"

I could say yes with truth, for I honestly thought that the little sandy boy was pining for his father and for America.

She went out on the portico and looked down on the land, sighing as if her heart had broken and the wind was whistling through it. "Beauty grows like a weed here," she said, "and so does disease."

"Will both the cows at home have calfs in spring?" asked Hel.

"Darling," said Miss Stella in her rare mother-voice, "do you really want to go home so badly? We can go back next week, if you like . . . in Aunt Joan's ship." She had come back into the room and taken the little boy's hands in her own, swinging them. He looked at her with eyes full of trust and dependence.

"Yes, it's very nice here," said Hel politely (watching me), "but I wanna go back."

So it was all decided in that moment, and Madam was the first to be told, but she was not surprised—only a little sad that Miss Stella would hardly see Miss Joan, and not see her youngest sister Natalie at all. "I really don't think that little Hel thrives with us, he has lost half-a-pound in weight," said Madam practically. She then set to work on the packing and other arrangements, doing it all so quietly and well that Miss Stella was able to leave the island without any fuss, without any stir, except the commotion she had made in our lives and our hearts.

※ The ship bringing Miss Joan was one of those chancy boats which just looked in when it pleased, picking up stranded passengers from the mainland of South America, and only dropping into our harbour if there was what the *Island Bugle* called "sufficient cargo inducement". It did not run to schedule, and we had no strong idea of when it would appear; save at the last, when a neighbouring island would send a message through, "*Caliope* en route your port".

When we heard of this message and knew that in a few hours Miss Joan would land, and that the next day would see the *Caliope* steam outwards with Miss Stella on deck, standing at the rails with Hel in her arms, Miss Stella said to me offhandedly, "I think I'll run over and say goodbye to Andrew and Cornélie."

She took the path towards Petit Cul-de-Sac and was away for a very long while—for such a long while that I set out to search for her, clumsy and unhappy though I am on the mountain tracks. I feared that she would miss the welcoming of her sister. But when I came upon her she was standing with her arms tight round a laurier cypre, seeming to listen, and gazing down into the valley.

※ The two elder sisters had their coming together after all, though it was my belief that Miss Stella would have escaped from it if she could. The Captain of the *Caliope,* being part-owner of his ship and having a coloured mistress in the town, decided to lie in port for two days.

It was never so easy for me to read Miss Joan's mind as it was to understand what was behind Miss Stella's talk, or even Miss Natalie's. First of all, her words were fewer, and she had a way of pausing in the middle of a sentence even as a child, looking straight into the eyes of her hearer, and seeming to change her meaning, perhaps to make it give less away.

Little Hel had begged to be allowed to sleep in the orchid house just once more, so Baptiste and Buffon had moved our bedding in there among the hanging plants again. He asked it, I thought, out of jealousy of his boy cousin. He had wanted to go home until he saw the other boy arrive, and then he started hanging about me, squawking a bit, talking about how he would miss white hen Félice and the cows Belle-mère and Doudoux.

The other boy, Ned, was a whole year older, he had put babyhood well behind him and his hair was cut like a prisoner's by the ship's barber. Although he was pale and tired, he did not cry, and he was never as curious as Hel: his surroundings did not surprise him—anyone could tell that he had moved house many times. He carried his own little pack on his back like a pedlar.

But his mother's luggage! She had three packing-cases full of books, one large and one small suitcase, and a string bag full of toys and toilet articles. She and her son stepped out of that hired car at the very door of L'Aromatique like a pair of boys (for she was straight and quick, wearing a navy cotton skirt and her hair quite short too): snatches of talk and her little dry laugh came to me as I introduced the boys to each other.

"Oh I had a wonderful journey! Do you know, I saw Natalie in Trinidad—I spent the night with her! She was giving a party, a sort of dance, and she was surrounded by handsome automatons (that's what she calls them herself). One of these Ha-has, for that's what she calls them for short, is going to fly her up here in his seaplane—when he can make the time . . . Mother, I even dipped into Barbados and saw the yacht club fluttering with little white craft and ladies' parasols. Ned and I came out of our dingy cabin and stared enviously . . . Father, have you sold the piano? I don't see it anywhere!"

She had darted into the house and now came out again and stood on the portico as if addressing a meeting.

"We only sold it after the wood-ants had eaten half of it and the mice the other half, and water had spouted in during the hurricane three years ago," the Master replied.

"Lally, how's your tumour?"—it was like Miss Joan to speak of my complaint as if I carried a child.

"Mamselle Bosquet, I hear you're an Anglophile nowadays and belong to the league for the suppression of patois . . . "

Christophine shambled out of her cookhouse followed by Olivet, and slyly but eagerly, waiting his turn with a foreknowledge of importance, Baptiste stepped forward.

"Oh, Christophine"—Miss Joan even went so far as to kiss that face which no one had ever seen washed by any water other than sweat and rain. "You still smell so beautifully of rum . . . Olivet, is this really you? You are so tall! But yes, I remember those teeth which I so much envied . . . "

Buffon, who had travelled up in the car with the luggage, rolled on the ground in a frenzy of jollification. Everyone had caught Miss Joan's excitement except the two boys, who stood regarding each other unsmiling, Ned with his hands in his pockets and Hel with a hibiscus in one hand and the other clasped in my own.

"And Baptiste . . . "—a loud squeak of boots mixed with Miss Joan's words. "My old friend. The only good letter-writer in the island. Yes, you were all hopeless. Only Baptiste told me the things I really wanted to know. Fancy *nobody* telling me the awful fate of the piano!"

The Master was paying the hired chauffeur. Suddenly Miss Joan looked weary, seemed to change her mood. "Where's Stella?"

I saw the cautious hesitation pull her back from asking, "Why is she going so soon—I don't understand!"

"She's waiting for you in your room—you two will share a room tonight, her last night, as Buffon may have told you," Madam said quietly.

You would not believe that two little boys could get sufficiently acquainted to start up a fight between tea and supper, but those boys did. Hel took the swizzle-stick off the cocktail trolley and hit young Ned with the spiked end of it. Ned did not hit back right away, but after he had rubbed the mark on his bare arm enough to turn it purple, he went up to Hel, tipped him out of his chair, and banged him on the head. I could not help but enjoy this, for it reminded me of how Miss Stella and Miss Joan had fought like little cats at the same age—of how they had been locked in such a struggle that they had bumped together from the top of the stairs at Maison Rose to the very bottom, covered with bruises, but still in a scratching grip.

All this made me wonder whether during that one short night of meeting, the girls would disagree. It was a great disappointment to me that I never heard a word of their conversation though I walked under the window after the boys were well asleep. I heard a murmuring and a murmuring, and it sounded peaceful enough, the only struggle being for who should say the next sentence: and the two voices, for all that they'd lived in those different lands, so much alike that it was a duet of mating sissizebs.

Just the same next morning I did my last-minute ironing of Miss Stella's dresses in the portico after I took them coffee and oranges. They were hard asleep still, though the sun was on their faces. The state of the room was something awful. Miss Joan's unpacking and Miss Stella's packing up had mixed all over the floor, table and chairs. I gave the tray a good slap down and said good morning. Both stirred. One of them said "Good . . . " and turned over. Young Ned had gone off sight-seeing across the estate with Baptiste; little Hel was digging with his wooden spade beside Madam. Mamselle Bosquet was sorting laundry; the Master had disappeared. The others were going about their business as usual.

When the voices came through, even the first words were the same as in the olden days.

"Stella, are you awake?"

"Not yet. Are you?"

"I'm coming to. Oh! am I at home? No, this isn't Maison Rose. I'm in Grandfather's house."

One of them laughed.

"Did you dream?"

"Didn't have time. The real is dreamier than the dream, anyhow."

"Throw me my orange."

"Lovely coffee. I expect the grinder still works."

"Joan, you're staggering. Don't tread on the things Lally ironed."

"American gingham," said Miss Joan. There was a sound of material being shaken.

"Now don't sound contemptuous like Cornélie. 'Machine-made! Oh my gracious!'"

"I'm in no position to be contemptuous."

"I know. Poor Joan. Not a rag to your back. That's why those things are lying on the floor. They're for you."

"Oh! Marvellous. Shall I try one on?"

"If you have the energy. Haven't you any underwear either?"

"Not much. But it doesn't matter in this divine heat."

"Of course it fits. We're still more or less the same shape."

"Your legs are longer," Miss Joan said after a pause.

"That's supposed to be a town dress. I seldom went to town."

"Well, I shall go. Baptiste will guide me. I want to see the people. The town smells just the same. Only I missed the open gutters as we drove by, and some of the cobblestones. I promised Ned that he would sail boats from the boat-tree in other people's bath-water. He'll be disillusioned. Ah, I like this white dress. I shall try it on too."

"Joan . . . "

"Stella . . . ?" the smothered voice came through the neck opening.

"Don't you recognise that dress?"

"How can I, when there isn't a full-length mirror in this room? Oh, the tucks! Mamselle's tucks! Did you ever find her embroidery lessons useful in your country? I didn't. I always wished she had taught me to knit, but of course we never had any wool here. Ned was always known at the clinic as the poor baby held together by safety-pins. Stella . . . ! This was *our* dress. All of ours. It makes me remember the catechism. And the Archbishop: 'Dear children of Gaard . . . ' Lovely dress. It was so old and severe for us at the time. Is it too young for me now, do you think? I'd like to wear it to a Government House *at home*."

"You are only twenty-five," Miss Stella said in a sad tone.

"I feel much older. How toughly I've had to live. Mamselle didn't allow for the family brain when she cut this out, did she? Well, did it fit?"

"Yes, it fitted. But Lally says we must not wear it with light thoughts in our minds."

"Light thoughts! I so seldom have them. Everyone thinks I'm too serious, except Edward . . . and the Labour Party. Here, get out of bed. Let's go out into the bushes."

"No need to do that. Remember we have plumbing now."

"I shall still use the crotons by the cliff sometimes. The old privy over the ravine terrified me. I was so narrow I used to feel that I'd fall through it."

"How alike our bodies are," said Miss Stella.

"Well, I'm certain that breasts are hereditary, though they sometimes skip a generation. Remember Grandmother Mowbray?"

"Yes: in spite of her eight children who died."

"We were in danger of becoming a matriarchy. But you and I have sons, at least! I wonder what the boys are up to? Blissful to know that there are other people to worry about them. Darling Stella—don't look so sad. Come along."

They went down the portico steps, pausing to make chaff with me, Miss Joan saying: "You perpetual old eavesdropper, Lally!" And I removed to the pantry until they returned, their temples wet from the cold bathing they'd done in the open air.

Miss Stella said: "I must really pack."

"If you have anything left. Stella, I don't really need all these clothes. All I want is the two gaudy ginghams and the confirmation dress."

"Oh, take them. I shan't go straight back to the farm. I'll stop off in New York for Hel to see a good Doctor, and Margaret will be so ashamed of me and so sorry for my shabbiness that she'll load me up with new dresses. I must see her anyhow. I've treated her very badly. She didn't really want me to marry Helmut, you know. And she is miserable without a romantic docile protégée."

"No one did," said Miss Joan. "With Edward it was quite the opposite. No one wanted him except me. It was such a relief to them all to see him stabilised . . . as they thought."

They were silent and busy for a while. I had long since finished my ironing, and sat on the top step resting, waiting for the boys' lunch-time. I was very tired: Miss Joan speaking about my tumour like that brought back the weariness of my old complaint. I'll just about last out these comings and goings, I thought.

"Luckily there are a few things that I can give *you*," I heard Miss Joan say at length. "These four exciting books. And Ned's warm coat for the chilly days on deck. I expect little Hel has grown taller here. And his scarf . . . "

"But won't Ned need them, when he goes back?"

"Ned is not going back."

There was another pause which surely was full of surprise and alarm, perhaps even full of jealousy. Then Miss Stella asked, in a strange way:

"Why, aren't you ever returning to Edward?"

Miss Joan replied: "Yes. But Ned is staying here."

"I don't understand."

"Oh, Stella, Stella! I haven't time to make you understand. We can't keep away from the others any longer—on your last day. Edward's life is always full of difficulty, failure and danger. I'm going back to him—of course. But I'm leaving Ned here for a year or two, until everything becomes clearer. So you see he will be too large for his overcoat then."

"Is it good to leave Ned? And have you told them here?" asked Miss Stella, and I knew she was echoing my fears.

"Mother knows. She has known from the first. It is the lesser of two evils, and it must be good when everything is so familiar and beautiful, and so warm! Do you know what I shall be afraid of, when I sail away?"

Miss Stella must have shaken her head silently.

"The cold. It terrifies me. I'm half-dead every winter."

"I don't mind it any more. I love snow."

"It's the grey cold. One day I shall die of it."

There was a great crackling of paper, something was flung into a box, and I heard next:

"One of my worse desolations is not seeing Natalie."

"Never mind. Natalie will be more worth seeing, or rather more worth talking to, in a few years' time. Do you know, although she's been married and widowed and become rich and all that, she hasn't grown up yet? You would hate her friends, Stella. She has the most awful friends in the world. I only hope she doesn't bring any of them here. She *really* cares about clothes and parties, too."

"She'll bring whom she pleases. After all, it's her place."

"And she has been generous with it. What would Father and Mother have done without her?"

"She never had our peculiar consciousness of living . . . that's the best way I can put it. The thing which makes us both so—so uncomfortable."

"And uncomfortable to live with, I dare say."

Another long pause, with more crackling and cutting of string, and two more objects were thrown into a trunk.

"My dear Stella . . . " Miss Joan, so seldom shy, hesitated. "All these garments I'm inheriting—they seem to mean something. It's as if I'm inheriting more than that. What is it? You know, sometimes I have what Edward calls a 'divination'. You puzzle me. You haven't told me anything, really."

"You'll come to it in time. Everyone, in fact, came to it at once. Especially Lally."

"I, too, came here to change things," said Miss Joan slowly and clearly.

"Well, that is part of what you have inherited from me. My changings. Look out for Lally: she'll put a curb on you, Joan— you old scientist!"

"You old romantic. You're as bad as the French Romantics. It's partly Mamselle's fault: no wonder she became more British than the British, in expiation."

✳ I saw Baptiste and Ned standing beside the cows, talking. Madam and little Hel joined them, and all advanced towards the house. The boys were trotting fast; they were hungry. I went into the girls' room and said:

"Your boys are coming in to lunch."

"Thank you, Lally," they answered together, as if in relief. Yet when I went out to dish up for the little ones, the girls hung back. The two names which were in the air, the Master's name and Master Andrew's, were almost spoken; but I doubt they were ever said. Miss Joan went up to her mother and put an arm around her neck. Miss Stella went to the boys and took a hand of each. Ned twisted away. Hel cried, " Ma-ma, why should I go away, and Ned live here with Lally?"

I couldn't help letting fall a tear into the transplanted weak-seeming poinsettia in the stone jar by the pantry window.

In the Town CHAPTER 10

"Lally, where is Ned?—Baptiste, I'm ready!" Miss Joan came towards us, clamping Miss Stella's left-behind straw hat over her hair. I was sitting beside Baptiste, who wore his Sunday clothes, on the bench which ran round the saman tree like a leather belt. Baptiste rose, but hesitated to smile.

"I don't really know, Miss Joan. But Mamselle says he is quite safe."

"Oh Lally! has she taken him away from you?"

It was so like Miss Joan to say right out the thing which I was feeling and keeping quiet. I had been obliged to take up my sewing and darning again, as Ned didn't cling to me the way little Hel did. Once he had got a map of the estate in his head, he was off like an arrow to some target or other. The only two who seemed to know where he was were Buffon and Mamselle Bosquet. Often when he had worn himself out exploring he would be found leaning against Buffon's boat, watching.

What charmed Mamselle Bosquet about him and made her go to the pains of teaching him patois words against her principles, was the fancy the Master had taken to this elder grandson. The second morning after his arrival, the Master had interrupted the boy in the middle of a sentence and said: "I

declare this boy hasn't a *t* to his words. Not one. He leaves them
all out. Where was he brought up?"

"In Balham," said the boy.

"The slums of Balham," murmured Miss Joan.

"In the slums of Balham, Grandad," the boy said, louder.
"And before that Wolverhampton. But I was born in Birmingham."

The Master gave a prolonged stare across the table, as if
doubting that any descendant of his could possibly have packed
such travels into five years of life. "By God!" he exclaimed. "The
slums of Balham! The other boy used to say 'I wanna'. That
was bad enough. But it is less pardonable for an Englishman to
discard a consonant than an aspirate. Micheline, you must take
him in hand."

Mamselle blushed for joy that he had called her Micheline
at the table. And Ned, proud of being referred to as an Englishman
already, reflected her red glow.

That was how the friendship started. After that the Master
would occasionally say something challenging in a growling tone.
The boy would stand up to him and answer back. Mamselle
Bosquet would clasp her hands happily under the table; Madam
and Miss Joan would smile at each other. But meanwhile Ned
grew less and less of a baby boy and more and more of a person.
I expect I had lost him before he arrived, even.

"Baptiste and I are going off to start our machinations," Miss
Joan declared.

"But why for do you want to walk into the hot dusty town
before midday?"

"Because . . . " Miss Joan appealed to Baptiste for an explanation.

"It's because of the people. We want to help them," said
Baptiste proudly.

"The people, the people. I don't understand the sacred way
you say that word, Miss Joan. I don't understand it at all. You
only know about a dozen of them, anyhow."

"It's politics," added Baptiste.

"There are a lot of labourers out of work. Baptiste says
they're starving."

"Well, we can't afford any more up here. So what's the use?"

"We can organise them," said Baptiste.

"Organise them for what?" I asked.

"To stand up for their rights," Miss Joan said.

"Poor people have never had any rights in this place. Every-body knows that. Most of them are poor because they are lazy."

"No, Lally, that's unjust," Miss Joan told me gently.

"And where would you be, Baptiste, if you didn't live off the Master's money, which is Miss Natalie's, or your poor mother's hard work?"

"I've been waiting for Miss Joan to start the organising."

"Look out you don't become a perfect Mr. Fiuminato. He's organised people into riots and misery in an island three times as big as this one. The people turned to him and he squeezed every penny from them and became a rich man."

"I fear you are of the old school, Miss Lally," said Baptiste.

"I should hope so too. Miss Stella was always wanting to change people she knew. But you want to change people you don't know! Where will it all lead to, Miss Joan?"

"I don't know: but we're beginning with the *Island Bugle*. We think it is misleading the population," said Miss Joan.

"Well, we'll have Marse Rufus up here like a ramping manicou."

"Lally, I promise to be tactful," smiled Miss Joan. She moved off and waved to me from a few yards away to prevent my answering back that she was the most tactless of the girls. Anyway I didn't want to bring her down too low in front of Baptiste. I took a little comfort in the thought that they wouldn't get very far with their schemes. Every sensible property-owner would be against them, and the nuns and the priests, and the Government officials. Perhaps after all Miss Joan would not break her heart over this business of changing people, the way it had happened to my darling Miss Stella. With her, perhaps it was something outside the heart: something she had learned out of books, something in the head.

It was through books and in the head that Miss Joan and Baptiste came close together, even as children. When I saw them go off like that I didn't feel the straining after them I suffered when Miss Stella escaped from my sight and power. I thought they might get into trouble, but it wouldn't be the same sort of trouble, and they could deal with it somehow, strengthened by their kind of religion.

Yet I felt jealousy against Baptiste, that he could hear and understand Miss Joan's special words, words which would never perfectly reach my ears. Sooner or later those words would come through to me; Baptiste would tell his mother, and Christophine, when she'd had more than a pint of black rum, would tell them to me. All the same, the meaning behind the talk would never come into my possession—nor would their intention.

It was no good my craving to be beside them as they strolled away. The things they so often spoke about were outside my understanding. Only later, when their words had turned into acts and results, would I feel the full thunderclap of my ignorance.

❊ "I wish you wouldn't walk three paces behind me, and keep on saying 'yes, Miss Joan', in that reverent way. You remind me of that old print of a slave holding a sunshade over a white lady, and it drives me to distraction. After all, we are contemporaries, and played together once," said Joan, stopping short in the track and waiting for Baptiste to come apace.

"I can't address you otherwise, but I'll try not to be too humble, Miss Joan," Baptiste said. "I can't forget that my mother is a servant in your house." (He walked on beside her diffidently.) "You wouldn't like me to become fast and familiar all of a sudden, the way they say we get when we're 'taken up'?"

"Baptiste, you're an educated person, and my friend."

"Yes, Miss Joan," said Baptiste obediently, contriving to straighten his neck so that he seemed inches taller.

They arrived at the swing bridge and both paused involuntarily, Baptiste stepping in front as if to shield Joan from something, and Joan studying the rapids penetratingly and curiously.

"It is mended now, and stronger than before," said Baptiste, mounting. "That's where he fell." A handrail of rope had been stretched across the river, which looked more swollen and untidy than ever. Both Joan and Baptiste held to the rope and paused again, while the bridge shuddered gently beneath their feet.

"Tell me what they say in the town about his death."

"People are too superstitious to say much aloud: they call him 'bringer of evil'. But I heard a rumour that Buffon had killed him for money, to oblige someone."

"Perfect nonsense. Buffon is far too much of a coward. You know that."

"Yes, Miss Joan, I know." They resumed progress and walked quickly through the last stretch of woods into the open valley road. Now hot dust began to clog Joan's sandals, and her face was heated and troubled.

"Baptiste."

"Yes, Miss Joan?"

"My father is a very sick man."

"Yes, Miss Joan, I know."

She could not get any further with him. A silent understanding hung between them.

"I haven't had a chance to tell you yet, but I'm leaving Ned behind when I go back to England. I want you to give him his first lessons—teach him to read and write. I will pay you for this, not much, but still something. I'll send you the money by post; so you will be more independent."

"But, Miss Joan—Mamselle Bosquet?" An expression of real alarm clouded Baptiste's brow.

"She can take care of his consonants and teach him French. You must do all the rest. Really. I rely on you."

"Yes, Miss Joan. You can rely on me. I will take the charge."

The lime-oil factory was in sight. A sound of machinery and a heightened citron smell told them that they had arrived at the boundary of the town. Cauldron-like puffs of steamy smoke evaporated in the bright air. A little gang of labourers with baskets of limes on their heads were passing through a gate. They stood still to gaze, and some of them greeted Baptiste, who waved and muttered embarrassed words. The others started laughing and speaking patois: she caught the jeering words "Backra" and "Negre".

"Never mind, they don't know that I understand, perhaps they don't even know who I am," said Joan serenely.

"Oh yes, Miss Joan—they know who you are."

"They must get used to seeing us together. After all, they are the people I've come to help," said Joan.

"Not those people. They work for Mr. Ormerod."

"Well, people like them."

Baptiste seemed to have gone doubtful and sullen. They could feel the derisive eyes of the labourers watching their fore-shortening figures from behind. The wide-open invitation of the botanical gardens' gates drew Joan inside. "Come, Baptiste, let's go to the drinking-fountain and have some water. I'm horribly thirsty."

He followed her in silence and stooped to break off a leaf as big as a bowl, which he twisted into a green cup. "You remember Miss Lally never used to let you drink from those public cups," he said.

Joan gave one of the heavy metal cups a push, and it swung on its chain like a bell, hitting another one with a loud clang. Baptiste had filled the leaf cup, and handed it to her with an air of great delicacy and hospitality, without letting a drop spill. When she had drunk she let the leaf fall on the grass. It uncurled there and Baptiste picked it up, re-formed the cup and filled it with water for himself. Joan sat on the grass and took off her sandals, beating the dust out of them. She soon saw that Baptiste was doing likewise, and cooling his feet in the overflow from the fountain. Without a word he filled the leaf cup and poured it over one of her feet. He then went back and fetched a second beaker-full, which he poured over the other.

"How marvellous that feels!" cried Joan. "Oh, I do thank you, Baptiste." She realised that she had fallen into an ancient acceptance of Baptiste's service, and added:

"Do sit down. We can go on in a few minutes."

"I like to stand," Baptiste replied. And in fact he leaned against the traveller's tree which stood ironically facing the drinking-fountain.

"This is the corner of the island where I was always happy," Joan said. "I played here every afternoon with my sisters, and with Andrew."

"You do not find it changed?" he asked.

"Only the way things change when they grow. The trees

are much bigger, but some of the bushes have shrunk—I expect because I was smaller then. I noticed bushes more than trees. The royal palm near the gate is dead . . . "

"It made its one flowering since you left," he said.

"And some of the other trees have disappeared. Would that be the hurricane?"

"Let us walk around, Miss Joan, and I will tell you." Baptiste brightened, as if the trees had some safe reference to the business in hand. Leading her like someone with a firm intention, he exclaimed: "Do you miss anything?"

Joan frowned. "Yes. But I don't know what it is."

"Well, there's the stump." A hacked-off trunk, the sap still bleeding from its cracks, clung to the ground as if to commemorate some vestigial memory.

"Come this way. Here is another."

The second stump was a little older. Faint traces of moss clung to its table-top. Seedlings flourished already in the cracks and nearby earth.

"And this one. And this."

"Baptiste, you are making me breathless. Who cut those trees down?"

"The Government," said Baptiste sombrely.

"Oh, no! Surely not the blue-fruit tree, and the gorgeous kennip tree? But those were *fruit* trees, Baptiste!"

"That's why," said Baptiste.

Joan gazed at the emerald grass which crept up to erase each evidence of massacre; she was visibly shocked.

"They cut them down because the children used to stone them and steal the fruit." As if to convince, Baptiste stooped and picked up a stone, which he flung far into a bamboo clump.

They had left behind them a smooth-turfed cricket pitch, with its enormous encircling cedars. Baptiste gloated over Joan's exclamations of incredulity. "I assure you, Miss Joan, that is the reason. The Government cut the trees down because the children stole fruit. And the children stole because they were hungry."

"Because they were hungry," she repeated in a voice not surprised, but dazed.

"Believe me. I used to teach school. There were children

who came to lessons who lived only on fruit. Stolen fruit. In the middle of the day they would sleep, or be sick."

"I believe you. Now I ask you to believe me, Baptiste."

"And what should I believe, Miss Joan, please?" Baptiste regarded her with such an air of reverence that she could have told him the most outrageous, the most preposterous lies—and he would have taken them to heart. But she only said in her brisk honest voice:

"In England, sometimes, I was hungry too."

※ Baptiste had spoiled the gardens for her with his revelation, and she had taxed his credulity to the depths. Nevertheless, Joan was reluctant to strike out into the main street, though their appointment at the *Bugle* office would soon be due, and she had promised to lunch with the Treasurer's wife. She loitered amid the familiar beauties and hiding-places of her childhood, conscious all the while of the tangled blue hill which overlooked her as indomitably as Lally. A gardener dressed in khaki passed by and saluted. He was young; the old head gardener who had chased her out of tree-branch lairs must have died. She searched the bluish fir-like tree where humming-birds used to nest: but found no treasure. It would have given her spirits a lift to discover on a tipmost twig one of those silken thimbles covered with lichen.

Baptiste took out of his pocket the draft of their posters and leaflets, and they sat on a bench to revise these.

"'The Unemployed Labourers Union.' A meeting will be held on—"

"Baptiste, I don't think we ought to call it a union. A union is for negotiating with employers, and these people aren't in employment. Shall we say 'association'?"

"Very well, Miss Joan." But he looked upset. The word *union* meant something to him: association did not.

"And how shall we get the posters out to the country districts? That's where the worst unemployment is. We want a really big meeting."

"I have friends, Miss Joan. And I am prepared to walk many miles myself." He stuck his feet out.

"Your lovely stout boots," said Joan. A smile of peculiar

gratified sweetness spread over Baptiste's face. "I knew they would come in useful in some great cause," he said.

"Then we'd better date the meeting a month ahead. As I remember, the roads are pretty difficult. It will take you and your friends some time to cover the territory."

"Yes, Miss Joan," said Baptiste. "But I think we ought to call it a union. These people won't come miles into town for an association."

"Very well then, Baptiste. I see your point. Oh, I wish Edward was here! He knows all this sort of stuff. To be truthful, Baptiste, I'm a bit vague about these things. Rules and so on. I bought a pamphlet on trade unionism for you, but the language is so stale nobody here would understand it. However, I'll give it to you when we get back to L'Aromatique. Edward, now . . . " She gazed far into the sea-going distance.

"Mr. Edward, then, was sometimes very poor . . . was he *persecuted*?" enquired Baptiste.

"No, I wouldn't say that, not to any great extent. But he was an idealist, and idealists seem to attract indirect persecution . . . Edward, you see, resigned his commission in the Royal Engineers to fight in Spain."

"I remember," said Baptiste.

"That finished him, as far as one side of his life was concerned, of course. And made it very difficult for him to find a good job."

"Like me," said Baptiste.

"Like you—that's right. I expect you're an idealist too. Anyway I'm sure Lally is wrong—you will never be a Mr. Fiuminato."

"Never," said Baptiste priggishly. "I too resigned my secretaryship of our trade union here, as I didn't think it was a true trade union."

"If only Edward could have come in place of me. But I was a woman and a mother, and had roots here; I was the right one to bring Ned. And how I longed to come!"

"Aren't you glad to be home?" Baptiste asked.

"Yes, terribly glad. But I worry about Edward. Has he found work yet? (You can see why my heart is in this unemployment business.) I feel I must go back before too long and work beside him—I almost said work for him. There's something great about Edward, Baptiste."

"I have seen no photograph of him," Baptiste said reproachfully.

"I'll give you one—I only have two. Edward . . . oh Lord, it's a queer thing to say, but still—Edward is an English gentleman."

"An English gentleman." Baptiste stubbed the grass with his boots reflectively. Joan could see that he was measuring Edward against his old conception of the term. Rising, as if to remind her of the passing of time, he remarked:

"I can only think of him as a man of courage."

Joan suddenly broke away from solemnity by saying in a laughing tone: "Don't think I'm belittling the Spanish war, Baptiste, but I used to think the bravest thing Edward ever did was to stick out evening after evening of dreary local Party meetings after he returned home."

Baptiste was silent; it was plain that this description of Labour meetings shocked him.

"Just the same, they were good people—our kind. We won't have meetings like that here," she adjusted. "Anyhow, I daresay Edward got a lot out of them—that's where he learned all the answers. He used to have some glorious scraps with Councillor Garter, who called him a bastard Fabian-Marxist."

"They called me bad names as well," said Baptiste. "Nigger agitator and foumi rouge—things like that. Your own uncle, too."

"My own uncle!" she cried, glancing at her bare wrist as if reading a watch. "To the *Bugle* office, Baptiste—I'd forgotten that he was waiting for us. To the *Bugle,* and a Roland for his Oliver!"

"Please bear it in mind, Miss Joan, that you promised Miss Lally to be tactful," said Baptiste.

To the gate of the *Bugle* office was affixed a notice stating that all kinds of printing were undertaken. Joan and Baptiste need not have doubted that their commission would be accepted. The moderately worded leaflet draft was taken down a flight of musty steps by Brother Peregrine for immediate setting up. Payment was made in advance, then the tough, broad little lay-brother guided them towards the editorial office.

In front of that door Baptiste paused and whispered that she had better go in alone. Surprised at this, she paused to argue with him. Then the door flew open from within and they were firmly pushed inside by the lay-brother.

Of all the things which had changed in the islands, the one which had changed most was Uncle Rufus. He looked clean and stiff in white linen, and had thrown away his hang-dog air of uneasy speculation. Joan realised at once that Baptiste had been right to hesitate. The temporary warmth of her uncle's greeting, the smack of his lips on one cheek and then the other, was speedily overcast by the glance of suspicion he cast on Baptiste while offering them chairs.

Joan was at home among undusted papers and books. She saw the piles of old yellow *Bugles* rising to the ceiling and could not help remembering how Christophine had once told her never to wrap up sandwiches in those sheets, since the setting chemical in their production was water provided by the Bishop.

"The things I believed when I was little!" she said to Uncle Rufus, smiling.

"I don't suppose they're much worse than the things you believe now," her uncle responded in an attempt at affectionate belligerence. "Come to improve us all, I understand."

"And I understand that you don't require any improvement—everything has turned out marvellously for you," she said. Indeed Uncle Rufus could not have worn more blatantly the air of one who had backed the right horse, and who was now determined to abolish all forms of betting.

"I'm a democrat. I fought against colour prejudice and I won. Listen here, my girl. Once long ago I asked your father for some helpful advice about this paper. He had just come back from the war and I had just started on my editorial career. But he high-hatted me! Yes, he high-hatted me, and that's something I've never forgotten. Treated me like a cheap journalist! But the situation is different now, for me and many others. I've helped to make a lot of people who were hardly accepted *respectable*. Nowadays one coloured merchant is worth two white officials . . . "

"Or a thousand penniless labourers," said Joan. She would have liked to add: "And nowadays your coloured relatives are more respectable than your white ones."

"It's a question of economics, not of colour," said Baptiste gravely, speaking as he imagined Edward would have spoken.

"Hold your tongue, you foolish Nigger, I've had enough from you already," Uncle Rufus declared, resuming his favourite role of popular bully. The curious thing was that as he got angry he became quite handsome, so that it was easy to understand why women fought over him. Joan could see her mother's family in him—strengthened, coarsened, intensely likeable. And after all, while liberal-minded people merely talked against the colour bar, Uncle Rufus had taken practical steps to break it down.

He got up and crossed the room, slapping at the jalousie blinds. This reminded Joan how she had peeped through green slats once during a bram in the town, gazing at Uncle Rufus as he danced with one clinging glistening woman after another, his movements heavy and free . . . the passeo band was playing

I love you awready
Moi aimé 'ou deja!

The memory was pleasing, but it also hardened her. She scowled at him when he said in a loud voice, standing between Baptiste and herself:

"This fellow only tries to annoy me because he wanted to run the trade union himself, and got slung out."

Was there some truth in this? Baptiste, for all his preparatory reluctance, was getting obvious satisfaction out of Uncle Rufus's rage. By this time they had all risen to their feet; something had to be done to save the negotiation. Joan said politely:

"We didn't come here to quarrel, we came on business. Just to ask whether you would put a notice of our meeting in the *Bugle.*"

Uncle Rufus accepted the sheet of paper dubiously.

"I'll have to go over the wording and give it my consideration after consulting with Father Toussaint. This paper exists for the promotion of good citizenship and religious doctrine."

"The labourers are starving and the merchants are making fortunes—is that good citizenship?" Joan asked hotly.

"We try to print only the truth," Uncle Rufus said, clasping his freckled hands. "Naturally we have to examine everything first."

"The truth!" Joan exclaimed. "What about Spain? Why did your London correspondent give up his assignment?"

"They say he committed suicide, Miss Joan," remarked Baptiste objectively.

"That's a positive lie, the fellow only got married!" shouted Uncle Rufus.

Words began to fly so hotly between him and his visitors that Brother Peregrine crept back, opened the door, shook his head twice, and deliberately upset a wire tray of papers. After stooping to pick up some of the papers, Baptiste addressed Joan: "Don't forget your lunch, Miss Joan; we are wasting our time here."

"Insolence!" shouted Uncle Rufus. Yet there was nothing left to do but to part in an atmosphere of embarrassed ferocity. Joan was comforted to notice that Baptiste did not seem intimidated.

"Do you think they will even print our leaflets?" she asked at the gate.

Baptiste shrugged: "They took our money." Joan straightened the straw hat which her vehemence had tilted to one side. Just then she saw Cornélie approach the gate and lay a hand on the latch. It was that same long thin hand, the shade of milky coffee, which had crept out in friendship between the bars of the convent fencing.

The face above it lit up only with a guarded gleam of recognition. It was Joan who profferred cordial pleasure, who took the familiar hand and exclaimed:

"Cornélie! At last!"

But Cornélie only said: "How do you do?"

"Come and see me," said Joan, determined not to be dashed by such coldness. As to Baptiste, Cornélie had never thought him worthy of her notice: he was nearly black, he was against her father, he was political. She ignored him utterly. He walked across the narrow street and stood picking cement out of a wall-crack with his pencil.

"Or shall I visit you?" Joan adjusted, as Cornélie opened the gate wider, preparing to place herself on its farther side.

"No, no—I will come. I'm glad to have seen you." Cornélie waved and gained the inner door.

"Miss Joan, I fear you have been wasting your time again," murmured Baptiste, as if to the sky. He carefully put away his pencil, to evade the sign of distress in Joan's eyes.

"She doesn't like me any more," Joan cried childishly.

"No, Miss Joan, I wouldn't say that."

"Then what would you say?"

"I would say, she was afraid."

"Afraid of what? I've never done her any harm."

"Miss Joan, it is nearly one o'clock." And indeed the clamour of the Catholic hour-bell seemed to smite the hot pavements like a bruising hammer.

"Oh, dear. I shall be late. Goodbye and thanks, Baptiste. I'll find my own way back."

"Mrs. Rubery makes a good strong cocktail, Miss Joan," said Baptiste comfortingly.

Callers ✖ CHAPTER 11

"**M**iss Joan, Miss Joan! Step outside and see a sight!"
What was she doing in her bedroom all that fine morning? Trying on her sister's left-behind clothes, I dared think, and taking in a stitch here and a stitch there; for all that Miss Joan said she was not interested in worldly things, she had been to several parties in the town, but always came back more serious than she went. I called her again. There was an extraordinary thing to see: the Master was leading a donkey across the cow-paddock. Buffon walked behind the animal, giving its rump loving slaps, and in front—capering and tumbling to rise up again with screams of joy—was young Ned. I saw the Master try to lift Ned and mount him, but fail; then Buffon heaved the little boy astride. The Master led the donkey by its bridle, and the little boy rolled and straightened himself, and cried out: "Giddy-up!" But the young donkey was now almost at the verandah steps.

"See my donkey, Lally? Grandad gave me him."

Now there was a revolution for you! The Master had never given anyone a present in years. He just didn't think to do it, he was so out of our world of giving and taking. Where he got the money from was a mystery; perhaps Mamselle's savings, if she still had any. But to me it was a good and wonderful thing to see that strange man loving any creature enough to make him a gift. The donkey was reined up (it was a nice clean fat little beast) and the Master looked me a bit shyly in the face, and gave me a very slight smile. My ears caught a rustle, and there was Miss Joan at the head of the steps.

"Lucky, lucky Ned!" she said, and her cheeks were stained pink. I had not the certainty of her thoughts that I claimed of my darling Miss Stella, but just the same I knew that she was thinking along my path. The pleasure in her face was because of the Master. For a moment I did not notice what she was wearing: then I suffered shock. She had on the white confirmation dress, quite carelessly, as if it could be an everyday costume. I had to clench on my tongue not to scold her out there in the open. Not that it wasn't looking well on her; her straightness saved it from looking frivolous. But it was not a seemly thing to do, and I was vexed until I turned to look at the donkey again.

"It was a plot between myself and Buffon," said the Master, handing the reins to him and turning away as if to hide himself again. "Don't forget to fetch the ice, Buffon, after you've given Ned a few rides. Tether him under the saman tree, well away from the cows."

"Yes, Master," said Buffon, his teeth showing so gaudy in a smile that anyone would think they would fall out, except for their roots as long as three-legged stools.

"Giddy-up!" yelled Ned again, and Buffon handed him the reins and slapped the donkey smartly, and the three of them dashed across the paddock in a noise of laughter. But the Master had vanished.

"Don't reproach me—Lally. I'll only wear it around the house very occasionally," Miss Joan said. "Not that it wouldn't be just the thing for a tea-party in the town. Oh yes! I know you wonder why I go to town so often. Well, I'm studying island society. I'm learning things."

"And you mean you don't have any fun from your gadding around?"

"Oh yes, Lally," she said in a peculiar voice. "I have fun. I hear talk that I haven't heard for ages. Talk about romantic love and fashions and scandals and island ways of living. It's all very illuminating, as Edward said it would be . . . "

"I hope you didn't come back here just to criticise our ways."

"Those are not our ways, Lally. Up here we live differently."

"Well, Miss Joan, I'd be thankful for a little help with my sewing today—that boy of yours is a terrible tearer of clothes."

"But of course, Lally," she said humbly, always ready to prove her industry. We gathered up the sewing-basket and ripped garments, and went off to the orchid house, where we sat silently working in two straw chairs, spreading the mended things on Ned's bed as they were done.

When we had been there some half-an-hour, Mamselle put her head in. "Seen the Master?" she asked me, nodding an anxious good morning to Miss Joan. We told her about the donkey, but she was not as pleased as she should have been. "I know," she said.

"But aren't you glad that he is happier, more normal?" asked Miss Joan abruptly.

"He is happier because *now* he gets everything he wants. But what will happen later . . . very soon . . . when there is nothing more for him to have?" Mamselle replied bleakly.

"Let us cross one bridge at a time," said Miss Joan.

"Ned seems to renew his spirits. There's something he sees in Ned that encourages him." She was proud.

"Perhaps." Mamselle faded from the doorway on that word.

"Now why doesn't Mother come out of her shell—she used not to be apathetic, she has changed. I think I shall go in search of her! Why should it always be Mamselle who concerns herself so? Has Mother given up fighting?" Miss Joan arose suddenly, tossing her thimble on the couch.

"Wait a minute—perhaps she likes better to be left alone."

"Oh, Lally, that's what you always say . . . leave things alone. Telling Stella to leave Father alone. And now me, 'leave your mother alone'. But I can't leave her alone! Don't you see, I'm on the side of all the mute suppressed people! Mother, who seems to have lost her old fierce pride, who *gives in*; and Olivet, who has one secret ambition, to call at Government House before she dies! Ah, I hope that she does! It won't be Baptiste's fault if she doesn't! Of course it's a curious ambition, but still . . . "

"And where is Baptiste—we haven't seen him since Wednesday."

"He's on his pilgrimage, Lally, as you might have guessed. He's taking word of our meeting into the mountains."

Miss Joan paused on the threshold, for a beautiful thing was holding her prisoner there. Just outside the orchid house was a frosted pink hibiscus bush, one of the rare ones which Old Master cultivated. A little fou-fou humming-bird had chosen the largest and most perfect of the flowers to drain of its sweetness. The flower was three times larger than the bird, which was only like a flashing black-and-emerald moth. The bird was fluttering and humming at such a speed that it seemed to lie still along the bright warm air, its tiny claws curled up; its long sharp bill was deep in the bedecked trumpet of the hibiscus. Seconds and seconds it remained suspended there, appearing rigid, then like a drunken spirit it reeled away and wiped the sword of its beak on some lichen. Shocked by this exquisite sight, Miss Joan sighed deeply and sat down again.

"For Stella," she said, "it was the hugeness of beauty and force which drew her—the mountains, the great trees, the violent torrents. But for me it is these marvellous small things, their amazing vividness. I could give up all the grandeur in the world for a thing like that humming-bird. It was worth crossing an ocean or two to see just that."

"Just enjoy yourself looking, then," I told her. "Leave these quiet women be, don't go rousing up their discontents."

"Lally, you can't suppress me. I'm a drawer-out of the crushed and retiring, especially when they are women."

"Now, Miss Joan, what would your English godmother say to that?"

"Ah Lally, now you've asked for it! My English godmother! Why, she was the beginning of everything! You see, you thought of her as of a formal wealthy lady living in the Surrey countryside. In a sense she was, I suppose; but she was something more. She was a thinker, and in her own way a rebel. She used to ramble all over England with Lady Violet something, preaching the Liberal cause. After a while she got too advanced even for Lady Violet. She went sharply to the left—"

"To the left," I repeated, looking doubtfully to one side.

"And took me with her, for that was about when I first really got to know her, and I was very young. She took the part of the people—"

"Well, all good Christians take that part," I said.

"In their different ways, Lally. When I say 'the people' you always make a sulky face. Oh yes you do! But Lally, do you know the only working-class white person I ever saw as a child was the Ridgate's English nanny, the fat type who eloped with a stoker?—I was perfectly amazed at the things my English godmother uncovered to me. Of course, it was she who introduced me to Edward."

"Who can't give you a rag to your back," I said, and I regretted the unkindness of this right away. Miss Joan flushed. She pleated the skirt of her beautiful white dress silently.

"Lally, don't be silly like the girls in the town. Clothes are not the only thing. Nor, incidentally, is romantic love." She got up again, and stared outwards. "Buffon and Ned and the donkey have disappeared. They haven't tethered up as Father ordered."

"Miss Joan, you have funny ideas about human nature. Don't you think Buffon helped to buy that donkey for his own ends? I'll lay you a wager he's taken it into the town, and your boy too, to fetch the ice-block. For years he's been complaining about dragging that lump of ice up the road in a sack, though I've continually pointed out how cool the drips make him."

"Dear Lally!" Miss Joan smiled. "Think of the money it will save, and the ice! I've often wondered why anyone should do anything so uneconomic as to buy a block of ice and cart it up on his head through miles of heat until it is reduced to one-third its size! Clever Buffon! Think of the time he will save."

I pursed my lips and let her go without speaking again. At any rate she was a quick darner, though a careless one; she had patched and mended nearly as many articles as myself. I went on with my sewing, loving her just the same in a vexed sort of way. I hoped that young Ned had worn his shady hat. True, he was a tough small boy, but the power of our sun would split the hardest skull. I was weary; my arguments with Miss Joan always tired me out; and I was upset because the *Island Bugle* which I carried in my pocket had a two-edged attack on that meeting which Miss Joan and Baptiste were hatching up. Not a direct attack, but just trying to make it seem foolish, make it seem somehow a gathering of malcontents, somehow against religion. Labourers ought to accept the misfortunes placed on them by Providence, the article said. Those who were stupid enough to attend the meeting would only return to their poor shacks hungrier and angrier than when they set forth. These little griefs made me sleepy. I closed my eyes and went off into a doze.

※   The voice that awakened me (and I do not know how long I had been asleep) was one which I had not heard for many months, it may be for many years: the voice of Master Andrew. At first I did not recognise it through my daze. For one thing, it was not only hoarser than in the past, more grown up, but it was also strangely weaker. The weakness of it struck a sort of terror into me so that I blinked my eyes in defence against what I might see. And I saw a very sad thing. I saw Master Andrew, taller than the Master himself, hanging strangely on to the planks of the doorway, and I heard him say faintly: "Lally! Where is she?"

"Gone—gone to America. Gone back where she belongs," I said to him, not meaning the harshness of this, but too slow to think of delicate words.

"No, no." He sank down, too tired to reach the chair, on the rushy floor.

I got up as quickly as my size and my tumour allowed. I helped him to a chair. "Yes, Master Andrew, my poor. She has gone. Didn't you know?"

We were two sick mortals, him and me, but it's my opinion that women are always stronger, even up to the death. I took his long thin hand in my brown ones.

He stared at me with a disagreeable impatience. "No, Lally. I don't mean Stella. I know. She said me her goodbye. I mean . . . where is Joan?"

It was now my turn to stare. "Master Andrew dear, did you half-kill yourself taking the path from Cul-de-Sac to see the second one, to see Miss Joan? Oh, you foolish mad boy! Yes, she's here . . . she was in this place a little while ago. She's with her mother now."

"Fetch her for me."

I stood up and continued looking at him, an awful pity weakening my heart. He put all his strength into his eyes, and with a fierce gaze, said again:

"Fetch her . . . please."

"Let me get you some water—medicine—a drink—"

"No, Lally. Get Joan."

His look gave some kind of speed to my heavy steps, and I took no time at all to discover Miss Joan. She was sitting beside her mother in the drawing-room. They were not speaking, but Miss Joan was holding her mother's hand as if to give her some of her own hardness. Break away, Miss Joan, I thought, you'll need that strength for someone else! "Come quickly with me, someone needs you," I said, and Madam had no curiosity, but as soon as Miss Joan's hand was released she seemed to sink into her old vague thoughts. Yet she appeared tranquil and happy.

Miss Joan had the sense to ask me no questions till we were outside. And then: "Who is it?" She was not excited.

"It's Master Andrew. His state is very bad. He came all this way to see you."

All the new colour that our sun and her hardiness had laid on those pale calm cheeks ran right out of them again. She touched my shoulder as if to press me back, and ran quickly to the orchid house. I had not even told her he was there. At the door she paused, checked in her swiftness like the humming-bird at the hibiscus. They must have greeted in silence, for I heard nothing. I did not dare to enter, but sat myself down in the shade of the wall where I could both hear their talk and see the waited arrival of young Ned and Buffon and the ice-block with that donkey. I was after all a part of the girls' lives. All that happened to them was my affair, was my whole life.

Miss Joan must have sat on the couch, for I heard Master Andrew stagger across and fall himself down beside her.

"You may lay your head in my lap, but only if you haven't any of that nasty oil on your hair," she said in her practical voice. "Otherwise Lally will quarrel with me, because of this dress."

He said in a sad complaining tone: "You would not come to see me. So I had to drag myself here."

"I did not come—on purpose."

He coughed dreadfully. And then, when he was quiet again: "What purpose?"

"A purpose—of leaving you in peace."

"And it happened in the opposite way. You left me in torture."

"Andrew, you are feverish, my poor dear, you are so ill. How could I torture you? I am only your friend."

His words were muffled as if he spoke through the stuff of that white confirmation skirt. "You deceive yourself, Joan. You are more than a friend. All three of you, you are part of my life, of my dreams. It *anguished* me to know that you were here, and didn't care enough to come to me."

"Stella was your dream," Miss Joan said quietly.

"Stella was my love. You are part of my dream. You are linked with Stella, with all the past." I could not tell whether his words were interrupted by a sob or by huskiness.

She spoke with kind comfort: "Well, here you are now, anyway. I will stay with you until you are well enough to go home. Lay your head more easily. There! Now I've smoothed the hair from your eyes, I can see your face."

"I can't see your face yet, I dare not," he said. "I can only feel your body—the strength of it. Lovely body, so like Stella's! I shall never go away. I'll lie here for ever drawing strength from you."

"You're delirious," Miss Joan remarked briskly.

"Yes, I'm delirious," he said.

For a while no words passed; time itself did not seem to pass. I stared out past the saman tree, but no one came. The house across the grass was utterly silent. Peace settled. And then Master Andrew started complaining again.

"Stella deserted me."

"She went to her duty," said Miss Joan.

"They sent her away. Lally and Mamselle and those interfering people, with their words and scares."

"Her boy was ill. He could not live here," said Miss Joan carefully.

"She chose her boy instead of me," Andrew said in a voice

of extreme petulance. "First of all she chose me. She began bringing me back to life. Do you hear that? Really bringing me back to life. Then she wrecked it all, she left me. I tried to carry on. I waited. Surely, I thought, she'll turn back! But no. She never returned. And you came, but you would not come near me. I felt accursed."

"I will not desert you," said Miss Joan.

"Oh yes, you will," said Andrew spitefully. "You too will go back to your precious north-country husband, whom you probably don't love—"

"Indeed, I love him," said Miss Joan boldly. "He is a brave man. And he is my companion."

"I have no companion."

"You have Cornélie."

"Cornélie is not a companion. She is everything else, but not that."

"You have your child. A very beautiful child, they tell me."

"A child! One loves a child, but what is there in a child that *binds* one to living?"

"The future," she said.

"I have no future."

"You are part of the whole future."

For the first time, Master Andrew laughed; a very thin laugh. "Oh, go on preaching at me! I revel in it! That's what Stella used to do!"

"My sermons will not be like Stella's. I don't think individuals so important. It only depresses me when they act like senseless egoists and won't admit they are part of a scheme."

"Now tell me, my dear Joan, what kind of scheme I am a part of? You tell me!"

There was a long, loving pause, in which I could clearly fancy Miss Joan's fingers stroking that wild black head. And at last, unwillingly: "A scheme of beauty." I was grateful that she didn't start that poor dying boy off on all that nonsense about *the people*. It was plain to me that Mimi Zacariah would try to haunt me if my girls made Master Andrew suffer any more; but then, they suffered too in their way. Only I could not argufy with Mimi any longer, she being dead. Some voice inside of me kept wanting to call out to Miss Joan: "Humour him!"

"The painful thing, Joan my darling," he told her, "is that now I want to live—desperately. I want to live so that I can do and see some of the things Stella kept urging on me. I want to experience the hardships of a cold country, and see the contrasts, to hear a big orchestra and even to dance again."

"I want, I want," she murmured in reproach. "You've always been that way—'I want'."

"Well," he replied angrily, "don't you ever want anything?"

"Oh, but I do," she cried, and then her voice seemed to fade. "I often do, bitterly. But I resist."

"I resist nothing," Master Andrew said. "Never have."

"But now," she remarked, practical again, "you must resist your despair. You must fight back."

"I can't fight alone. It's the fearful loneliness, since Stella went. I lie awake and fancy I hear dogs barking in the town all night long."

"You doubted that I love Edward," she said. "But that's exactly what I love in Edward. That he can fight, alone or with me, friendless or with his comrades."

"Oh, Edward!" sang out Master Andrew in derision. "Forget Edward, can't you!"

"No," said Miss Joan firmly. "I can't. But then I never could forget you either."

He seemed for some reason satisfied with this, and a silence followed. At length: "But you are near to me now. Edward, thank God, is leagues away."

"Not really," said Miss Joan.

"Hold me closely, then, against Edward's nearness and against Stella's distance."

"Stella is near too. This is her dress, our shared dress. I had the most curious feeling this morning, putting it on. I felt: 'I am putting on Stella'."

"And so you did," he said, his speech almost choking him. "So you did."

"I am myself," she said. Then, changing her note, and speaking as though to a child: "Let me raise you so that you can breathe freely and look out of the low window. Look out and see the loveliness of which you are a part. Today I saw something so special . . . " She told him about the humming-bird; and her telling was almost as beautiful as the thing we had lately seen: it was English poetry.

"But now I only see your face," Master Andrew said. "It is a firm little face, harder than Stella's, nearly like a boy's face. No, I won't look at it for too long, because it's too uncompromising, it gives nothing away. I prefer to stifle against your little breasts, and to pretend . . . I can't breathe properly anyway; so let me smother myself divinely."

"You are a poor spoilt boy," Miss Joan said, with a sigh.

"A dying man," he said. "And if you were Stella, you would cry out in protest, 'Live for me!' But you don't care."

"I care, but differently," she said. I could hear the tears springing up in her throat. Some came into my own foolish old eyes then. When I wiped them away I myself gazed outwards at the scene around me, trying to see what there was in this common everyday outlook of mountains and blueness which filled my girls with passionate admiration. All I could see was a riot of gold and purple and crimson (Madam's flowering bushes) and the two huge mango trees, the shining silver fern against a damp wall, and the purple shadows on far hills. Nothing unusual, except to those who had lived like exiles in grey shadows. I turned my head to gaze and gaze, and when I heard faint hoofs I did not raise myself in welcome, for I knew it was the donkey coming up the slope, and I was vexed with Buffon for keeping little Ned in town that long while. It was with shock and surprise that I heard a little-known voice behind me saying, "Good-day to you", and saw the black robe falling over the mule's flanks: it was Brother Peregrine who reined up beside me, almost at the door of the orchid house.

※ It was a new thing for the clergy to be visiting in the forenoon just before lunch, and I had a foreboding when I saw Brother Peregrine draw up. The two in the orchid house must have felt it too, for they ceased talking.

He was a good modest holy man, with hard-working hands and a blank face, and he spoke to me politely.

"I have come from Father Toussaint with a message for one Baptiste Delgaud," he addressed me. "Would you be so kind as to call him for me or conduct me to him."

"I'm sorry, Brother. He isn't here. He's gone on a . . . " (what was it Miss Joan had said was his object?) "he's gone on a . . . pilgrimage."

"Ah. H'm. To what shrine, I would ask you to tell me?"

"Not a holy pilgrimage, Brother, not a real one—just a tour. On business."

"Well, in that case, I am disappointed, and will have to disappoint the good Father."

"Will you give me a message for Baptiste, Brother?"

"When is he coming back?"

"I don't know." I certainly was in ignorance. "Miss Joan thought he would be away for several days."

"Miss Joan: ah, h'm." Brother Peregrine pondered. "Might I have a brief word with Miss Joan—she is the second daughter, is she not—before I go?"

I was afraid. I edged to the door of the orchid house as if to guard it. The worst thing for our happiness and the family reputation would be for Brother Peregrine to find those two together. The Brother gave a faint shrug, raised his black brimmed hat, and turned his mule's head a little, so that the large horseflies on its eyelids buzzed outwards for a second before resettling. Meanwhile Mamselle had come to the verandah, and stood looking down; and some way behind her I caught the light effect of Madam's dress.

"She is not here." What good fortune it is that the black face cannot show a blush! But I spoke like a guilty woman. As if God would punish me, Master Andrew began to cough painfully and without ceasing. He coughed until he strangled for breath, and Brother Peregrine, in great alarm, dismounted from his mule and left the animal roaming loose. He rushed into the orchid house. Mamselle, as pale as death, fled back into the dining-room for brandy and water. I could not move a foot. I was too full of horror. It seemed to me that Brother Peregrine had to struggle with that gasping Andrew to tear him from Miss Joan's arms; after forcing him to sip the brandy he lifted the poor boy, who hung like a scarecrow, on to his mule, Mamselle Bosquet lending a hand.

"Leave him to me now," said Brother Peregrine as sternly

as the Bishop, giving Miss Joan the coldest and most accusing of looks. "This man is very ill. Let me take him home."

"Leave him here with me—you will kill him!" Miss Joan cried bravely. But Master Andrew, though he tried once to stretch out a hand to her, was in no condition to resist. Supported by the sturdy Brother, he sagged over the mule and was slowly led away.

Miss Joan crossed her arms over the white bodice to hide the stain which lay between her breasts like her own heart's blood. She passed through the house before her mother's eyes.

Miss Natalie  Arrives

The People CHAPTER 12

Rain fell for the rest of the week, seeming to draw a solid veil over everything, so that we all remained in peaceful watery suspense. Olivet dared to struggle over to Petit Cul-de-Sac on Miss Joan's behalf to make enquiries about Master Andrew; but she brought back little news. He lived, he coughed, that was all.

When the rain stopped I could hear at night the interminable hum of big and little insects. I lit my oil lamp and turned it low so as not to waken young Ned, who now slept in my room; we all avoided the orchid house since that dreadful noon.

The fireflies were encouraged by the rain and came out in their hundreds, settling on the orange groves like shining blossoms, diamond-flowers. The bigger jewels of the La Belle beetles, those things which looked so hideous in the daytime but at night showed two emerald eyes and blazed from under their bodies, shone out in rivalry against the fireflies. One of these La Belles flew in and settled on my Bible. I could see the print brightly under its light. On the slope of the mountains swollen cascades of streams roared softly. The moon was only a humble circle above all the other shining things.

I knew that Baptiste and Miss Joan were in the pantry talking. It was not a good thing for a young white lady to be talking in the pantry with a manservant. I had told her so. But now it seemed to me that she was in such disgrace already that one thing more would matter little. Baptiste had taken off the boots which were stuck to his swollen feet. He sat on the floor stretching his cracked toes. Miss Joan sat on a stool with some papers in her hand. They were making ready their speeches for tomorrow's meeting. Peeping through the hatch window, I saw Miss Joan's face. It was serious, but not more sad than usual: if anything, it was a little more stubborn.

Those two were talking against the weather, and about politics. Baptiste, for all that he looked worn, was full of hope. He told Miss Joan that many people had promised to come.

"I reminded them that you were the granddaughter of Old Master, who cured their sores in the old days," said he.

"Oh Baptiste! Do you think that was ethical? He aimed at justice for the people too, but I doubt if he would have sanctioned our methods," said Miss Joan, wrinkling her nose.

"I beg pardon, Miss Joan, it's said and done now," he replied. "But I also told them that you were a Labour Party official of importance, back in England."

I listened closely to see if she would tell Baptiste what she had once admitted to me—that she was quite no account in English politics, just a hack-worker really. And she did. She distressed him by saying that she was only a ward secretary and wrote up the minutes—as petty as any Government Office clerk. "And when I left the district for a few months, while Edward was away, I doubt if they missed me at all, though it was all so fraternal while I was there. I expect they promptly forgot me. Human nature, Lally would say."

"Maybe they were afraid of you in some way," said Baptiste in a complimentary tone.

"Oh Baptiste! Maybe they were. I never thought of that."

"You put thoughts into heads," said Baptiste solemnly.

"A dangerous thing to do. Heavens, I am glad you are back! You understand it all. What do you think Brother Peregrine wanted?"

"To stop the meeting," said Baptiste.

"Well, it is going on. Nothing can stop it. We aren't doing any wrong."

"Only putting thoughts into heads," said Baptiste.

"In the hope of putting food into stomachs," said Miss Joan.

"Which is more difficult," Baptiste added. A long silence fell. Then, trying to enliven Miss Joan, Baptiste said: "When I climbed those roads, I thought of Mr. Edward. Ah, I thought of Mr. Edward! I thought of him climbing the roads of Spain, under fire. And I kept on going, contacting my runners and scouts, but the pain in my feet was terrible. I thought of what you wrote me, of when there were no bandoliers left and he had to carry bullets in his pockets . . . swimming the River Ebro with those precious bullets in his pockets, trying to keep them dry . . . crawling through the churchyard for the Batea attack, dragging a machine-gun between the tombstones; and when he helped to build that bridge in Catalonia, with his poor wounded hand, and his lorry-driver was hit and the lorry went into the water, breaking the bridge. And he an English gentleman all the while!"

"You recite it like an epic poem!" Miss Joan cried. "Edward would be grateful for that. You, at least, are one of those who do not forget . . . "

"No, Miss Joan, I never forget. To me that war was the only war that was ever important, and it always happened yesterday."

"But tell me the other epic—about your long hard route-march," she urged him.

"No, no, not again—my feet ache too much. There's one thing I saw though . . . Do you believe in symbols, Miss Joan?" he asked.

"If I did, I should be very gloomy tonight. Such a sad thing happened after tea. A humming-bird flew in through my bedroom window and beat itself to death against the ceiling, the wonderful little darling. I expect they resent captivity more than any other kind of bird, they are so quick and restless."

"What I saw was a tree that was not a tree . . . something taller than a tree, but it was a parasite, a bromeliad Old Master called it. I saw it on the top slope of Morne Gauchin. A tree, old but still tender, had this great glossy spike towering above it, sapping it like a disease but growing to be even stronger and more beautiful than the tree itself. I sat with my feet in the stream and considered it for a long while."

"Baptiste! Was the bromeliad a beautiful thing?"

"Very beautiful, Miss Joan, and very fine, for all that it lived without its own roots in the earth."

"Ah . . . I don't suppose I shall ever see a bromeliad. I haven't the time to climb so high."

"They live also in the lower slopes," said Baptiste mysteriously.

"My poor little humming-bird," murmured Miss Joan.

"Miss Joan, don't fret yourself. The bird is dead, but Master Andrew is alive as yet. How can you think so highly of one who lives for himself alone?"

"It's not that I think highly of him. It's just that the thought of him lies heavy on me . . . " As she spoke, Miss Joan crossed her arms over her bosom, and lowered her head.

"He will not be much missed," said Baptiste.

"Oh yes, Baptiste, he will be missed—he will be missed!"

"But not by me," said Baptiste sullenly.

At that moment Buffon slunk into the pantry in a sort of backward crawl. He was in such deep shame that he hardly dared lift his eyes. Baptiste gave him a cold glance.

"I come to 'pologise once more, Miss Joan," he mumbled. "I never tie-up that donkey outside a rumshop again, *jamais, jamais.*"

"Not with Ned mounted on it, I hope," said Miss Joan. She folded up her papers.

"The world is crazy, the world is a band of *foumis rouges,*" declared Buffon.

"You mean you are crazy," said Baptiste rudely.

"Everyone crazy," said Buffon. "Except Madam," he added.

Miss Joan got off her stool. She frowned.

"You don't need to wear filthy rags in Madam's pantry. You earn good money. Naked bellies are for those who have no work, and stinking bodies for those who cannot buy soap," said Baptiste in an offensive tone.

Buffon merely smiled foolishly, and pulled at his one earring. "Well, I stink. Fish stink too, but they are good just-same."

"I will leave you two to discus the point," Miss Joan said. She opened the door to the passage and I tried to hide my bulk in the shadows. As she stepped outside a voice on my right whispered to her and a hand pulled at her. "I must speak to you. Please. I must. Take me into your room and shut the door against that listening old nurse."

I could not see the look of surprise or alarm on Miss Joan's face. I only saw that she drew Cornélie away in complete silence. They went into Miss Joan's room and shut the door tight; and then they must have talked in near-whispers, for not a word more did I catch, and I was too tired and cramped to leave my bed empty any longer.

Although I knew what Cornélie would require of Miss Joan, and I halfway knew what Miss Joan might grant, it was as hard to imagine the tone of the chosen words as it was to catch shades of meaning between Madam and Mamselle Bosquet in the old days, before they came together. What made it all the more difficult was the way those girls had reversed their ways of life. Now it was Cornélie who had land and new dresses and considered herself to be in society; and it was Miss Joan who enjoyed the company of common people, and had no fixed station at all. Like all the gently bred young ladies in the island, Cornélie's only reading was her missal and those shiny fashion magazines with little stories where you had to hunt for the endings among the advertisements—stories that always ended happily. Miss Joan's eyes swallowed enough print to give her congestion of the brain—troublesome and serious print I used to think it must be, but she wouldn't be weaned of it any more than Christophine would give up rum.

Seeing that they don't speak alike, I told myself (and that night it was hard for me; I closed my eyes without even a prayer), it's as well that the thing between them is so woman-simple that they'll be able to understand each other without looking it up in a dictionary. Master Andrew never opens a book either, I said to the china cockatoo. How does he come to hanker after my two darling babblers who feed on print, poetry and politics? The worry of this question sent me to sleep without a blessing.

▨ Cornélie's head-veil was sopping wet, and leaves were caught in its folds. Her feet were dripping. She removed her sandals and placed them on the window-sill. Drawing a damp hand across her forehead (almost like the first motion of the sign of the cross), she seemed to gather courage for a fierce quarrel.

"Andrew is dying. You are killing him. Why did you come back here? You and your sister!"

"Cornélie. Listen. I have done you no wrong. I am your friend—believe me."

"No wrong? Coming back here was your wrong. He loved me, he loved Roxelane, until you returned to the island! You and Stella!" She cried out the word "Stella" in a desperate hiss.

"I can't answer for Stella, but for myself—"

"You are both together in this. You have taken him back to the past, you have ruined us. Brother Peregrine had to tear him from your arms!"

"Am I then never to visit my family, because I am part of a sick man's dream? My poor Andrew! And I so neglectfully kept away from him . . . "

"'My'! Andrew is not yours. He is mine, do you hear, mine!" Cornélie went back to the window-sill and took up one of her sandals, beating it against the wood. Then she saw that a dead humming-bird lay there, and shuddered away, dropping the shoe.

"He is yours. So why do you come to me?"

"I come because I can bear it no longer. I come to accuse you. And also . . . Andrew calls for you, in the small moments between his coughing. You must save him!"

"Cornélie, calm yourself. You are asking an impossible thing."

"It was impossible for Andrew to stagger down the path and see you—but he did it. And it nearly finished him."

"No, Cornélie, it was Brother Peregrine who nearly finished him—dragging him away on that mule!"

"Don't speak against the holy brother!" Cornélie's eyes were spears of anger. "Everyone knows you are no lover of good religious people."

"I remember a time" (despite her expression of distaste, Joan's voice was tender) "when we used to smile at each other between the convent bars. In those days, Stella and I used to think that you would become a nun, a Mother Superior even.

You were so lovely and serene. The thing which has come between us is a beautiful but terrible thing—human love."

"Human love! Why do not you and your sister cling to your own men? Natalie is the only nice member of the family. She lives for pleasure."

"I cling to mine. Honestly, Cornélie" (Joan laid an uneasy hand on the moist shoulder of her cousin) "I cling to mine, in my own way. I would not rob you of anything."

"You treat me like a common coloured girl!" cried Cornélie bitterly.

"Oh, no—Cornélie; never *that*! I've always respected you. Such an attitude would be against my philosophy, anyhow." Joan flushed.

Cornélie was not appeased. Fear and suspicion overlaid the anger which showed in her face, now a pale lemon colour after its sleepless vigils.

"When Stella first came here, I preferred that he should die, rather than that she would have him. But now that I seem to be losing him, it makes me desperate to see him die, not loving me and so Godless. Oh Joan! Won't you help him to live a little longer, so that he may find God?"

"And what would Father Toussaint say to that—*my* saving Andrew for God? I can't give him life, Cousin Cornélie. I'm not an obeah woman like old Majolie. I have so little vitality to spare, anyhow. I'm all given over to other things—matters outside personalities and private griefs. My meeting tomorrow, for instance. I need all my strength for that."

"A meeting!" Cornélie sneered through her piteous rage. "A rabble."

"Yes, a rabble: but a rabble of poor labourers whose sorrows are as keen as yours."

"No, no. They can't feel agony like mine. They are only illiterate peasants. And anyhow" (Cornélie quoted from her father, from the *Bugle*) "the condition of the coloured people is improving every year."

"Of the coloured merchants, the educated people, yes. They are taking the responsibility over from us—we are now the poor whites, we have no longer any power. But I don't notice any greater tenderness in their attitude towards those landless, shoeless devils . . . "

"We leave them to God," said Cornélie quietly, though she had listened to Joan's words with gathering impatience.

"And I leave Andrew to God—and to you," said Joan.

The two girls stood apart in stubborn resistance. Both had clasped their hands tightly together. Joan was the first to unloose hers. She pressed her throbbing eyes, then said: "I am deeply sorry, Cousin Cornélie."

"You have no heart," said Cornélie bleakly. "If you could see him, hear him fight for breath! You would let a man die, because of your stupid old meeting."

"Yes, I have a heart. But my heart is Edward's. Perhaps the meeting is my manner of clinging to him. Anyhow, you asked me in the wrong way. You insulted me, and begged me at the same time to save Andrew. Now, if you had asked me for your own sake, for the sake of our old kindness . . . "

Reminiscence swam in Cornélie's large black eyes, so that they almost became like the loving eyes of the little girl who had peered through convent bars. "Cousin Joan," she whispered, "I do ask you now to come—for my sake."

"It is too late." Never had Joan been more tired, adamant, and dispirited in one breath.

"Ah no—it cannot be too late! Come to him—for my sake!"

There was a heavy pause, full of trouble for them both. Then Joan said, making a great effort:

"Very well. I will come. But I come for Stella's sake."

※ The next morning, Christophine gave me news that a great whale had been washed up in the harbour and was drawing crowds who hoped to share in the oily richness of its great swollen carcass. At the first word of this Buffon had dropped all his duties and disappeared. Christophine had also heard of a more important matter: another beautiful accident of nature. An ox had been run down by a lorry near Mr. Ormerod's vanilla estate, and there had been a slaughtering, so good meat was to be had by the nimblest seekers. Lacking the service of Buffon, Christophine had tottered into town to wrench her share off the butcher's slab. L'Aromatique was emptying fast. Miss Joan had not returned at all from Petit Cul-de-Sac, but had sent word by Old Majolie that she would meet Baptiste on the savannah at five o'clock. I took hold of the Master's spy-glass and tried to see a far distance into the town, and indeed I saw a great movement of persons hastening towards the sea-front, but whether they were the labourers for Miss Joan's meeting, or the treasure-hunters for the whale, or the servants hastening to buy a cut of beef, I could not tell; I was left isolated with my curiosity. Madam and Mamselle had gone for a walk, and Master Ned had ridden his donkey to the Master's secret hiding-place. I declare that (saving Mamselle) Ned was the only mortal the Master had ever encouraged to visit him there. Even Olivet had gone, after cooking an early lunch. She had joined Miss Joan at Petit Cul-de-Sac, to help with the tending of Master Andrew.

The big one-storey house was blessedly empty. At last I was able to walk through the rooms and think my thoughts without stress or strain. It came to me that too much had been happening in that house of late, too much for an old body like mine, and too much for my ears which can hear the rustle of a gekko on a wall. I said aloud to myself: "Peace!" But in my pocket was the telegram which the cable-office boy had dropped in my hand: Miss Natalie saying that she was flying over in a seaplane *with friend* the following afternoon. Well, at any rate she's not a serious one, my sense told me. She will dance into these rooms and make fun of all their tragedies. She will mock them a little, splash their dark thoughts with her nonsense. I used to take her to task for it, but goodness knows we need a little nonsense now. Peace! The house was as still as the dead hush before a hurricane strikes. I went into Mamselle's room and had a good look around.

Mamselle's room was always the neatest place in the house. She had her own little ironing-board and flat-iron, and her clothes never had wrinkles in them, for all that some of them were over twenty years old. It was still a virgin's room with a sort of dryness in it; she never put flowers on her table, and her holy-pictures were well dusted, while the books that she never read these days were under glass in a little bookcase. In a corner of the bookcase I saw the box she had taken from Mr. Lilipoulala's valise. I feared that she might catch me at it, but I turned the key and took that box out. I opened it. It was the last one, and it was nearly empty.

I knew now why she had said to me last night, "In the end there is nothing left but prayer." I put the box quickly back, and polished where I had touched with my apron. Miss Joan, I was sure, would not agree with Mamselle's words: she thought that prayer was a weak substitute for action—she told me so herself.

I went into Madam's room, which was calm and wide; it still seemed like the room of a mother, the mistress of a household; some of the girls' little old things were scattered about it. I sat in the rocker and lulled myself. Action is all very well, but I am past it, I thought. And my Methodist prayers are quickly said and have no mystery. I tried to imagine what Baptiste and Miss Joan would be saying in their speeches. Well and good, I had told Miss Joan, for you to inform those ragged people that in England the unemployed get money from the Government. Our Government hasn't any money—we have to borrow from England. And if England has to support her own out-of-work people, why should she look after ours too?—Oh Lally, I know all that, she said, tossing her hair, but some day everyone will realise that we can't leave these people to rot away uncared for.—Well, who's to do the paying? I asked her.—Some of our islanders are very rich, she said, and see how the priests live, on the fat of the land!—O Lord alive, you're going to have Father Toussaint against you, and Marse Rufus, and all! I warned her (Me rocking in Madam's chair, where once she had sat with Miss Stella, then with the other little ones, nursing them.)—Lally, if the only thing we do is to wake people up and start them thinking about the misery of these penniless labourers, we are doing right, said Miss Joan.—But it's my opinion that the only ones she and Baptiste will wake up are the labourers with their hollow bellies.—Starving dogs can bite, I told her. Did you ever hear tell of the Rationalist speaker who got hounded to his death in this very island, for saying troublesome things? He jumped over Beausavoir cliff, after they stoned him! Besides, I said to her, you are letting down those town friends who had you to tea.

Rock . . . rock. I was very tired. But I had to heave up and go to the verandah, for I couldn't keep away from the spyglass. I twisted it around and looked into the town. My eyes were not as keen as my ears, but the mass of the people appeared like a thick shadow which had shifted. It had moved away from the whale and the butcher's shop. Now I could see quite plainly that the mass had gathered on the savannah. I swept my gaze over the paddock and I saw Ned jump off his donkey. He tied it up like a little man and came running into the house. "Lally! Grannie! Am I late for lunch?"

"No, Ned you can eat any time. It's a cold lunch today. Salad and such. Where is your grandfather?"

"He's coming, Lally." Ned had changed his way of speaking: he talked much better now, he began to talk like us. "Grandad walks slowly. And how my donkey canters!"

I looked at the boy curiously. Why didn't I love him as much as little Hel? Perhaps because he was too independent and big, not enough of a clinger. Yet in that moment I loved his manliness. He was a plain boy with a square face, and his eyes were green and seldom blinked; he had heavy eyebrows and his ears stuck out a bit; his upper lip was sharp, and looked brave. "May I have a look through the spyglass at my mummy's meeting?" he asked me cleverly. When I lifted him down from the rails again he sighed and said: "I wish I could be there. I used to go to all the demonstrations when I was a baby."

"It's no place for you. Come now and sit at the table. You and I will eat together, as no one else is here."

"Lally," he said, chopping up his tomato, "do you think it wrong for people to fight?"

"What sort of fight?" I asked him with care.

"Any sort. I was really thinking about Grandad's war—the old one. He wishes he had never gone."

"Lord God Almighty! You don't mean your grandfather talks to you, Ned? *Confides* in you?"

"Yes, he talks a bit. He tells me what he is frightened of."

"He tells you!"

"Grandad is frightened of machines. Do you know what, Lally? If he hears a car it makes him tremble. Didn't you know?"

"No, Master Ned. All these years and I've never known. What more did your grandad tell you?"

"He hates crowds. Don't let's tell him about the meeting.

It's all because he was in that fight. He went up in the air in a very old-fashioned aeroplane. Of course, it crashed. People were all around him, on a battlefield. So he likes to be in his little secret place, where nothing can get at him."

"Well, for peace and pity's sake!"

"I don't suppose the plane was anything like the ones in Spain. Those were quite modern. But they all belonged to the enemy, my dad said."

I heard a step, a slow step. I was so amazed at Ned's words that I hastened to say, taking the telegram from my pocket: "Now I'll tell you a secret. Your Aunt Natalie is coming tomorrow." I did not say that she was landing in a seaplane—not then.

"Oh, goody. She's rich, isn't she?"

"Yes. And she's pretty, too."

"Prettier than Mummy?" Ned looked stubborn, just like Miss Joan.

"Considerably prettier," said the Master, coming to table in his best mood. "But don't be upset, my boy. Your mother has her own qualities, her special *gamine* charm . . . "

"I beg pardon, sir, for sitting to table with Master Ned. But there was no one in for lunch."

"Oh, don't apologise, Lally. You're one of the family. Where are they all?"

"Here we are," said the voices of Madam and Mamselle, surprised, like myself, at his great good humour.

The Master stared across at Miss Joan's empty seat. On his face was a look which gave us permission to tell him anything. He seemed so strong!

"Joan is holding a political meeting," said Madam gently.

"Well, just as long as she doesn't hold it up here," said the Master. He spoke no more after that.

※ Just the same, part of the meeting did come back to L'Aromatique on the heels of Miss Joan. It was a mercy that the Master had shut himself up in his room and lain down in his old haze. The sight would have shocked him dreadfully. A great horde of those worthless no-work labourers followed after Baptiste and Miss Joan, singing in a dreary way. They sat down in the paddock holding out their hands for food. Some of the women had babies who were crying. Miss Joan asked her mother's permission to give them whatever food we had in the larder, and we all helped to share it out, for they would not go away until they had eaten. They were so hungry that they ate raw sweet-potato peelings. In the end, when it was drawing dark, though some of them had only swallowed a few mouth-fuls, they got up and left. One or two of the rough men asked for drink: Baptiste satisfied them with rum and water. Olivet opened some fresh coconuts and gave their women the milk. They left crying blessings on our heads. But I did not trust them a little bit. Long after they had gone I went about the house with a hurricane lantern, shining it around outside to make sure that none of those vagabonds was hiding in a corner to mur-der us in our beds.

The Lucky Child — CHAPTER 13

I went in and had a look at her after breakfast. She was too tired to get up. Her eyelids were heavy and red, but she had not been weeping. "Oh Lally! Must I eat? Only a cup of coffee, please. Then let me go on sleeping. I'm weary to death."

"You need strength, Miss Joan. Just this little slice of toasted breadfruit. It's all we have in the place, after last night."

She ate it obediently but unwillingly, as I watched her. "What news of Andrew—has Olivet been over?" she asked.

"He is better. He slept all night."

"Good." She drank the coffee.

"Soon," I said, "you'll hear something this house has been lacking for many a week. A laughing sound. Your sister Natalie is coming today."

"Good," she said, but vaguely.

"That lot of ragamuffins you and Baptiste dragged up here after the meeting didn't go away empty-handed. They took Ned's donkey. And one of the lime-juice vats. And a hen."

"Never mind, Lally. We'll get them back."

"Not with the police against you, you won't."

"Oh Lally! Leave me be! I'm so tired."

There was a hand at my skirt. Ned said "Mummy!"

"Mmmmmm," Miss Joan murmured.

"Mummy, it's awful: my donkey has been stolen."

"Oh go away, Ned. You'll have it back some day."

"To my way of thinking," I told them both, "those people were so hungry they'd likely as not chop that donkey into steaks and fry him up." Ned began to cry, and blew his nose in my apron. I took the poor boy out and tried to comfort him, ashamed of my words. I told him that the meeting-rabble had also stolen white hen Félice, Hel's pet. He felt better when he heard this. "Lally," said he, "did you mean that about the steaks or did you say it to punish Mummy?"

"Both," I told that strange boy.

Of course it was like careless Miss Natalie to choose the middle of the hurricane season for her flying journey. But the day was fair and sweet. "Golden morning!" cried out Buffon to Ned and me. It was golden for him, anyhow, because he had managed to obtain some blubber and also got a piece of sirloin which he sold to Christophine at a profit.

Mamselle was agitated, and well I knew why. She was like a fluttering tropiale which sees the shadow of the hawk. Her only escape was to chatter around Madam, who answered little. The Master had gone to his private den, but Ned, still upset at the loss of his donkey, didn't join him there. Baptiste, like Miss Joan, seemed exhausted, and sat silent in the kitchen watching his mother prepare the new-bought vegetables, which kind Olivet had fetched from town.

All morning long Master Andrew was on my mind. I wondered, could I raise the power to make that troublesome passage to his house? But I did not like Majolie; and that, more than my own weakness, kept me away. I tried to find little things to amuse young Ned.

When we heard the hoofs Ned was excited. He thought it was his donkey, which might have broken away and cantered home. But there were two sets of hoofs: we soon saw the reason. Brother Peregrine rode in front, and not many yards behind him, on a chestnut mare, rode Father Toussaint.

"Ned!" I cried. "Run quickly to your mother's room and get her out of bed!" At the same moment I hastened to the kitchen to warn Baptiste.

"Ned, did you tell your mother?"

"Yes, Lally. She's coming. She says it means the meeting was a success."

"Ned, you're too young to be mixed up in politics. Go away somewhere."

"Lally," said the little boy, "I've always been in politics. Since I was born, I mean."

✳ Father Toussaint was a good man, and a powerful man. The gentlemen over in Whitehall believed that they were governing our island. That was not the case. Father Toussaint and Marse Rufus were the real rulers. People challenged them now and again, but those people always lost. After the Rationalist speaker went to his end, there was a piece in the *Bugle* which began: "Would to God that the AUTHORITIES help the community in all manner of civilisation by COMPULSION if necessary. We must stamp on these irreligious vipers before they can raise their heads to poison us."

I didn't want to set myself up against the good Father. I knew Miss Joan was being unfair to him; he had done a lot of good wise things for the poor people. He said that we must accept the poor, and give them real charity out of our hearts and purses. The Bishop, who was a very old man, and homesick for Lorraine where he was born, always supported Father Toussaint and Father de Vriet. They had helped to build the new hospital wing. Disease, Father Toussaint said in his sermons many times, sprang from sin. I'd like to know what grave sin I have committed to inflict me with this tumour. Perhaps my sin has been loving Madam and the Master and their children too much. For that love grew in me through the years, and not a mortal soul, let alone a man of God, could dislodge it.

The priest and his Brother reined up. They dismounted. Both removed their different shapes of black hats. "Good morning, nurse," said Father Toussaint. "This time I hope we shall be fortunate in finding Baptiste Delgaud at home."

"Here I am," said Baptiste. He had put on his white jacket. But his feet were still too painful for the boots, so they remained bare.

"Ah, good. May I have a private talk with you, Baptiste? I

do not see much of you, since you lapsed as a communicant. This is a pleasure."

Poor Baptiste! He looked disturbed. He cast a glance around for Miss Joan. But she had not come out yet.

"Take the Fathers into the orchid house," I said to Baptiste. Brother Peregrine gave me a wry glance. I clasped Ned's hand and went to Miss Joan's room. Not that I thought Baptiste would give in to them in any way. He had been fighting his lone fight for too long.

"Well, did they ask for me?" said Miss Joan drowsily. She pulled a blue cotton dress over her head, and slapped her short hair with the hair-brush.

"No, Miss Joan. But Baptiste looked about for you. They wanted to see him alone. To my thinking, you and I could go and sit on the grass outside the orchid house."

"And listen to every word! Lally, you're a scream—you're a dear old riot." Still, she followed me out, and we sat down in silence. We did not hear much. Murmur, murmur. They were talking very gently to Baptiste, in a persuasive way. I could only hear the words "goodwill", "tolerance", "education". And after a while: "His Lordship . . . offers you the job, if you have the wisdom to submit yourself to his guidance."

Baptiste came to the door of the orchid house and looked out. He was smiling. He looked straight at Miss Joan. Then he turned back and said clearly: "No, Father Toussaint, I fear I cannot accept. I already have a job to do. I have a pupil."

"So," said Father Toussaint. "So. Well, Baptiste, I hope you never regret throwing away this opportunity to earn an honest living, to be a worker, and what is more, to have your past overlooked. Brother, I think we may depart. But before we go I'd like to have a word with Buffon, one of my dutiful parishioners. It happens that I have had information from Port-au-Prince—"

"Buffon is in the town," said Baptiste hastily. The three men, two pale priests and one tired-looking Negro, emerged into our strong sunshine.

"Ah, good morning," said Father Toussaint to Miss Joan. Brother Peregrine looked aside.

"In Port-au-Prince," Father Toussaint continued "there are rumours that the family of Mr. Lilipoulala is not satisfied with the circumstances of his untimely death. Buffon was of course the witness who found our unfortunate friend's body. I cannot, naturally, urge upon him to relate his innermost secrets to the authorities. The secrets of the confessional are sacred. But Buffon is a good Christian, and I can point out to him his duty."

Miss Joan stood upright in the sun, straight and blazing. She looked the good Father full in the eyes. "You paid me the compliment of listening to my speech yesterday," she said.

"Yes, yes! It was not bad: you said many true things. But you are in too much of a hurry. In another hundred years, now, the people will be ready for that sort of talk. At this moment, such a speech does great harm."

"You are not the only judge, Father, of what is harmful to the people," she said boldly.

"I am not a judge at all, only a poor priest," said Father Toussaint kindly. "A poor priest on his rounds. Now I must go over to Cul-de-Sac to comfort a dying man.—Yes, Brother, please mount.—You are the second daughter, I believe? You are Joan, whom I knew as a child?" His foot found the stirrup.

"Yes, I am Joan." She spoke so proudly, that one might have thought she was saying, "Yes, I am Joan", to those Bishops at a trial in the olden, olden days.

"It is a pity," Father Toussaint said, bending from his mare, "that I was unable to speak to your sister Stella before she went away . . . "

"Oh . . . " Miss Joan seemed for once taken aback. "Do you think that she would have had much to say to you, Father?"

"That is a matter for supposition."

"If you have anything to ask, I will answer for Stella. I have taken her place."

Brother Peregrine turned his mule's head and stared coldly and uneasily at Miss Joan.

"You have taken her place. Yes, so I have heard. Allow me to say, child, that you have courage."

"Thank you, Father, I have some courage. And what is more I have faith—more faith in life than you have yourself. Andrew is not dying. He will live."

"Is it not presumptuous that you and your sister should feel you have the power to sustain life . . . or to withdraw it?" Father Toussaint flicked the mare playfully, covered his head, and added: "Goodbye."

"Goodbye, Father," Baptiste said, and I echoed the words. But Miss Joan was silent. Ned waved, but she did not lift her hand. She knelt on the grass and put her arms around the boy. He was puzzled, and eager to break away. Miss Joan released him and turned to Baptiste:

"You see the choice, don't you, Baptiste? You see the alternative he puts before us?"

"Yes, Miss Joan, I see it. Either we shut up and he holds his peace, or we go on speaking and he makes scandal."

"Scandal!" she cried. "That's a trivial word."

The Master had come out on the verandah. He was looking up into the sky. In all our talking and anxiety, we had not heard the buzzing noise. It was a noise of engines, eastwards to sea. Ned jumped up and ran towards his grandfather. I wondered, will the Master flinch, and duck, and run away to his haunt? He seemed to hesitate until Ned came up and caught him by the sleeve. "The spy-glass, Grandad, the spy-glass!" the boy shouted. "Here comes Aunt Natalie's seaplane—let's watch it land!"

※ I had been neglecting the holy word since the girls came home. Of late instead of taking up my Bible in the afternoon I'd fallen to thinking of the tales we used to read them when they were small. Well I remembered that story of the little mermaids who rose up from the sea and had a look around to see what was going on above water. There were three of them, just like mine; but Miss Natalie hadn't wandered far and she wouldn't be the one to have her fish-tail and tongue chopped off and suffer dreadful pangs for the hopeless love of a prince. Miss Natalie was more like Betsinda in *The Rose and the Ring*; indeed I remarked on this right away when I saw her darting straight from that seaplane into Miss Joan's room, her hair like flying gossamer. I told her, and she sang out:

> *"I can dance and I can sing*
> *I can do just everyt'ing!"*

. . . Betsinda became the Princess Rosalba and the rose passed from hand to hand, and with it the magic and the loving.

Once in the olden days Miss Joan's godmother had sent her out a box from England, and when that box was opened the tissue paper smelled of the mystery of big cold cities, and nestling within it was a wax doll dressed in silver. Now that English godmother might have been a clever lady for politics but she had no notion about climate at all, for the doll was brought out into strong sunshine to be adored and admired by my children and Mimi's two and Christophine's brood. The fairy creature was left out there by the coralita vine to stare up at a sun which blue glass eyes from a factory ought never to have regarded at midday. But the only child who wept and wailed when she saw the melted pink wax was little Miss Natalie. She was the only one who really cared for dolls and babies: and now look at the turnabout. Her sisters have a son apiece and all Sir Godfrey left her was a fine name, money in the bank, and a big house with pictures of the Royal Family in the best bathroom.

"Lally, give the Ha-ha a drink," she called out. "He's entertaining Mother just now."

The Ha-ha was Miss Natalie's new handsome automaton. He was young, brown-haired, and most obliging. He also was rich, and it was his private plane which had brought the pair of them to us. But he was not exactly entertaining Madam. He was frightening her—telling how Miss Natalie had co-piloted the seaplane beside him. "I taught her," he said (he was a Canadian called Eric something). "She's pretty good now. My plane is a funny little amphibian with two engines on top—I expect you saw us fly overhead. It flips out wheels to land usually, but in this rugged place it landed in the sea, and Natalie got out competently and picked up the moorings. We can take four passengers sitting frontways, and we have two little seats facing the tail. I hope to have the pleasure of giving you a ride some day! This time, of course, we only brought ourselves."

"Oh dear . . . I hope you fly very carefully," Madam said.

"Only at about a hundred and twenty miles an hour. It's perfectly safe. There were lots of baby cumulus clouds about, and white flashes of flying fish below. Just before we landed we were flying between cloud and a gorgeous rainbow. Felt like an arrow going straight through its target."

"We appreciate your bringing Natalie home. But it's still

the hurricane season, remember." That was Madam's Sunday-afternoon voice, which I hadn't heard for a long time: we so seldom had visitors.

"I promise to take her back to Trinidad before anything blows along," said the Ha-ha confidently. Then he and Madam sipped their iced punch in silence. I went back to the girls' room and saw Miss Natalie stripping off the pleated tussore shorts she had landed in. She pulled open the clothes press. "I jumped into that plane straight from a set," she told Miss Joan. "Got anything old and cool I can borrow? Buffon hasn't lugged our things indoors yet."

"Don't take that one—Olivet just washed and pressed it for me," said Miss Joan.

"Well! I like that! As far as I remember, it's my very own, this white dress! I was the last to inherit it."

"It was made for Stella," said Miss Joan.

"Oh, I've got dozens of things you or Stella can have in exchange. I fancy myself in it. It goes well with this house—has a faint cemetery flavour. I remember walking between the tombstones in it."

"*Don't!*" exclaimed Miss Joan.

"Good Lord—you have a cemetery flavour too! That face . . . Joan, darling, what's going on around here? Why is everyone so edgy? Is it Father?"

"No, Father is better—for the time being."

"Then it must be Uncle Rufus casting his shadow. I met him while we were waiting for a car. He didn't offer to drive us up. He saw me, and shook hands sourly, but someone has put him into a dreadful rage."

"I have," said Miss Joan.

"I knew it. You and your absurd goings-on. The nerve of you, thinking you can oppose people like Uncle Rufus and Father Toussaint and Father de Vriet and the merchants! And what's it worth, anyway? What's it *worth*?"

"That's what I am considering," was Miss Joan's reply.

"Come out and drink with my Ha-ha. He's a pet. One of the nicest. Quite brainless, swims marvellously, and so sporting. A bore, of course, but then I'm always bored with men who love me madly. Now listen, Joan: I could shake you. You've brought the grey blight of your English theories all the way across the Atlantic Ocean. Why not give yourself over to the sunshine—let it burn all that away. You upset me in Trinidad, gazing at me with those earnest eyes, asking: 'But for what do you live?' For what indeed? Just living, that's enough. Dancing, that's enough. You people, you and Stella, won't *allow* yourselves to be happy. You agonise. Stella tears herself apart just loving people, and fearing for them. If you only knew how fortunate you are, both of you . . . "

"Tell me why you think us fortunate. You've always been the lucky child."

"Just being alive, and healthy. And your sons."

"Ah, the boys . . . "

"Then you have your own permanent men, sheer devoted blind idiots, by the sound of them—"

"Well, why don't you marry again? You have lots of followers!"

"I shall never marry again. But don't go thinking that I adored poor Godfrey, and broke my heart when he died. I didn't like him much. I married him for money."

"Lally," called Miss Joan, reaching out and kicking the door. "Ask Olivet or someone to fetch us a drink. Two drinks. Three, if you like."

I went to the pantry myself and fixed the girls a couple of strong rum swizzles. I fixed one for me, too. I needed that drink. When I brought the tray in, Miss Joan invited me to sit down. "Lally knows everything," she said to her sister. "She might as well be in on this chat."

"And you can lip-read or mind-read as well," said Miss Natalie, smiling at me. "Now, Joan. Why didn't you and Stella marry nice safe naval officers or doctors? Why did you have to marry a Communist and Stella a German farm yokel?"

"Edward," said Miss Joan furiously, "is not a Communist."

"Well, Communist or Labour Party type, it's all the same out here, as you know," said Miss Natalie. "Such dreary world-changers! Leave things be, that's my motto. It's yours, too, Lally—isn't it! I play at everything, of course. But my playing has its value. Where would everyone be without my money?"

Miss Joan seemed to make an effort. "Father would be in a

loony-bin, Mother in a paupers' home for poor-whites, and Mamselle Bosquet at the bottom of the boiling lake, I suppose."

"Yes, and you and Stella would never have had the chance to come here and agonise, for some well-off coloured people would own L'Aromatique. So brighten up. I'm vulgar; I want my pound of flesh. I like dancing around between the tombstones in a white dress, but I want my zombies to be grinning ones! Well! I made you laugh, anyhow."

Miss Joan had taken her drink in one gulp and flung herself on the bed. Her shoulders were shaking.

Miss Natalie went on: "If you are responsible for all those ragged diseased-looking types cluttering the town no wonder Uncle Rufus is upset. Much better stick around up here drinking cocktails with my Ha-ha."

"Lally," said Miss Joan, quickly sitting up, "where is Baptiste?"

"He's in the kitchen with Christophine, I should think. Or else he's gone off after Ned's donkey."

"Young Ned," said Miss Natalie, dreamily swilling her glass around as Miss Joan hastened from the room. "Ned. Where is *he?* Tell me, Lally. You know everything."

"Ned went out with the Master. He's somewhere around by the nutmeg trees," I said.

She went over to the mirror and looked at herself. "Yes, I'm Betsinda today, in this dear old dress," she said. "Lally, shall I tell you a secret? It's about Stella. She never went back to that farm, you know."

"Mercy alive!" I cried. "Where did she go then? Have you got her hidden away in Trinidad?"

"No, no," she replied swiftly. "She got as far as New York. But she didn't go any further. Didn't want to; and I advised her not to. 'Why not have the hell of a good time and forget it all,' I wrote her. As far as I know, she's doing just that. Living with her friend Margaret, doing the rounds."

"But Hel," I asked, "little Hel? Surely, Miss Natalie, his father would fetch *him* back?"

"She'd never let Hel go," Miss Natalie scoffed. "What do you think we are, Lally? As weak as reeds? Hel is in New York too. 'Let that German-American type come and haul you both back, if he really likes you better than his animals and his old Mutter,' I wrote to Stella. She saw the sense of it, of course."

"Well, I don't," I was bound to say.

"Lally," said Miss Natalie, "you're like an early-Victorian white spinster. Since when have we been ordered around by dumb Teutonic males?" She spun like a wax doll with flaxen hair, like a glass doll with gossamer hair, and danced out through the door, pausing to show me one of her impertinent smiles.

※ I knew in a moment that Ned wasn't with the Master, for the Master had quietly entered the drawing-room, and to entertain him Miss Natalie's Ha-ha had begun again to describe the seaplane flight. When I carried their filled glasses in I saw the Master clutching to the sides of his mahogany chair, white knuckles showing. With the rum swizzle in my head, I nearly said to the Ha-ha, "Oh, hush!"—But I'm still in some ways a servant, so I withdrew.

The Ha-ha was to have the orchid house for his sleeping place. I went in search of Olivet to make up the bed. When I couldn't find her anywhere I set about it myself, and was carrying out the new sheets when I saw Miss Natalie returning up the slope, looking lost. "Ned has totally disappeared," she said.

"Listen, Miss Natalie. Ned's upset. You'll never find him. This is a good place for people to lose themselves in. You'd oblige me greatly by helping to fix the room for your Canadian."

"Oh, let him sleep on the grass," she said pettishly, taking the sheets from me and throwing them into a verandah chair. "Lally, you old know-all, come for a little walk with me and tell me all the crazy things that have been going on around here. I'm burning with curiosity. Where is Mamselle Bosquet?"

"Praying," I said.

"Not for Father, surely?" asked Miss Natalie, in a tone of surprise. "I've never seen him look better."

"For the time being," I said.

"The time being? Why does everyone say those sinister words?"

"By the end of the week," I explained to her, "the Master will find out that Mr. Lilipoulala is dead and that there's no more to be expected from that quarter."

※ Miss Natalie was pulling me along and I found that we had taken the bridle-path to Petit Cul-de-Sac. I didn't resist her. Mimi Zacariah had been pulling me along that path anyway, in my mind, these several days. "Isn't this the track to Cornélie's house?" she cried out (as if she didn't know!) as she halted in her skipping and darting, and waited for me to catch up.

"Miss Natalie, I can't go any faster. Give me grace to sit down, if you please."

We sat together on a fallen flamboyant log. That youngest girl took a sharp stick and started digging away at the soft rotten part, causing wood-ants to come pouring out. "To think," she said, "that these marauders always choose the most beautiful trees to undermine. Just look at the devils!" She slashed the scuttling army and a strong hateful smell came up.

"Do you intend to go the whole way, Miss Natalie?"

"The whole way!" she laughed, and threw her stick into the gulley. "The whole way! Oh Lord, Lally, the world is full of people expecting one to go the whole way!" Then she sobered up. "Actually, I don't know, Lally," she said, low. "That rather depends on you."

She had always been a weak little girl, a frail one. The many times I'd nursed her through attacks of malaria! I'd spoiled her, of course, but I knew she had strength behind her softness. In some ways she was not as wilful as the others—she was satisfied with indoor things, and she'd see reason. She always knew the value of things, she knew the price of hair-ribbons right from the start, and had helped me to press hers out against coming parties. She hadn't played those rough games with Master Andrew as a child, nor had she made friends with Cornélie— she'd just watched, clinging to my skirts, biding her time, waiting to grow up. Even after she grew up, she was foxy and pretended to be more of a child than her years.

She noticed my broody look and said, coaxing:

"Now why didn't you come and live with me and be my housekeeper, like I suggested? It would have been nice and restful for you."

"Restful! With the dance band camping out in your garden day and night, and Government House on the telephone, and ladies with high voices coming in to lunch every day? Restful!

No, Miss Natalie, I'm a nurse born, and the only thing that brought me back to service was the children. If you had a baby, now . . . "

She looked at me straight, and if ever there was something to show the difference in the girls, it was their tears. Miss Stella's were hot loving wild tears, Miss Joan's were shamed drops quickly brushed off, but Miss Natalie's tears were slow unwilling pear-drops of glass that rolled untended down her cheeks and broke on her dress.

"Oh, what a party I had the night before we left!" She denied her tears. "What a show! Every good-looking man in the Caribbean area was there. Poor Eric Ha-ha, he *was* in a moody state! I danced half the night with a distinguished Scotsman, some sort of scientist—a psychiatrist, I believe. He just dipped in from his yacht. The strange thing was, I didn't even invite him. He just came to call at nine o'clock in the evening. Said he had called at L'Aromatique, too. Everyone was beastly rude to him there, from what I gathered. But he wasn't really interested in me, though he could dance the rumba like a creole. It was Father he was after."

"Yes, he called on us. Mamselle sent him away."

"Mamselle! that praying mantis! What a nerve she has!"

"True, Miss Natalie: she has a nerve. But it's breaking."

"Oh, I'm sick of all these old wrecks. Give me someone young and tough like Eric Ha-ha! Lally, I apologise. I didn't mean it, really. And I certainly don't include you: you're a pillar of power. . . . Have you rested? Shall we go on?"

"To where?" I asked.

"The whole way," she said. "To Andrew's."

"Day before yesterday," I told her, "Master Andrew was a wreck too. He was near dying. But he came alive again."

"Must have heard I was coming," she said, stretching and brushing off her dress, then holding out her small light hands to raise me.

"Indeed no, Miss Natalie. I doubt that anybody told him. He came alive again for Miss Joan."

▨ They had lifted Master Andrew into his deck-chair and placed him under the banyan tree in the clearing. The long red-brown ropes of that strange tree swayed slightly in the breeze. Roxelane's pail and spade were flung down by one of the little caves the tree-roots made. Master Andrew had his violin on his knees, but his hands were laid on it unmoving. His eyes were open and he saw us come out from shade into sun and cross the clearing. He saw us, but I mistrust that he knew which of the girls it was. He saw only the white dress at first. Then his eyes raised themselves to study the head and hair, the hair like spun sugar, and he smiled in a dazed way.

Miss Natalie ran, ran—seeming to float towards him, pausing in the air a few yards away till her feet brushed grass again and her skirt swirled.

"My darling Andrew!" she cried in a small soothing voice, the laughter only halfway subdued in it.

"*Your* darling now, am I?"—Oh yes! His voice was better. He was stronger. Majolie came from the outhouse, smoking her clay pipe and scowling. She barely said me a good morning. "Lally, my good friend," said Master Andrew, "help yourself to a seat. Majolie, get Miss Lally some coffee. Coffee for everyone."

"Not for me," said Miss Natalie. "I've been drinking rum swizzles. I've just arrived home, and I came straight to you. They tried to scare me that you were on your last legs, but I didn't believe them."

"Stand away a little—let me take you in. You have an American accent. Horrible!"

"I got it from my friends. I move in the smart set," said Miss Natalie.

"Well, I'm not on my last legs, but I'm hardly on my legs at all. Cornélie has gone to her father's house. She took Roxelane there early this morning, before the heat rose, because the poor baby isn't well. They are all terrified that she has my complaint. Fifine carried the child downhill. So I'm just sitting here calmly thinking of my sins and waiting for Father Toussaint."

When he spoke fast his voice sank and grew breathless; but he did not cough.

"I won't stay, if that old raven is coming."

"Stay for a little. You're another kind of angel . . . When you crossed the grass I thought you were a vision."

"I'm Queen Rosalba," she said. (And the rose has passed

to you, well enough, I thought. But maybe he is too ill to notice.)
"Did Joan send me a message?" he asked.

"No, she was too busy plotting to save the poor."

"I'm poor. She saved me," he said simply.

"And I'm rich. I'll take over." Miss Natalie's face was crystal-mocking in the banyan shade.

"I really must be better today. I can smell your lovely perfume."

"That scent! It comes from Spain. I expect it's what all the prostitutes in Barcelona use."

"Oh, quit that silly worldly talk," he said. "Are you sure Joan sent me no message? Will she come and see me today?"

"She might come and preach to you for half-an-hour before sunset, if I remind her to. Why don't you ask me if *Stella* sent you a message?"

Now as I took the welcome cup of coffee from old Majolie, not caring if she had filled it with poison, for I was so thirsty, my hand stiffened: I watched that poor boy's face to see his heart ride into his eyes. The blind spoilt girl went on talking, teasing him. (He loves her, say no more! He loves Miss Stella, be careful! For all that Miss Joan dragged him back from the gates of death, it's my first darling he loves!) But he was recovered enough to pretend:

"How could that be? She abandoned me long ago."

Miss Natalie lowered her lashes, the only dark lashes in the family, looking startling on that transparent cheek and under the fair silk hair. Beautiful she was, the loveliest of the three (I was bound to admit it), but with a kitten's naughtiness in her glance.

"Poor Andrew—did she leave you for that thick-headed German?"

"Miss Natalie plagues you," I interrupted. "She knows better. And you ought to know better, too, than to upset a sick man," I told her crossly.

She was ashamed. Just a tiny bit ashamed. "Stella didn't go back. She only went as far as New York."

"What good is that to *me!*" Andrew exclaimed. His tone was so strange that old Majolie came forward with the palm fan, making an excuse to flutter around him with it, fanning the air fiercely as if she would brush Miss Natalie's scent right off the island.

"How should I know? But at least it means that she's hovering; she's not tied to anyone."

"I hate hovering! Oh, go away, Majolie, sacrée vache! That's all I ever do now—hover between dying and being alive."

"Then stop hovering and get yourself well and strong, so that you can dance with me again." Miss Natalie took the fan away from old Majolie. Humming a calypso tune, she made some feathery steps over the rough grass. She seemed to lose herself in her dancing, and he lost himself in watching her. She had forgotten all about us—or did she know the magic of her dancing as she wandered lightly to the music of her own humming, playing with the fan?

Tired at last, she sank down near enough so that Master Andrew could lift his weak hand and crisp his fingers in that soft hair.

"Did that make you feel better?" she asked.

He did not answer.

"Will you get well and dance with me again?"

Still he did not answer.

"Why fret your heart over your illness, and over Stella and Joan? They have husbands and children. Think of me, for a change—I'm *here.*"

"Yes, you're here," said Master Andrew, dreaming somewhat.

"I'm here and I'm there—space means nothing to me. I practically own a seaplane now. Climb into it soon, very soon, and I'll get my friend to fly you anywhere you like. We'll find a cure-place, a specialist."

"Lucky girl," he whispered.

"Lucky Andrew, now I've come back," she said.

"Why do you wear your sisters' dress, if you're so rich?"

"And it's a holy dress, not at all for dancing and carrying-on in," I told her.

"It's my dress now. I can do what I like with it. I had it last."

But Miss Stella had it first . . . I was saved from uttering those words by the sound of Father Toussaint's hoof-clops in the valley.

✳ You wouldn't think that a young lady—"my lady" as those foolish servants in Trinidad called her—would bother to fascinate an elderly priest. You wouldn't think it—except of Miss Natalie. She was not at all taken aback when Father Toussaint dismounted before we had time to escape. He had been riding fast. The chestnut mare was damp with sweat. After greeting us briefly he went over and took Master Andrew's hand. It struck me that he was feeling for a pulse, like the Doctor did; and I daresay he found it jumping up and down like a sissizeb after crumbs. Majolie brought him a silken cushion for his deck-chair and scraped the ground with her nose.

"He seems better," said Father Toussaint, addressing us all.

"He *is* better," said Miss Natalie, letting the full light fall on her face as she smiled delicately at the good Father.

"Yes, I am alive," said Master Andrew.

"And have you been able to think over the things I discussed with you?"

"I have thought a lot."

"Please don't make him think any more," said Miss Natalie, cooling Father Toussaint's heated face with a few slow sweeps of the palm fan. "He's all thought and no flesh already."

He stood it from her very nicely. Now if Miss Stella had said that—or Miss Joan . . . But when Father Toussaint spoke next, he called Miss Natalie "my child".

"My child," he said, "mortal life is brief, even for the strongest of us. The things I asked Andrew to consider affect not only himself, but Cornélie and the baby Roxelane."

"He thinks I ought to marry her at once," said Master Andrew calmly.

"They are living in sin. This is a grievous wrong to Cornélie, whose conscience is troubled and whose religious life is damaged by such a situation." Father Toussaint spoke low but firmly: he had said it many times before—anyone could hear that.

I was the nearest one to Master Andrew. So I believe it was to my ears he addressed a whisper which was his most secret thought: "It was not sin . . . until Stella came."

"Nearly all the people in this island were born in sin, as you say," remarked Miss Natalie, losing her formal air of reverence.

"What would you do for parishioners otherwise?" Father Toussaint gave a dry chuckle, which quickly passed; he added gravely: "Cornélie is a very special case. She is a good young woman lost to the Church. At one time we had high hopes of her."

"I know," Miss Natalie said, reflecting.

"I understand from the Sisters in Trinidad that you are so kind as to continue your late husband's donations?"

"Yes, Father, that is so," said Miss Natalie, making a nun-face at him.

It was like a game. Miss Natalie and the holy father were playing for points, with Master Andrew and myself looking on.

"But you have no . . . how shall I put it, knowing your family? . . . You are devoid, so to speak, of a philosophy?"

"Well, Father, I have an open mind—Lally thinks it is a vacant one, I'm certain" (she curled her lips at me) " . . . empty anyhow. I just do what is expected of me."

"Unlike your sisters," he said.

"Unlike my sisters," she replied quietly.

"Ah." It crossed my mind that Father Toussaint was relieved, if not gratified, by these words. As we all sat silent, I saw a mountain trembleur fly out of the lime-trees. This rarest of birds, its stiff tail held high above its little body, its wings trembling and drooping, resembled nothing so much as the human heart flying out of a troubled breast, agitated and shaking, hunting for something to feed on. Master Andrew and I dropped our eyelids together as it vanished.

"The Bishop used to take me for short drives in his carriage when I was little," said Miss Natalie, giving herself another reference.

"Ah," said the Father in a misty distant voice.

"Tell me, Father, do you think Cornélie is more important than Andrew?" Miss Natalie suddenly asked.

"All human souls are important to God," said Father Toussaint.

"But to *you*?"

"It is not my place to choose between one individual and another," he said.

"Yet you think that I'm more important than Stella and Joan?"

He weighed these words. Then, giving Miss Natalie a bright hard glance, he stated: "Not more important, my child—simply less *formidable*." He paused before speaking the last word. And he spoke it in the French way.

She pursued her subject, recalling to me how Mamselle Bosquet used to describe them in the olden days: *Stella la touchante, Joan la téméraire,* and *Natalie la tenace*; Mamselle had explained to me these titles.

"I believe you really do think Cornélie is more important than Andrew—more worth saving."

Father Toussaint seemed aggrieved at her pressure and said in a fretful voice: "She is one of my flock. Her father is our valued friend."

"Then that makes it all so beautifully simple," Miss Natalie declared, bestowing on the good Father her most radiant and guileless smile. "You want to save Cornélie's soul, and I want to save Andrew's body. So what is the obvious thing to do? I should take Andrew away for healing and remove the cause of sin."

"It is not so simple," objected Father Toussaint, but mildly.

"It's simple enough, and it is urgent, Father." She rose and the whiteness of her dress blotted Master Andrew from my sight. "He's tired. He needs to sleep. It *is* simple isn't it, my darling? It *is* possible?"

"Yes, it's possible," he said, turning his head sideways.

It seemed plain to me that Father Toussaint had accepted the possibility also: he helped old Majolie to support Master Andrew indoors, and took kind leave of us soon afterwards, without further argument.

But of course deep men like priests have a lot of afterthoughts, as I warned Miss Natalie on the way home. My warning had a bad effect on her—she dashed ahead of me so that I panted to keep up, and when I called her to halt and reproached her for this, she began a lot of silly talk about dinner-parties and tennis parties and the style of her friends' dresses; then she lagged so slowly, picking at leaves and buds, that I had time to wonder which was aching most: my heart or my stomach.

Flight ❀ CHAPTER 14

T he rest of that day went well enough, though it went by
without Miss Joan. She had gone into the town with
Baptiste to speak again to those country labourers without
work, who hung about the sea-front like beggars waiting for a
miracle to happen. What she said to that band of no-goods I
never yet found out, but they started drifting back to their
homes slowly. Afterwards Afrodidy's son at the cable office told
Olivet that Miss Joan had sent off telegrams to England. Miss
Natalie and the Ha-ha went for a river swim; young Ned went
with Buffon to see the great whale's bones and look at the seaplane. Madam, worn out by being sociable, retired to her
rocking-chair; the Master went to his hiding-hole. Christophine
and Olivet stayed in their black close kitchen. I myself took a
little nap, but when I raised myself up to look into household
matters, Mamselle and I were the only ones to be wandering
the rooms. Although I have suffered because Mamselle treated
me in the past as no account, on this day I approached her as
a friend. I told her what Miss Natalie had said about the Scotsman in Trinidad, the man from the yacht. And she and I stayed
talking for a very long time.

The evening passed calmly and well, only the crickets going

tsik-tsik and the croakings and dronings of the other insects filling in the long gaps between people's words. I saw a spider as big as a mouse with legs four inches long, roaming around the Ha-ha's pyjamas; but I didn't stoop to hit or crush it. Let it ramble over him in the night, the sooner he takes himself off the better, I thought. I daresay it curled itself up in an orchid-cup, and spent a quiet night as we all did. It was not a night for fears and frights: the moon was near full, and its light was so intense that all flower colours were as brilliant as in the daytime. The big plumes of the palm-trees waved and waved through the long hours, like old Majolie's fan.

Next morning the sky was bluer than the mountains, for a change, with the lower slopes green and blossoming. The only ugliness was the screeching of pea-hens, for our grand peacock was losing his tail feathers and looked sickly: they were upset, and pecked at each other. The Ha-ha had got out his camera and gone off to take pictures. Baptiste had received word from one of his scouts that Ned's donkey had been traced. The thief had been beaten by his comrades and the donkey turned loose. For a while the poor creature had lost itself in the mountains, but now it had been found again, and a young boy would be bringing it back later. There was no mention of white hen Félice, and it was my conviction that Hel's pet would never have her feathers washed at the hydrant again. Ned came to tell me this, and he sat contentedly looking at a picture-book beside me as I sewed. We were under the saman tree; looking across the paddock, I saw the figures of four women: Madam, Mamselle, Miss Joan and Miss Natalie. They were holding a conference, and now and then the pairings would change: Madam would walk with Miss Natalie, and Mamselle with Miss Joan. All their characters showed in their movements, Madam firm but slightly hesitating now, Mamselle jerking her head bird-like, Miss Joan plunging a little ahead, straight and upward-looking; Miss Natalie, for all the concern on her face, unable to resist breaking into a little dance-step at intervals. After a while they seemed to come to some conclusion, and the older ladies returned silently to the house. My girls came across to me.

Miss Joan began: "While I saw the usefulness of your ideas of shanghai-ing Father and bearing him off in the seaplane to that yacht, I couldn't quite support you. After all, he's an individual and still has a certain amount of free will . . . No, Natalie, I think Mother was right. Someone must tell him, and let him make up his own mind."

"His poor ruined mind," said Miss Natalie. "I'm sure Stella would have agreed with me."

"Stella? Would she? I know she had pretty autocratic principles about dealing with troublesome people, and incidentally I couldn't agree with her less on that point: you don't solve anything by violence. But still—Father! She loves him, you know: perhaps more than we do; and she is very much like him."

Ned, who was listening attentively, frowned up at his Aunt Natalie, and remarked: "I love Grandfather."

"Run away to him, then," said Miss Joan. "But don't tell him we are talking about him. Grandfather is very sick. We feel he ought to go away and see a doctor."

Ned went away, but his legs dragged and he looked back twice. He seemed to me to be carrying his puzzlement with him.

"Sometimes I feel we ought to clear out and leave all these poor old people to go to the devil in their own way," Miss Natalie said. "Taking the children, of course. And Andrew."

"Well, you can clear out—why not?" replied Miss Joan. "You are the free one of the family."

"I hold the purse—that's all," said Miss Natalie. "But perhaps I am as much bound as anyone."

"Let's try and get it straight then. Someone tells him. One of us, I think, as we are younger and can stand his raging despair better than Mother or Mamselle. We persuade him to leave the island, to save himself—"

"And I warn the Ha-ha. Poor Eric! He didn't know what he was letting himself in for!"

"Nor did I. This isn't the struggle I came here to engage in—"

We must move fast. That Scotsman leaves Trinidad next Thursday."

"Yes, we must move fast." But Miss Joan spoke so heavily that all movement in her was slowed down, weighted.

"Supposing he will not come away?"

"Then we must leave him, as Cornélie would say, to God."

"Cornélie!—Oh heavens! I am reminded. I promised Andrew to give you a message . . . "

"Natalie, Natalie, have you seen him already?"

"Yes—I move fast."

"Ah." (I looked into their faces, and tried to read their thoughts: but it was all very difficult. It was all mysterious, because of the contagious alarm in the air.)

Miss Natalie seemed to be battling with herself. At last—

"He asked you to go and see him."

"I can't. I can't. There's something I have to settle with Father Toussaint. Something terribly important."

"I take it, then, that you don't think he will die . . . at least, not immediately?"

"No. I think he will live." Miss Joan straightened her neck and thrust out her chin.

"Well. I'm sure you intuitive people are very wise, but still. He looked pretty bad to me . . . He looked a lot readier for a sanatorium than Father. I tried to deceive him about my thoughts, of course."

"I don't oppose you in that. You're quite right. If Andrew doesn't go away, to Switzerland or somewhere like that, he will certainly die soon. At best he can only be halfway cured."

"He must go away," said Miss Natalie.

"Well . . . I leave that to you. You have the money, and the power. Go and see him in my place. I must—I simply must—go to town."

Miss Natalie looked at me for guidance. But I had no decision to give her. It was all beyond me now. The whole thing was a question of loving. The thing was a question of loving enough. I had heard the strain in Miss Joan's voice when she said: "I leave that to you." I recalled Miss Stella, her arms tight around the laurier cypre, saying goodbye to that tree which was never a man. I recollected Cornélie's look of dreadful anguish when she crept in through the rain that night. Would she let him go? Is the end of all loving letting the dearest go?

"I will go now to Cul-de-Sac," said Miss Natalie, leaping up lightly and forcing a look of sauciness to her face.

"Give him my thoughts. Tell him I hope he will accept—will go away, heal himself . . . " Miss Joan laid herself down on the saman bench and put her head in my lap, on my percale skirt, just as Miss Stella had done once. The strong one: but she was weakened by her anxieties. "Just to rest for a few moments, Lally, darling," she said.

※ It happened that the girls did not have to tell the Master after all. He was sitting on the verandah after lunch with young Ned when a car, a fast new car, came swiftly up the last lap of the private road, and Marse Rufus got out quickly. He moved forward as if to corner the Master, whose trembling started when he heard the vibration of the engine.

"I hope you are in condition to hear something important, John," said Marse Rufus—insolent as he never dared to be in the olden days.

"I am very well, thank you," the Master answered. Ned went to him, and putting an elbow on his knee, leaned there.

"You must stop your daughter from agitating the unemployed labourers into a state of unrest. There'll be hell to pay if you don't." Marse Rufus almost shouted.

"My daughter is of age. I cannot prevent any of her activities," said the Master, and there was pride in his voice. It was not that he approved. Not he. But something had happened to him since the girls came back, and since he grew to trust young Ned. He was conscious of his family.

"Your daughter—running around with a common Negro—"

"I ask you not to insult her. You are in no position to say such things: and she is your niece, by the way. She happens to believe in different things than you do. Or even different things than I do. She may or may not be right." The Master shrugged with something of his old arrogance.

"Dragging the name of her grandfather, my respected father, in the dirt! Those people came in from the mountains because they owed him gratitude. And they stayed to hear subversive propaganda! Pay for the unemployed! Things like that—stuff straight from Moscow!"

"I know nothing about it," said the Master. But he did not speak timidly. He spoke in distaste. He even raised up the spirit to smile slightly at Ned. In that moment he did not seem like an old man any longer.

"Stuff straight from Moscow!" yelled Marse Rufus. He smelt very faintly of whisky.

"Stuff straight from England," said the Master coldly.
"And the other girl—your daughter Stella. She was another unscrupulous one. The harm she did—"

Having heard the shouting, Madam and Mamselle Bosquet had emerged from their rooms. They stood appalled in the portal of the drawing-room.

"The death of Mr. Lilipoulala," continued Marse Rufus on a note of rough menace. "The death of Mr. Lilipoulala . . . the circumstances . . . an investigation . . ."

"The death of Mr. Lilipoulala . . . " The Master passed a hand across his brow. Ned looked up at him. Sweat was on the hand which the Master laid on Ned's tiny fist.

This was the point when Madam too denied her age and her weakness. She came forward. She came forward swiftly, and stood between her brother and her husband.

"Go away, Rufus," she said. Just that.

He gaped at her, not used to this hardness from her. It was a long while since he had seen her. He stared at her new white hairs and trembling lips.

"Go away," she said.

Marse Rufus still stood there, seemingly rooted.

"Leave us. It is you who do the harm," she said. "Go back to the *Bugle* and write it all up. We have nothing to lose."

Marse Rufus backed down the stairs, now really acting like someone drunk. He nearly crushed my foot as he passed. He got into his car. But he did not drive right away. We saw him sitting there staring at the wheel. I felt almost sorry for him. I thought of him then as of Cornélie's father. The grinding noise of the starter was our relief, though it set the Master to shivering and shuddering again.

Even then Marse Rufus didn't drive off. He sat there with the engine running. I was afraid that he would get out and come back, that he had in mind to talk about Master Andrew as well. But no: suddenly with a jerk the black car moved forward, circled the drive and disappeared. For some moments we could hear its noise. If he drives so fast, he'll run into Miss Joan, and kill her stone dead, and that will be the end of it, I thought. Yet I knew that Miss Joan would take a lot of killing.

I was ashamed to look up at the group on the verandah,

feeling myself in some way guilty—a part of the things that had happened. I shut my eyes, hearing the Master say (but I did not know whether he spoke to Madam or to Mamselle Bosquet): "Am I so poor a creature, then, that you *dared* not tell me?"

※ After Marse Rufus had gone the Master sagged to the ground like a flamboyant log, so I took Ned to have a look-about for his donkey—a weak excuse but the boy humoured me; we left those poor ladies to turn the Master's study into a sick-room, with Buffon to lift and lay him on his couch.

Ned climbed up a tree for a better view and I took my little doze: he woke me when he saw his mother and Baptiste coming up the road, and almost at the same time Miss Natalie came out of the leaves from the track to Cul-de-Sac. They had not been absent for long; and all three of them wore expressions which told of matters being settled in some way or other. Ned wanted to run to them, but I held him back; the three came together and paused in their walk for a brief conversation.

Baptiste went off to the kitchen and Miss Joan went straight to the house, before I could warn her of the morning's happening. It was Miss Natalie who joined me, wearing her beauty like a triumph. "Lally, I fixed it. Andrew is coming away with me in the seaplane. Ha-ha will fly us to Trinidad, and I'll take care of Andrew in my home until he is strong enough to make the second journey, to Canada. Eric's uncle is a Senator and will get Andrew into the best tuberculosis clinic in that country."

As she was speaking, Eric Ha-ha came strolling up with his camera, looking like an advertisement for good health and good humour. He stood some way off and made a photograph of Miss Natalie as she sparkled there in the sun. Then he approached us and listened to her, seeming to agree to every word said; he would have swallowed a tête-chien snake for her sake. He smiled and blushed when she cried out, "Eric is our rescuer, our knight on wings!" She always had that gift of making men foolish.

"But has Cornélie agreed?" I couldn't help asking.

"Cornélie put him into my hands. She saw it was the only hope. I tried to persuade her to let little Roxelane come too, for the doctors to examine; but that she wouldn't do. She said

Uncle Rufus would be against it. Cornélie is quite calm; she has taken refuge in her religion. When we have left, she thinks she will go into retreat."

"Into retreat—and that's what I'll do myself," I said to that third girl.

"Joan has gone to arrange about Father. Eric darling, chuck that camera over to Lally. I'm sick of this mopish estate, aren't you? Let's go to town. Let's go to town and have the hell of a good time, or I'll go crazy. We must get up some steam for tomorrow's operations."

And you'll need all your gaiety, I nearly told her, taking on that poor boy with his coughing and choking—you who would jump in disgust over some spit on the sidewalk.

Young Ned slid down from his bough. "Oh let me come to town with you and see the whale's skeleton again!"

"Morbid boy," she said. "As if there aren't enough skeletons up here. All right, come along then. You can go and brood over that decaying sea-monster, and Eric can tune up the seaplane and see officials, but I . . . I shall sit in the club and hold court; people will whisper around me that I'm one of *them*, but they won't dare say it aloud, because I have money! Ah, it's essential to be rich, isn't it, Eric Ha-ha? All these drippings and dronings and reformations, they don't get you anywhere without good solid cash!" She had pink stains of excitement on her cheeks. Ned looked at her wonderingly, and took the Canadian's hand. The three of them bade me goodbye and swung down over the crest of the hill. There's always a lot of sense in what Miss Natalie says, though she says it in a troublesome way, I thought. Then I fell to dreaming of Miss Stella, who never talked sense.

※ The hours spun round feverishly to the time of flight, the day of parting.

The Master went to town on a stretcher, having refused to be put into a hired car like Master Andrew. Buffon and Baptiste and Eric Ha-ha and one of Baptiste's mountain friends were the carriers. They moved along gently and slowly, so that Madam and Mamselle would not be left behind. It was like a procession of the dead, that was my opinion. But Miss Joan said to me, giving me her arm at the difficult bends, "It's not like a

funeral, Lally. The seaplane will be flying them back to life."
"It's a parting," I told her. It seemed certain to me that
something final would happen, that the seaplane with its anxious load would run into the fiercest of hurricanes and become
a few splinters of metal and board—the youngest mermaid
would be cast into the deep sea, while the spirit of the Master—
who could say where that turbulent spirit would find rest? And
who could say how far along the road to heaven Cornélie's
prayers and Father Toussaint's intercessions would bring Mimi's
poor boy whom so many women loved?

The moment of greatest trial came when we reached the
shore and the Master was set on his feet. Master Andrew had
been put aboard first, lifted from the row-boat to the seaplane
very quietly, he casting only one deep backward look towards
Miss Joan, while Cornélie wept softly on the shoulder of Mamselle Bosquet. Sitting already in that contraption was the hospital nurse, Coralita-bigmouth's daughter, whom Miss Natalie
had hired. Madam stepped forward as if to offer the Master her
strength. But he hung back. He gazed at the seaplane in terror.

"I won't get into that—I can't!" he muttered. "Why did you
bring me here? Didn't you know that I swore never to have to
do with diabolical machines again?"

The sea was sucking between the stones, and a coconut fell
loudly. "You can't go back now," Madam said.

He sat on a rock and covered his eyes. He was shaking all
over. A little crowd of townspeople had gathered to watch us.
They hung around laughing and whispering in patois at the
Master's cowardice. He glowered at them with his trapped look.
Indeed, he was trapped—between the seaplane, his family and
the jeering crowd.

Mamselle Bosquet, releasing herself from Cornélie, came to
the Master and said in a pleading voice: "John! It's your last
chance! Everything is finished! Make the effort!"

Eric Ha-ha had started up the engines suddenly and those
loud awful things like electric fans were whirring and roaring
above the body of the plane. Miss Natalie leaned forward, her
head in a silk pilot-cap, and her eyes for once dismayed. "Father! Hurry! You *must* come!" Miss Joan said nothing. But she
gave her son a little push.

Ned went up to the Master and reached out his small hand. "Come, Grandad, they're waiting," he said. He tried twice to take the Master's hand, but it trembled away from his grasp. At the third attempt, the little boy got hold of that poor quaking bunch of fingers and held them as tight as he could.

"Grandad, come. If you're frightened I'll go with you. I'll sit beside you." Of course he wasn't doing it quite high-mindedly; he'd been wanting to go along with them for hours.

The Master rose. The boy's words had stilled his shivering. He seemed not to hear us speak, or even to hear the roaring, any longer. Buffon and Baptiste heaved the Master and the boy locked together into the boat, and into the cabin of the seaplane. All this while Miss Joan stood silent. She had not protested or tried to hold Ned back. But I thought I could hear the thumping of her heart above the roar. There was a great dash and spray of water, the machine made some little skips like a game of ducks-and-drakes on the bright sea, and they were off. A hand waved. The terrible machine split through low cloud and sailed out into the air.

❋ We went back to our rooms at L'Aromatique, needing peace. Whatever the hopefulness of that flying away, and whatever the final bravery of a man who dared to do at last the thing he feared most, I knew that for those older ladies something was over for ever. Yes, I knew it. And I think Miss Joan knew it too, though she had the thought of young Ned uppermost in her mind.

The house was empty of men. It was a house of women, like the Maison Rose in the old days. I'm bound to say that such a situation was not disagreeable to me, in my condition. Madam had said to me that the girls would bring life to the place. They had brought more than that—they had brought sons and torment and love complications beyond the endurance of an old dark-skinned Methodist like me. I picked up my china cockatoo and said to it, you and I will be going back to our one-room shack after we've heard of the Master's landing. But I did not know then that I would remain to hear young Ned say in the presence of his grandmother, "Grandad held my hand all the way. I didn't like to take it away, as it made him not frightened. When we landed he was still holding me hard and cold . . . only the Doctor could undo him." No, I didn't think to hear it said in such dreadful innocence, though I had known the Master's going was for ever. I should have had the wisdom to guess that if a man's heart is once cracked in some strange way, a sudden buffeting between fear and courage in the high winds of the sky would split it clean in two.

So in that peaceful pause of ignorance I took up my Bible; too many human conversations had caused me to neglect the holy word. When Miss Joan tapped at my door I pretended not to hear. She opened the door cautiously. "Don't get up, Lally, go on resting. I didn't mean to disturb you—just came to tell you something important."

I wanted to say to her, wait and tell it to your mother; I'm weary of talk. But one look at her face, so eager and strong, weakened me.

"We've quite worn you out, poor darling." She was tender. "I only came to reassure you about Stella—about Mr. Lilipoulala. I had it all out with Father Toussaint yesterday. We reached an understanding."

What could I answer, but *tsik, tsik,* like the crickets?

How two such different souls as that second girl and the good Father could reach an understanding, was outside my comprehension. She must have seen the unbelief on my face, for she said:

"Father Toussaint was educated in a Jesuit school, and I was educated by Mamselle. It was not so difficult."

For all that, her face showed that it had been difficult enough: and I could see that she wanted me to be inquisitive. She had a nervous tattle-tale air, but didn't look defeated.

"Tell me the way it happened, then," I consented, sighing a bit and easing up my hard pillow with the crochet border.

"The Presbytery," she said, "had just the opposite feeling and smell to Maison Rose in the old days or this house today: a smell of men dedicated to God. I was received in an ante-room with the doors wide open to the courtyard, and all the time I was talking to Father Toussaint, Brother Peregrine was squatting on the flagstones by the granadilla trellis churning ice-cream in a wooden pail. It was a very interrupting noise at first, until I got used to it . . . I bore it in a flattered way until I found out that he was not making it for me, but because of the Bishop's birthday! Later on he brought in a dishful apiece for Father Toussaint and me: and oh, Lally, it was made of coconut milk and covered with black specks of pounded vanilla: it tasted as I used to think that snow might taste, when I was a child . . . "

"Yes, but what went *on*?" I asked her.

"Wait a minute, I'm coming to that. The atmosphere of that room, and the taste of the ice-cream, was part of what went on . . . It wasn't only the smell of dedication. That room had also the look and feel of Europe—of France. The chairs were plush and mohair, and the curtains had a pattern of fleurs-de-lys. Sitting there opposite Father Toussaint, I felt adrift from town life. We were the two cleverest people in the island, and we both knew that."

"Miss Joan," I said, "where's your modesty?"

"Oh, I was modest enough! First of all we spoke of long-ago things. I told him about that terrifying book we all doted on (even Baptiste loved it, though it was full of magic and fancy): I mean the tale about the Black Necromancer and the Red Necromancer. I told him how Stella would never go for rides in the Bishop's carriage because she called him the Black Necromancer; and he said—"

She picked up the bottle of hair-oil that I grease my plaits with, uncorked it, and sniffed hard.

"He said, 'And as we sit here today, am I the Black Necromancer and are you the Red one?'—You see, he can be sly and joking too. Then we went back even further into the past, and he spoke of the time when my forefathers regarded Negroes as chattels, while the Catholic Fathers right away esteemed them as precious human beings."

"And what did you say to *that*?"

"I said to him, 'Yes—you backed the right horse, like Uncle Rufus. Think of all the property that has been left to the Church since those days, out of gratitude!' He didn't know whether to laugh or be severe. So he said, 'My brothers did not make a *temporal wager* three hundred years ago. Out of gratitude . . . perhaps; but also out of piety. Piety is a plain word, yet it is not in every vocabulary.' We began to eat the lovely ice-cream, then he suddenly looked up and said: 'I sometimes wonder if you are a *bien-pensant.*'"

"But was anything ever said about the important—the terrible things?"

"No names were spoken. The only time Stella's name ever fell between us was when I said that about the Black Necromancer. To tell you the truth, Lally, at one moment I felt that I would scream—I so much longed for him to come to the point. I looked out of the open door and saw Father de Vriet walking up and down, swinging his rosary like a horsewhip."

She put a smear of my hair-oil on the back of her hand. "I think this would be rather good for chilblains," she said. But I held back from scolding; it was just that the telling hurt her.

"Of course Father Toussaint had me there to drive a bargain; and he reminded me that he'd already made one concession . . . over Andrew. Now I'll tell you a strange thing, Lally. I can't explain how he did it, because there were no words you could actually catch on to; but I had a clear indication that Father Toussaint no more regretted the sudden end of Mr. Lilipoulala than we did, though he gravely disapproved of the way it had come about."

"But how much did he know, Miss Joan?" I asked, out of anxiety for that first of my children.

"He knew an awful lot, Lally. I think he knew everything."

I could not help but exclaim: "That treacherous long-tongue Buffon!"

"Poor Buffon, he gets blamed for all sorts of trouble. Why not Mamselle?"

This suggestion upset me so that I could not speak.

"Well, however it was," she continued, "all this leading-up business filled me with alarm because I couldn't think of anything important enough to cancel it out with. But when we finally came to a show-down it was quite simple. He only wanted me to make a promise. Father de Vriet and Brother Peregrine had come into the room by then, and they stood there like witnesses. Their black gowns made enormous shadows on the walls . . . "

"Don't slay me with this waiting!" I begged of her.

"I promised not to engage personally in political activity in the island. I promised, in fact, to devote myself to my husband and child."

Miss Joan smiled; and her smile was for once as provoking as Miss Natalie's.

"You've always been a one to keep your promises, Miss Joan." I spoke a little sharply.

"To the letter, Lally; to the letter."

"Then how about your promise to Baptiste—and the labourers?"

"I have reached an understanding with Baptiste too. He is perfectly satisfied."

"Miss Joan," I said, raising myself on my elbow and putting down my Bible, "tell me—what did you say in those telegrams to England?"

"Lally," she said, postponing her answer, "can't you see that unless people like Father Toussaint and Baptiste and me come to some sort of rough understanding, there's no hope for the world?"

"That's as may be. A household is worry enough for me without fretting about the world."

"As to the telegram . . . " she went on, off-handedly. "Oh! I sent a telegram to Edward, asking him to come here."

I considered this. Another man in the house of women and another difficult man too, by the sound of him! How could a man with four fingers missing be any good as a planter? But I didn't want to crush her, because she loved him.

"What will he use for money, to get here on? I thought he was so poor?"

"Natalie gave me the money," she said.

I now began to see it all, how Baptiste would be satisfied and in what manner Miss Joan would keep her promise to Father Toussaint, though there's never been anyone in the island to get the better of Father Toussaint or Marse Rufus indefinitely. (I promised, she'd said, to devote myself to my husband . . .)

"And what did Miss Natalie get for a bargain?" I asked.

"She got Andrew," said Miss Joan.

"Well, she won't hold him for long, even if he gets well. Wait until he gets better in Canada and finds out how near Montreal is to New York."

"Oh Lally!" she wailed. "You still love Stella the best."

She had opened my other door that gave on the portico, letting in the everlasting green, the double blues of mountains and sky, scent of many flowers, tallness of palms, and a whole carnival of little insects.

"I love you all, Miss Joan," I said. "Goodness knows why, because you're killing me fast, but I love you all." Just to prove it, I gave her my china cockatoo for young Ned. "Ned," I said, "is the hardy one, he's the one who will outstay us all, living here perhaps to repair some of our mistakes." Then I turned back to the holy book to teach Miss Joan that I, too, had my wider reaches beyond the family.

ABOUT THE AUTHOR

Phyllis Shand Allfrey was born on October 24, 1915, in Roseau, Dominica. Her father, Francis Shand, was Crown Attorney of that island; she was educated privately there but later left to work in New York City and to travel in Europe. She married an Englishman, Robert Edward Allfrey, with whom she had a son and a daughter. The early years of their marriage were divided between Britain and the United States. Later they adopted three children. In London, Phyllis Shand Allfrey became involved in the Fabian Society, the Labour Party, and the Parliamentary Committee for West Indian Affairs. In 1953 she won second prize in a world poetry contest, judged by Vita Sackville-West among others, and soon after she completed *The Orchid House*, which was published in England and the United States that year. She also published four collections of poems and wrote numerous short stories published in newspapers, magazines, and anthologies.

In 1954 Allfrey returned to Dominica where she was soon caught up in political activity. She founded the Dominica Labour Party, was elected as one of the federal representatives for Dominica, and was made Minister of Labour and Social Affairs in the West Indian Federal Government. During her tenure as Minister, from 1958 to 1962, she lived in Port of Spain, Trinidad, the federal capital. When the Federation was dissolved in 1962, she returned to Dominica where she became editor first of a weekly paper, the *Dominica Herald*, then of a small opposition paper she founded with her husband, the *Dominica Star*. Phyllis Shand Allfrey died in 1986.